Praise for the Asperger's Mysteries

———— *The Question of the Absentee Father* ————

"The reader has the satisfaction of getting a mystery, a romp, and a respectful treatment of a neuroatypical protagonist."

—*Publishers Weekly*

"Fans coast to coast can take pleasure in seeing Copperman's quirky hero."

—*Kirkus Reviews*

———— *The Question of the Felonious Friend* ————

"The investigation is entertaining, but the cleverness of this book is its treatment of the personality disorder, which manages to be funny and at the same time accurate and respectful."

—*Ellery Queen's Mystery Magazine*

"Samuel Hoenig…takes on a real puzzler in Copperman and Cohen's winning third Asperger's mystery."

—*Publishers Weekly*

———— *The Question of the Unfamiliar Husband* ————

"Captivating."

—*Publishers Weekly* (starred review)

"Samuel is a fascinating character … His second adventure will captivate readers."

──────── *The Question of the Missing Head* ────────

A Mystery Scene Best Book of 2014

"[A] delightful and clever mystery."

—*Publishers Weekly*

"Delightfully fresh and witty…Pure heaven."

—*Mystery Scene*

"In this well-crafted story, the Asperger's element … provides a unique point of view on crime-solving, as well as offering a sensitive look at a too-often-misunderstood condition."

—*Booklist*

"Copperman/Cohen succeeds in providing a glimpse not only of the challenges experienced by those with Asperger's, but also of their unique gifts."

—*Ellery Queen's Mystery Magazine*

"Cleverly written and humorous."

—*Crimespree Magazine*

THE QUESTION OF THE

OF THE

DEAD

MISTRESS

THE QUESTION OF THE

DEAD MISTRESS

AN ASPERGER'S MYSTERY

E.J. COPPERMAN

JEFF COHEN

MIDNIGHT INK
WOODBURY, MINNESOTA

FIRST EDITION
First Printing, 2018

Cover design by Shira Atakpu
Cover illustration by James Steinberg/Gerald & Cullen Rapp
Editing by Nicole Nugent

Midnight Ink, an imprint of Llewellyn Worldwide Ltd.

Library of Congress Cataloging-in-Publication Data
Names: Copperman, E. J., author.
Title: The question of the dead mistress / E.J. Copperman.
Description: First edition. | Woodbury, Minnesota : Midnight Ink, [2018] |
    Series: An Asperger's mystery ; #5
Identifiers: LCCN 2018014116 (print) | LCCN 2018015717 (ebook) | ISBN
    9780738755267 (ebook) | ISBN 9780738750613 (alk. paper)
Subjects: | GSAFD: Mystery fiction.
Classification: LCC PS3603.O358 (ebook) | LCC PS3603.O358 Q44 2018 (print) |
    DDC 813/.6—dc23
LC record available at https://lccn.loc.gov/2018014116

Midnight Ink
Llewellyn Worldwide Ltd.
2143 Wooddale Drive
Woodbury, MN 55125-2989
www.midnightinkbooks.com

Printed in the United States of America

For Terri Bischoff.

ACKNOWLEDGMENTS

It's always hard to thank everyone who helped with the creation of a book; inevitably some are omitted not because of a lack of respect but due to a faulty memory (or two). But no book since the printing press has ever gotten to a reader without help from someone other than the author. And that is just as true here as ever.

Samuel Hoenig's journey began with our idea and that's the fact. But it was Terri Bischoff at Midnight Ink who saw something special in Samuel and wanted you to read his thoughts and exploits. There is no higher level of gratitude we could feel. Thank you, Terri.

Great thanks also to Josh Getzler and the team at SKG Agency for getting the book to Terri to begin with and for continuing to believe in us and champion our work throughout the publishing world. We're nowhere without you, Josh.

Thanks to Nicole Nugent for her diligent editing and to Shira Atakpu for the cover design. The cover illustrations by James Steinberg/ Gerald & Cullen Rapp made you look, didn't they? Thanks very much.

We would have nothing to do at all without readers, librarians, booksellers, and reviewers. Thanks to all. We'd name names, but then there would be no room for the book.

It's been a blast bringing Samuel to an unsuspecting world. His growth reflects that of so many we know with ASD or related personality traits. We are proud of all of you and hope you found Samuel's stories entertaining and respectful. Don't ever think the world is against you; they just don't understand yet. Give the neurotypicals a little time and a little patience and they'll discover the wonderful person you are. It's not always easy but it's always worthwhile.

—E.J. Copperman and Jeff Cohen
May 2018

ONE

I RECEIVED AN EMAIL message.

To be more accurate, my business, Questions Answered, received the email message. But since the business's personnel consists entirely of myself and my associate Ms. Washburn, such a communication would undoubtedly arrive where either she or I would discover it. In this case, because our company account was set up before Ms. Washburn joined the firm, it came to me.

I have a question that I desperately need answered, it read. *May I come in for an appointment?*

Since my business is located in a storefront that is part of a strip mall on Stelton Road in Piscataway, New Jersey, and there is no requirement of a prearranged appointment, the message was a trifle baffling to me. I looked over at Ms. Washburn, who was at her desk eight feet to my right in the repurposed pizzeria.

"I have received an email asking if the person can come in for an appointment," I said. "We do not require an appointment to ask a question."

"Is the person a man or a woman?" Ms. Washburn asked.

"The message does not specify."

Ms. Washburn waved a hand, a gesture she has told me is intended to deem the previous statement (or, in this case, question) irrelevant. "Just tell them they don't need an appointment and can come in anytime we're open," she said.

I had believed that should be the proper methodology so I nodded thankfully at Ms. Washburn for confirming my theory. Then I sent a reply to the email that conveyed the information we had discussed. I went back to my previous task, which was determining the reach in millimeters of the average orangutan. A client was interested in such a statistic to surprise his wife, he said. Ms. Washburn was skeptical, and I was also making some inquiries to determine if the man had ulterior motives. So far I had found none.

The email reply came much sooner than I would have expected. It read, *I'm coming now.* Since I had explicitly stated there was no need for advance notice, I found the new message superfluous. I looked briefly at the door to our office in anticipation, but no one entered immediately.

Thirteen minutes later, after I had glanced at the door sixty-seven more times, a woman walked to the doorway of the Questions Answered office. She stopped for a moment, contemplating the hand-drawn sign on poster board in the window (something Ms. Washburn had been suggesting rather forcefully that I have replaced), then shook her head and walked through our entrance. The bells over the door rang and Ms. Washburn looked up.

The woman was in her early forties, I'd guess, although my estimates in such matters have often proven to be inaccurate because I rarely look at an unfamiliar person's face for more than a second. Her manner was somewhat nervous; she looked at Ms. Washburn and then at me as if trying to decide which one of us could answer her question more accurately. Clearly that person was me, but the woman couldn't have known that unless she'd done research into our business.

She walked to the center of the room, almost equidistant between my desk and Ms. Washburn's. "Who should I ask a question?" she said.

I immediately knew she should have said, "To whom should I ask a question?" or "Of whom should I ask a question?" Over a period of years it has been proven to me that such a correction made aloud would simply slow down the conversation and fail to make any change in the speaker's grammar going forward. So I did not make the observation.

"Why don't you ask both of us?" Ms. Washburn said, gesturing toward the chair I keep for clients in front of my desk. Ms. Washburn walked in front of my desk and leaned on it as she continued to stand, smiling at the potential client. "This is Samuel Hoenig and my name is Janet Washburn. Have a seat."

The woman nodded. She sat in the client chair and did not try to use the one I reserve for my mother, an easy chair to better soothe her back and leg issues. I appreciated the fact that our prospective client had not assumed she could sit in the place I keep for Mother despite the fact that Mother had not visited the office in five weeks.

"My name is Virginia," the woman said. "But please call me Ginny."

"Thanks, Ginny," Ms. Washburn said. "Call me Janet."

Virginia glanced in my direction. "May I call you Sam?" she asked.

"No, thank you." Ms. Washburn had taught me to add the *thank you* because she said my answer until that point had sounded "abrupt." I thought it was direct and to the point. "I am Samuel Hoenig. What is your question?"

Virginia's look averted eye contact, something I understand because I do the same thing many times per day. But her motivation was not, as far as I could discern, caused by Asperger's Syndrome or any other autism spectrum disorder. She simply did not want to see our facial reactions when she spoke.

"I think it would be best to give you a little background first," she said. At that point I was tempted to interrupt because it has been my experience that clients want to convey more information than I actually need to answer a question. But Ms. Washburn, probably anticipating my thought process, shook her head negatively in a very subtle gesture. I doubt Virginia noticed at all.

"I have been married to Brett Fontaine for seven years," Virginia began. Already I did not see how the information was relevant, but I waited. "They say men cheat at the seven-year itch, so I guess he was right on time."

"You believe your husband is having an affair?" Ms. Washburn asked.

Virginia's eyes closed, either to hold off tears or conjure them. "I'm not sure that's how you would describe it," she said.

I do not respond well to coyness. It is a tactic that would never occur to me and as someone with Asperger's Syndrome (which technically is no longer a clinical diagnosis but best describes my personality traits), I find it a waste of time. What Virginia was doing was simply meant to prompt a question that did not need to be asked, but Ms. Washburn provided the question anyway. It is invaluable to me to have Ms. Washburn in the office to help me through moments such as these.

"What do you mean?" she asked Virginia.

"Brett is involved with another woman," Virginia answered. "I can tell that from his behavior. But whether or not you would consider it an affair is, well, sort of out there. I think it qualifies as infidelity, but I don't think anyone else would believe me."

I had heard enough. "I'm sorry," I told Virginia. "We are not a detective agency. We answer questions. And we are not equipped or inclined to follow your husband so we can take what you would consider 'incriminating' photographs. I can direct you to a very reputable investigation agency not far from here." I looked to Ms. Washburn, who reached into her pocket for the business card of a firm we recommend under such circumstances.

"No," Virginia said. "I don't need a detective. I need to have a question answered." She seemed quite determined and certain in her assertion. Ms. Washburn took her hand out of her pocket. "It's just that I don't know how to phrase it."

"As simply and directly as possible, please," I advised.

Virginia nodded and for the first time in the conversation looked me directly in the eye, which made me vaguely uncomfortable. "Okay, then," she said. She took a visible breath in and sat up straighter than before. "Mr. Hoenig, is my husband having an affair with his dead girlfriend?"

TWO

"No," I said.

Ms. Washburn turned her head rather abruptly to look at me. Virginia Fontaine did not avert her gaze again. I sat in the chair behind my desk and glanced at the computer screen; it was estimating more orangutan reach probabilities as I watched.

"No?" Virginia repeated. "Do you mean you won't answer my question?"

I did not look back at her because I didn't want to. "I am answering your question," I told her. "No. Your husband is not having an affair with his dead girlfriend."

Ms. Washburn, who knows me better than anyone besides my mother and in some ways better than even her, pursed her lips. "Samuel," she said. I do not process tone of voice very well, but I have known Ms. Washburn for some time. She was admonishing me, but I could not understand what I had done wrong.

"How can you know?" Virginia demanded. "You've never even met my husband and you don't know the details of my situation. Do

6

you just answer questions like that for all your clients and expect them to pay you?"

"I do not expect any payment from you, Ms. Fontaine," I said. "And you may rest assured that any client who walks through that door will get my full attention and an accurate answer to his or her question. In your case the answer was so obvious that it seemed foolish to continue with the interview. No. Your husband is not having an affair with his dead girlfriend."

"I'm going to ask again, Mr. Hoenig," Virginia said. "How can you be so sure?"

"Because it is physically impossible for a living man to have a mutual relationship with a dead person," I said, marveling at the idea that I even had to point out such an obvious fact. "If your husband is being unfaithful, I would assume it is with a living person. But the notion that he might be carrying on an extended affair with a deceased woman is literally impossible to consider."

I fully expected Virginia Fontaine to rise out of the client chair, thank Ms. Washburn and me for our time, and leave. Instead she settled back and folded her arms across her chest, a gesture that I have learned through study is meant to show at least a small degree of defiance or unwillingness to cooperate.

"Mr. Hoenig," she said, "I would appreciate it if you would hear me out. I know how crazy the suggestion sounds and believe me, two months ago I would have thought a person who asked that question was just as crazy as you think I am now."

"I do not believe I am qualified to diagnose any mental illness," I said.

Virginia did not respond to my statement. "Let me tell you how I reached my conclusion, why I'm certain that Brett is in love with a woman from his past who happens to be dead, and if you still think there's no point to your taking on my question, I'll leave and never bother you again. But I think you'll be interested and I think you'll answer this question for me once you hear what I have to say."

Ms. Washburn made a tiny sound in her throat. When she first did so it alarmed me because I thought she was choking or in some way ill. Now I know it is a subtle device meant to attract my attention. I looked in her direction and she nodded, her eyes darting in the direction of Virginia Fontaine. She was suggesting I listen to the prospective client's story. I saw little point in the pursuit but mentally acquiesced to Ms. Washburn's silent plea. She is often, if not always, a better judge of human emotion and social interaction than I am.

"Very well, Ms. Fontaine," I said. "Why do you believe your husband is carrying on with a dead woman, and why do you think such a thing is possible?"

Virginia's eyebrows lowered at my tone, I suppose. It can be an expression of disapproval or contained anger. I have seen the face charts.

"I know what it sounds like," she said. "I'm not crazy." I let that remark go despite having refuted it once already. "I know Brett well. Better than anyone else on this planet, after all this time. And I started picking up signs that he was looking in other places a few months ago. As you would imagine, I assumed he was simply bored with our marriage as men tend to be and would be trying to find someone he could have a fling with."

Ms. Washburn settled more heavily on the front of my desk. "Didn't that bother you?" she asked.

"Of course it did. I didn't feel that kind of boredom. Sure, you live with a person for seven years and you get to know their patterns, in life and in bed. I'm well aware of Brett as a lover and I know what he's good at and what he's not."

I was uncomfortable with the way the conversation was going. I did not like to discuss matters of sexual relations with anyone, least of all a woman I had met less than five minutes earlier. But I reminded myself she was a potential client and wanted me to hear her story despite my having answered her question as soon as it was asked. My strategy became, then, to listen to her increasingly detailed explanation, have her ask the question again, answer it the same way, and then politely usher Ms. Fontaine out of the Questions Answered office. Interrupting would simply prolong the process. I did my best to look attentive and nodded for no particular reason.

Ms. Fontaine seemed to take that as encouragement. "About three months ago I noticed he was less present when we were eating dinner or just watching television. He didn't seem to be part of us anymore, just him. I tried to say something about it, but Brett said he was under stress at work and his mood didn't have anything to do with us."

"What work does your husband do?" Ms. Washburn asked. She had retrieved a client intake form from her desk drawer and was securing it on a clipboard. Apparently Ms. Washburn believed we were actually going to accept Ms. Fontaine as a client.

Virginia answered, "His specialty is in refurbishing existing properties for better use by students and then providing the property with clients." Her tone was flat and rehearsed as if she had recited it many times before.

Ms. Washburn's eyes looked confused. "What does that mean?" she asked.

"Brett works in the real estate business," Virginia repeated. "He buys houses that are run-down, fixes them up, and then rents them to Rutgers students. There isn't nearly enough housing on campus so there are always kids looking for an apartment close to College Avenue especially, but also in Piscataway near the Busch and Livingston campuses." Again there was the impression that Virginia had been carefully schooled in her husband's business affairs and how to describe them.

"Do you work outside the home?" I asked. It didn't really bear any significance on the question being asked, but I felt it was important not to assume that Ms. Fontaine was a woman whose husband was her entire existence. That was increasingly rare according to statistical analyses I had read.

"Yes," Virginia Fontaine said. "I am a researcher for a pharmaceutical company in Piscataway. We live in Highland Park." The Questions Answered office was located in the town of Piscataway, and Highland Park was a small suburb of New Brunswick only three miles from where we were sitting.

But I wanted to conclude this interview and get on with my work. "You were saying that your husband had been acting differently than usual and said it was because of stress at his job," I reminded Virginia.

She nodded, which I found slightly confusing. There was no need to inform me that I had been correct and I had not asked her a question that would require such a response. I made a note on a pad I keep on my desk to ask Ms. Washburn about the gesture when Virginia had left.

"I can't say I stopped thinking about it just because Brett denied anything was going on," she continued. "I mean, what man is going to confess to an affair with something as skimpy as that for evidence? So I did something I'm not very proud of doing. I looked at his phone one day when Brett was in the shower."

Ms. Washburn's left eyebrow lifted, a sign she was a little surprised and possibly disturbed by what Virginia had said. Ms. Washburn was fairly recently divorced from a man who had in fact had more than one affair while they were married. With living women.

"What did you discover?" I asked.

"First I saw a series of text messages with his friend Peter Belson. I think they met when he went to Fairleigh Dickinson in Madison and I knew Peter from years before I married Brett. In fact, Peter is the one who introduced us. These texts didn't seem to be that odd, but they kept talking about Melanie Mason, and Brett had told me about Melanie a long time ago. She was his college girlfriend."

"What were they saying about her?" Ms. Washburn asked. She had no doubt seen similar communications as part of her divorce proceedings, although I knew she had never investigated her ex-husband's personal phone or computer records.

"At first it was real general, just stuff about remember this time or that time. But then Brett started asking Peter if Melanie had been faithful to him when they were together, if Peter knew of anything Melanie had said about him, about Brett, after they broke up. He seemed really worried about it, almost obsessed with what Melanie might have said or felt about him, and they broke up maybe twenty years ago."

"Did he text Melanie?" Ms. Washburn asked.

Virginia looked slightly startled. "No. I thought I made that clear. Melanie is dead. She died in a car crash three years ago."

It was late in the afternoon. If we did not conclude this business swiftly I would be unable to complete the orangutan computations before it would be time to go home for dinner. It was necessary to, as they say in the film business, "cut to the chase."

"So why do you believe your husband is cheating on you with the ghost of his deceased college girlfriend?" I said, perhaps with too insistent a tone, to Virginia.

"Because she started talking to him two months ago," she answered without hesitation.

THREE

Ms. Washburn sat down on the chair I reserve for Mother, knowing full well it was fine as long as Mother didn't arrive, which would have been completely unexpected. Since my father had recently returned to our home, Mother was spending much less time at Questions Answered and as I stated, dinnertime was not far away. Mother would not be dropping by. I think Ms. Washburn's move was a gesture designed to ingratiate her more with Virginia Fontaine, to bring them to the same eye level.

"Melanie Mason spoke to your husband three years after she died?" It was Ms. Washburn's way of clarifying the situation, getting Virginia to explain herself, which I appreciated. Virginia had an irritating habit of saying just enough to elicit a response.

Now she nodded. "Brett doesn't mind if I look at his emails. Sometimes he doesn't check the home account very often and he misses things, so he appreciates my checking in. When I started seeing all the texts about Melanie, I'll admit I was thrown off and I checked for my own purposes. And sure enough, there were emails from Brett to his friend starting just around the time Brett was getting more distant. He said he went to her grave and she talked to him. I also found a Facebook page in Melanie's name that was still active. Brett was one of her friends listed."

I doubted some parts of that story (particularly the idea that her husband was content to have her look through his personal devices and his social media contacts), but I did not challenge Virginia on them. I thought it best to discuss the matters with Ms. Washburn when we were alone. Sometimes I misunderstand certain aspects of social interaction. I was not inclined to embarrass myself now. I still wanted to dismiss Virginia's claims and move on.

"Are you certain the emails you saw were not simply figurative?" I said. "Sometimes people say things they do not mean literally."

"I did some research," Virginia answered. "I do that professionally and I understand online accounts. Brett said he heard her voice. He told at least three of his friends but not me. What does that tell you?"

It occurred to me that with her obvious expertise in research, Virginia Fontaine might very well be able to answer her question as efficiently as Ms. Washburn and I could, but again I restrained myself from saying so. Ms. Washburn has informed me that sending clients away is bad for our business.

"What was the content of the emails and the Facebook messages?" I asked.

"Times, places, dates," Virginia said. "They were clearly setting up times and places to meet. There was no explicit talk about what they'd do when they got there, but I don't really think they were discussing Brett's job."

I assumed that was a sarcastic remark although the concept is not an easy one for a person like me to grasp or recognize. If it had been meant literally, that would undoubtedly come across in the ensuing conversation through context.

"Are you absolutely certain that Melanie Mason is dead?" Ms. Washburn asked.

Virginia regarded her carefully. "There was a funeral, but Brett didn't go. There were obits I looked up online. She died in a crash on Route 22 in Union three years ago. The driver of the other car was investigated for driving under the influence but they determined the accident wasn't his fault. Seems to me if she's not dead, she's gone miles out of her way to make it look like she is."

"Besides the online communication, is there any other evidence you have that your husband is carrying on an affair with Melanie Mason?" I asked. "It would be far too easy for someone living to assume her accounts and get in touch with him that way."

"I followed him last week," Virginia said, once again avoiding eye contact. "I'd seen a Facebook message from Melanie saying they should meet and he made an excuse about an eye doctor appointment and left. He didn't go to the eye doctor. I know because I followed him in my car."

There were sixteen minutes before I would have to leave to have dinner with my parents. "And you saw your husband meet with a dead woman?"

Virginia turned to face me and her expression was defiant. "I saw him meet Melanie Mason on a park bench near the Metuchen train station," she said. "They got into her car and drove away and I lost the nerve to follow them. I saw her."

"And she was alive." That would answer the question as asked. No, her husband was not having an affair with a dead woman. The woman was not dead. I began to calculate the amount of time we'd spend on this question and wonder whether I should reverse my previous decision and charge Virginia Fontaine for this consultation. She had not signed the client intake form.

"No," Virginia said. "The woman I saw was Melanie Mason and Melanie Mason is dead."

"I think the facts would tend to disprove that statement," I told her. "You saw your husband get into a car with a living woman. No matter how close her resemblance to the person you might have seen photographs of in your husband's phone or online, that was not the deceased Melanie Mason."

"I could see right through her," Virginia said. "She was transparent. She was a ghost. She's dead."

"I think you are mistaken or lying," I said.

"I'm not."

Twelve minutes left. There had to be some way I could get this woman to leave soon without being socially inappropriate. "Do you have any evidence that proves what you say?" I asked.

"That is sort of why I'm here," Virginia said. Appearing to have an idea present itself to her, she reached into her rather large purse and extracted a cellular phone quite a bit larger than the one I have. I tapped on my hip pocket to ensure that mine was still where I'd left it. It was. I worry about such things.

"Take a look at this." She pushed on the screen of her cellular phone seven times and swiped across it twice. Then she turned the phone around to allow Ms. Washburn to see. Ms. Washburn looked puzzled. Virginia then turned the screen in my direction.

Eight minutes before it would be necessary to leave. I am very punctual. Ms. Washburn says I am obsessive on the subject.

I found it necessary to stand and walk around my desk to get a better view. Virginia offered to hand me the cellular phone, but I prefer not to touch things if I am not sure they are clean. I had no opportunity to look inside Virginia Fontaine's purse and did not want to risk it.

Upon consideration, the image on the cellular phone's screen was a photograph no doubt taken with the onboard camera. It showed a man, from behind, about to seat himself behind the steering wheel of a current-model Subaru BRZ. The driver's door was open and he was standing inside the door about to step inside. The passenger door was open as well, but there was no one standing next to it or seated in the passenger seat, although the angle of the photograph made it difficult to be certain of that last impression.

"I do not understand," I said. "How is this proof of your claim?"

Virginia Fontaine came close to rolling her eyes but stopped herself. "That's my husband," she said. I did not see how that answered my questions. "I followed him and took this picture when he and Melanie were getting into the car."

"But no one is getting in on the passenger side," Ms. Washburn correctly pointed out.

"Exactly!" Virginia spread her hands to indicate we weren't getting it. "I'm saying I saw her there and she didn't show up in the picture!"

I glanced at Ms. Washburn with no doubt that my eyes were showing my complete confusion. Was this some odd neurotypical behavior that I did not understand? Her expression assured me she was feeling exactly the same way. That can be very comforting to a person like me. At least my emotions were not inappropriate.

"That really doesn't prove much," Ms. Washburn said to Virginia. "What we're seeing is a man getting into a car with both doors open."

"Well, why would the passenger side door be open if nobody was getting in?" Virginia's tone indicated she was on the verge of exasperation. There were four minutes until I would absolutely have to leave this office and I could empathize, something that is not easy for me to do under normal circumstances.

"I have no idea," Ms. Washburn said. She slumped back in Mother's chair.

"Well, that's what I'm talking about!" Virginia put her phone back in her purse and made a sound with her hands that wasn't exactly clapping. She pushed her right hand, down, over her left palm and slapped it to make a noise. I guessed it was meant to be a gesture of triumph, but I could not determine exactly what Virginia had done to merit such a feeling. "The passenger door would never be open if nobody was getting in but you can't see anyone in the picture. So it's a ghost, right?"

Two minutes. "If I say yes, will that answer your question?" I asked. I have been told that sometimes a small "white" lie is preferable to the truth if it hurts no one and accomplishes a goal. My goal was to leave. Now.

Ms. Washburn, understanding my concern, stood up from Mother's chair. She looked at the coat rack we have situated near the unused pizza ovens toward the back of our office space.

"Of course not," Virginia said. Ms. Washburn's mouth flattened out into something almost approximating a straight line and she began to walk toward the coat rack to retrieve our jackets. "If the picture proved Brett is having an affair with Melanie, I wouldn't have come here to begin with."

"Then I do not understand what you are asking," I said. "And I must apologize, but our office hours are—"

Virginia did not let me finish the sentence. "Mr. Hoenig," she said, "will you find definitive proof and answer my question or not? *Is my husband having an affair with a dead woman?*"

There was no time left. Ms. Washburn handed me my jacket and I let it hang on my right forearm. "Fine," I said. "We will take you on and answer your question, but you must fill out your client intake form at home tonight and bring it back here tomorrow." I extended the clipboard holding the form, which Ms. Washburn had left on my desk. "Is that acceptable?"

"Yes," Virginia Fontaine said. "Oh, Mr. Hoenig. I'm so grateful that—"

It was my turn to interrupt her sentence. "I'm sorry, but our office is now closed. You must leave."

Without another word Virginia Fontaine turned and left the office. Ms. Washburn and I were not far behind her in our departure.

On the way out Ms. Washburn looked at me. "Maybe we'll get lucky and she won't come back."

"Then we will be without one clipboard."

FOUR

"I GET WHY YOU caved in, but I still think taking this question is a mistake."

Ms. Washburn was driving, so she knew I was uncomfortable with a prolonged conversation possibly diverting her attention. But she was watching the road intently and her hands were properly positioned on the steering wheel. I had spoken to Ms. Washburn while she drove on a few previous occasions and we had never been involved in an accident. I did not object now.

"I don't believe I 'caved in,' and I agree that this question is not something we should investigate. But the fact is we can answer it quickly because there is no such thing as a ghost, which makes the question moot as soon as it is asked. The difficult part will be convincing Virginia Fontaine to accept the factual answer."

Ms. Washburn was oddly quiet for a long moment, which I attributed to her concentrating on the drive. We were less than a mile from my home. But when she spoke again it was with a strange timbre in her voice. "So you don't think there are ghosts?"

The question surprised me. It never had occurred to me the issue was at all unsettled. I had very little time to process Ms. Washburn's point and I knew she expected a response from me. It was very concerning indeed since we were at a new and uncharted place in our personal relationship.

Ms. Washburn had kissed me, which I found unexpectedly pleasing but somewhat unsettling, only a few months before. And I had reciprocated by asking her if we could kiss again less than one month earlier. We were now at a stage where we did kiss on a fairly regular basis but we had not defined our connection. I did not know if we were "dating" or if we simply expressed a type of physical affection that had no larger context.

Writing the previous paragraph was extremely difficult for me. I sincerely hope anyone who reads it will not be offended or disgusted by its contents. It is a part of the overall story being told or I would have omitted the subject entirely.

As it was, I did not know exactly how to respond to Ms. Washburn's question except to answer truthfully. "There is absolutely no evidence that people have some presence in the world after they die," I said. "Without empirical evidence there is no reason to believe such things happen, and there have been countless studies on the subject. Not one has managed to find proof of the existence of, as people call them, ghosts."

She was pulling the car into the driveway of my home when Ms. Washburn said, "I saw a ghost once."

That was a surprising statement and again I fumbled for a way to respond. We both got out of the car, since Ms. Washburn would be joining my parents and myself for dinner that night as had been previously arranged. That gave me a little time to formulate an answer to her claim. We walked toward the front door after I looked in the box on the front porch and found a few unremarkable pieces of mail.

"I believe it might have been something else," I suggested.

"I don't think so," Ms. Washburn said as I opened the front door. I could not read her tone, and that was unusual.

Before I could say anything else, my mother spotted us from the kitchen door and headed in our direction. Her surgically replaced knee had fully healed and her gait was a bit slower than it had been, but smoother and she was clearly not in pain as she had been. "Why look who it is," she said as she approached.

That too was somewhat disconcerting. "Were you expecting someone other than Ms. Washburn and myself?" I asked Mother. She had embraced Ms. Washburn, who smiled when she saw Mother.

"It's an expression, Samuel," Ms. Washburn said. Mother released the embrace, did not offer one to me because she knew I preferred to limit physical contact, and asked for Ms. Washburn's jacket, which Mother quickly hung in the front closet. I took off my own jacket and hung it on a coat rack near the front door.

"Of course we were expecting you," Mother said. "You show up here every day at exactly the right time."

"It's always good to see you, Vivian," Ms. Washburn said. "Samuel and I were just discussing ghosts."

I had not expected Ms. Washburn to continue the conversation with my mother, and my face must have betrayed my surprise and discomfort. "Ghosts!" Mother said. "How interesting! Why did that happen to come up?"

My father, Reuben Hoenig, appeared at the entrance to our living room having come from the den. He looked at Ms. Washburn and myself and grinned. "Look who's here," he said. I had discovered in the weeks since my father had reinserted himself into our family after many years that he and my mother tended to react to stimuli in very similar ways. They used the same expressions and independently offered the same thoughts with rather alarming frequency.

This time I understood that Reuben had not anticipated seeing anyone other than Ms. Washburn and me. I nodded hello to him. My father had left my mother and me to seek financial security when I was four and had returned only recently. I was still somewhat wary of him and had told Dr. Mancuso, whom I see once a week, that I was not entirely certain Reuben would stay with my mother for any extended period of time. Dr. Mancuso had suggested that nothing is certain in life, which did not in any way make me feel better.

"It seems Janet and Samuel were talking about ghosts," Mother informed him.

"Really!" My father seemed to find the subject amusing if I was reading his expression properly. "Seen any lately?"

I thought, given Ms. Washburn's revelation of a few minutes before, that my father's question was somewhat insensitive. Still, I understood his skepticism since there is no such thing as a ghost. I decided against admonishing him for his remark and said nothing.

"Come in to dinner," Mother said. She has a talent for defusing difficult situations, which I assume she cultivated while raising a child with a personality that did not conform to the accepted societal norms.

When Ms. Washburn is joining us for dinner, which had been more frequent an event, Mother sets the dining room table or asks Reuben to do so. That was the case this evening.

"I thought I'd make something a little bit different tonight," Mother said, and a small knot of anxiety formed in my stomach. People like me do not welcome change and I have an especially sensitive spot where food is concerned. I am not fond of changes in the menu, particularly at home. I consider our house a sanctuary from the rest of the world. "Don't worry, Samuel. There will be chicken and pasta for you." Mother, I realized, would not make a new dish without giving me significant time to process the information before the meal.

22

My stomach returned to its normal state. And it was hungry.

Mother had brought out a dish she called Chicken Paprikash, which seemed to please Ms. Washburn and Reuben. A separate platter with the baked chicken and plain rotini pasta to which I am accustomed was placed near my table setting. Normally I would be somewhat embarrassed by the special treatment, but both Ms. Washburn and Mother are close enough to me to understand my seeming eccentricities. Reuben's opinion did not yet matter to me. I was still evaluating him.

Meeting my father for the first time in my memory had not been an emotional experience. The circumstances required some quick action and his demeanor at the time was affected by medication he was being forced to take. Since then we had not experienced much time alone, largely because I had not sought my father out. I preferred to keep my routine as it was, and the somewhat baffling nature of my relationship with Ms. Washburn was definitely a higher priority.

The conversation tonight veered away from ghosts for much of the dinner. In fact, it was seventeen minutes before the subject was broached again, this time by my mother, the person I would have least expected would find it interesting.

"I assume this talk of ghosts has something to do with a question you've been asked, Samuel," she said. "What's the story behind it?" Mother does like to keep current on the doings at Questions Answered. It had been her idea I open the business and she had provided a small loan (since repaid) to secure our storefront on Stelton Road in Piscataway.

I was not eager to delve into the realm of the supernatural so I hesitated. Ms. Washburn seemed less reluctant. "A woman came to the office and asked Samuel whether her husband is having an affair with a dead woman he dated in college," she explained. "Samuel doesn't want to take her question, and I don't blame him because I don't think he can research it objectively."

Mother's eyes widened and her mouth dropped open. She had never heard Ms. Washburn or anyone else suggest I could not be trusted to answer a question because my mind was already made up on the issue. Frankly, I was somewhat shocked myself.

"I am being objective," I told Ms. Washburn. "There is no empirical evidence that would begin to confirm the existence of ghosts or any other manifestation of an afterlife spirit. I would be taking Ms. Fontaine's money to answer a question that she could easily answer if she were being honest with herself."

Ms. Washburn did not look the least bit angry when she looked at me, which was reassuring. It is true that I could not reliably read her expression, but it was not one of irritation. "I have seen a ghost, Samuel. I am the empirical evidence."

Before I could dispute her claim with the point that she was at best anecdotal evidence, Mother asked, "What did you see, Janet?"

Ms. Washburn faced her. I noticed Reuben at the other end of the table looking at Ms Washburn with particular interest. "It was when I was a teenager in Leonia, Vivian. A bunch of my friends and I were walking through a cemetery late at night. I stopped at one of the gravestones to read it. The woman who had died had the same birthday as I do. She died on that date, too, exactly a hundred years before I was born."

"That is an impressive coincidence," I began.

But Ms. Washburn stopped me before I could explain that it did not prove anything about ghosts. "While I stood there I saw her rise up out of the grave and look at me. She smiled, and then she walked off in the other direction. I wasn't even scared, just surprised. She seemed like such a nice woman."

"What did she look like?" Reuben asked her. He had put his hands together and was holding them in front of his mouth. "Could you see through her?"

Ms. Washburn considered the question and shook her head. "Not really. It was more like she was floating, but almost solid. Like she had looked when she was alive, I guess."

"You guess?" Reuben seemed not to believe Ms. Washburn. "You never looked up a picture of her from when she was alive?"

"It never occurred to me," Ms. Washburn answered. "We didn't have internet access when I was in high school."

Mother shook her head, prompting Reuben to sit back in his chair and look admonished. It was interesting that she could do so much with such a small gesture. "Janet dear," she said. "Are you sure that's what you saw?"

"Absolutely," Ms. Washburn said without hesitation.

I realized Ms. Washburn had never told me very much about her past before she married the man from whom she was now divorced. "Ms. Washburn," I said, "the night you and your friends were in the cemetery. Why were you there?"

"Why?" she said. "I don't understand, Samuel."

"Most people do not socialize in a burial ground. What was the purpose of the visit?"

"We were kids. We thought it would be spooky and fun. I don't see what difference it makes to what I saw." Ms. Washburn's eyes were searching mine, but I could not determine what she was trying to find.

"Was alcohol involved in the evening?" I asked.

The eyes narrowed. "Are you prosecuting me, Samuel?" Ms. Washburn said.

I had not expected the question so I took a moment to respond. "I am not an attorney, Ms. Washburn. You know that."

"You sound like one."

I considered kissing Ms. Washburn to better reassure her of my affection, but my parents were in the room and I was not comfortable with the idea of doing so in front of others. Instead I said softly, "It was not my intention. I simply wanted to determine if there were factors that might have led to you having this hallucination."

Ms. Washburn sighed, but before she could answer me Reuben decided to insert himself into the conversation. "Just because she saw a ghost doesn't mean she was drunk, Samuel," he said. "She might have been on drugs. Were you using, Janet?" Sometimes my father exhibits signs that my Asperger's Syndrome might originate genetically on his side of my family.

This time Ms. Washburn sputtered. She faced Reuben. "*Using*?"

"Don't be silly, Reuben," my mother said. "Shall we clear the table?"

But Ms. Washburn was not to be deterred and neither was I. She turned toward me. "You think I was drunk? You think I don't know what I saw?"

"I believe that there must be an alternative explanation for what you saw," I said. "I don't deny for a moment that you saw it."

Ms. Washburn is a remarkably patient and understanding woman. She knew from having observed me over an extended period of time and under diverse circumstances that I was not trying to make her feel badly about herself or diminish her in my estimation. She knew I was not suggesting she was a bad person. But I was not accepting her account of the night in question at face value and that made her feel, if I can recall the social skills training, isolated and unaccepted. Neither of those things was true but human emotions do not always take facts into account as much as they should.

"I get where you're coming from, Samuel," Ms. Washburn said. "But it still hurts."

"I am only trying to confirm the facts," I told her with what I hoped was a gentle tone. "I am not passing judgment on you."

She lowered her head a bit. "We had been drinking," she said. Then she raised her head again to look me directly in the eye, something that unnerves me a bit even when Ms. Washburn does it. "But that doesn't change what I saw. I wasn't that drunk."

Mother stood, her surgically replaced knee slowing her down but not making her grimace as the biological one had before she'd submitted to a replacement. "Help me clear the table," she said to no one in particular. I stood to help her as is my habit. Ms. Washburn did not stand and that was odd; she is usually the first to help, often telling Mother not to bother.

"You don't believe me," she said quietly.

"I do believe you saw something," I answered as I picked up dishes very carefully to avoid touching any uneaten food. "I do not agree with your interpretation. There are no ghosts, so clearly what you saw was something else."

I took a few steps toward the kitchen door but Ms. Washburn's words stopped me. "Just like Virginia Fontaine," she said. "What are you going to tell that poor woman when she comes back tomorrow expecting you to help her?"

Reuben Hoenig stood up and removed some of the smaller items—saltshaker, napkin holder—from the table. My father assists in tasks around the house but does not volunteer for anything very taxing. He had been forcibly given prescription drugs for a prolonged period of time and was still not fully recovered physically or mentally. I had suggested he see Dr. Mancuso and he was considering the suggestion.

"Samuel should be honest," he said, grunting a little as he moved. "He can't answer the question if he doesn't believe in the premise of the question. She needs to find someone else who can."

"No one else is in the business of answering questions," Mother pointed out.

I brought the dishes I had collected into the kitchen and laid them into the sink, but I was thinking as I went. My father had a valid point, but so did Mother. Without Questions Answered, there was almost nowhere for Ms. Fontaine to turn for help, despite my belief that her problem was not one I could help her solve. I do not solve problems and I am not a psychologist. I answer questions.

On the way back into the dining room, where I saw that Ms. Washburn had stood and was picking up drinking glasses and utensils, I realized there was one more option for Ms. Fontaine that had not been previously considered.

"I know what we should do about Virginia Fontaine's question," I told Ms. Washburn.

"You've already decided," she countered. "You're going to send her away and let her figure it out for herself."

"No," I said. "I think we should tell her we will accept her question."

I heard Mother walk through the kitchen door behind me. She stopped at the threshold and did not continue into the room. I did not turn to look at her face so I had no idea what she might have been thinking.

"You can't do that," Ms. Washburn said. She walked very close to me to get a clear path into the kitchen and it distracted me for a moment. "You don't believe her."

"But you do."

Ms. Washburn looked at me with questions in her eyes. That is a metaphor.

"I don't see how that makes a difference," she said.

"I do," Mother said from behind me. "Samuel is saying you should answer the question on your own."

Ms. Washburn looked astonished.

FIVE

"Is this a good idea?"

Ms. Washburn was sitting at her desk in the Questions Answered office and looking at me. But the question now had come from Virginia Fontaine, who sat in the client chair we had moved to the front of Ms. Washburn's desk. And Virginia was asking me, not my associate, if our plan to have Ms. Washburn work alone on the question was legitimate.

"It is the most logical solution," I said. "Ms. Washburn is an experienced researcher and has worked with me for some time. She knows the methods we use and has often been instrumental in answering the question when I was stopped in my tracks." That last sentence was possibly an exaggeration but was not untrue. "I trust her implicitly and believe that under your circumstances she will do a better and more complete job in answering your question than I would." That was entirely honest and true.

I think Ms. Washburn might have wiped a tear from the eye faced away from Virginia Fontaine.

The client looked at me, then at Ms. Washburn, then back at me. "I thought she was your assistant."

29

"No. Ms. Washburn is an associate here at Questions Answered and completely qualified to answer your question. Since I am not a believer in the existence of what you would call ghosts, I am not qualified to answer your question. Ms. Washburn does not share my belief." I did not mention that I did not consider my stance a belief but a fact. There was no utility in raising that issue again. The two women would disagree with me and we would be back where we were before I assigned the question to Ms. Washburn.

For a moment I thought Ms. Fontaine might balk, feeling she had been "cheated" by not having the proprietor of the business serve her directly. But she nodded at Ms. Washburn and said, "That seems reasonable. What's our first step?"

I knew that I should focus my attention on my own work. I had given Ms. Washburn the assignment and she had, after some initial and I thought unfounded reluctance, accepted it. It was now her responsibility and not my own. But I was curious as to how she intended to attack the question because I had no ideas at all in that area. So I was looking at my own computer display to reassure Ms. Washburn she was not under scrutiny, but I will admit that I was listening to the exchange between my associate and our new client.

"The first thing is for me to look over your intake form because that will have information on it that might help me formulate a plan," Ms. Washburn began. "Thank you for getting it back to us so promptly." It was four in the afternoon, which I did not consider prompt, but I had determined not to intervene in any way while Ms. Washburn ran her operation.

"Not at all a problem," Virginia said. "I was happy to do it." That seemed unlikely but again, there was no reason for me to mention that.

Ms. Washburn scanned the form, one she had seen many times before. She knew where to look for pertinent information, looking past the cursory data like address and contact information. There would be time enough to enter that into our system later. She stopped at the third page, as I would have predicted she would.

"You've been married for seven years but this was not your first marriage," Ms. Washburn noted from the form.

"That's right. I didn't think it was relevant but I was married briefly when I was much younger." I glanced briefly at Virginia, who was not looking away. "My first husband, William, died very suddenly and very young."

"I'm sorry to hear that," Ms. Washburn said. I did not see why she would express regret, as she could not have had any role in the death of Virginia's first husband. "You don't say on here how he died." I have discovered that sometimes a question is phrased in the form of a statement, which took me a great deal of time to recognize. I still do not understand it.

"It was an accident," she said. "We were living in New Brunswick. He was on our fire escape and fell off. We lived on the third floor."

"Oh my!" Ms. Washburn said. That is another expression I have never fully grasped. Oh, her *what*? That question is not answerable in my experience. "That must have been horrible for you!" It was considerably worse for her husband, I would think, but surely there was some emotional pain from the experience. "Were you there when it happened?"

"No. I was at work. The police called me. A lot of people saw him fall so the cops were there very soon."

Any number of questions suggested themselves. Why was her first husband not working when she was at her office? What was he doing on the fire escape? Had there been any suggestion of foul play?

"How long was it before you got married again?" Ms. Washburn asked. Not my first impulse but a perfectly legitimate line of inquiry.

"It was six years," Virginia answered. "I met Brett at a farmers' market in Metuchen and we just struck up a conversation. He asked me out and I would normally have turned him down, but he seemed so genuine and kind that my defenses were down. We were married only nine months later."

Ms. Washburn nodded and wrote something on the form. "And there's never been any hint before that he might be cheating on you?"

Given that Virginia Fontaine had come to Questions Answered to determine whether her husband was having an affair with a dead ex-girlfriend, her shocked facial expression was something of a surprise. "Never!" she said a little too loudly. I wondered if she was that upset by the suggestion or, to paraphrase Shakespeare, protesting too much. If Ms. Washburn were to ask me later, I would offer the latter idea as more likely. "There was never even a suggestion!" She sounded weirdly offended.

Ms. Washburn wisely redirected her questioning, keeping her head down and giving a nod. "Okay. Then we'll focus on this incident alone. Before all this came up, had you heard your husband mention Melanie Mason before?" She looked up to gauge Virginia's reaction, which was a more calm and businesslike one than to the previous question.

"Yes. Of course he'd told me about her. They dated in college, broke up just before he graduated and then got back together briefly a year or so later. That was probably around the same time I got married to William."

"And what was William's last name?" Ms. Washburn asked.

"Why?"

Ms. Washburn, I could tell, was trying not to register any emotion but she did cock an eyebrow at the unexpected response. "Because I need to have all the information if I am to research your question successfully." She had heard me say precisely those words to many of our clients. For some reason people walk into our offices and ask a question but don't seem to think we need any further data to help answer it. It is very odd, and something I consider a neurotypical behavior.

Virginia Fontaine seemed to accept the answer without liking it, if I had accurately interpreted the look in her eyes. "William Klein. He was an IT technician with a transit company based in New Brunswick."

Ms. Washburn wrote the information down, got the name of the companies for whom Virginia and both her husbands had worked and then looked her client in the eyes. "Do you think Brett has been in love with Melanie all these years?" she asked.

Virginia did not hold the eye contact, indicating the question was a painful one. "I don't know," she answered after a moment. "I guess it's not the kind of thing you think about after someone dies. I know it's not a consideration when I think about William. He's dead. There really isn't a workable path to having a future with him so I moved on. Brett is my husband now and I love him."

"How did your husband—Brett—manage to find and contact Melanie?" Ms. Washburn asked. It was a question I would not have considered because I do not believe such a thing is possible so it is useless to explore such avenues. I had made the correct decision in assigning Ms. Washburn this question.

"I have no idea. I figured that would be your problem."

Ms. Washburn took a moment, pretending to be writing on her clipboard while I knew she was evaluating the meeting and deciding what would come next. I'm sure Virginia did not see the hesitation, which did not last more than two seconds.

"I think the most direct course of action right now is to follow your husband," Ms. Washburn told her client. "If he is somehow cheating on you, with his dead girlfriend or anyone else, we'll find out soon enough."

"There's no one he would consider doing this with except Melanie," Virginia insisted.

"All right, but until we know for sure we need to have proof of everything. I understand that as a wife you know your husband better than anyone, but in our area we need to make sure there are absolutely no possibilities we're overlooking." Ms. Washburn was explaining the Questions Answered method as well if not better than I could. "My question is: If he is involved with anyone other than Melanie, do you want to know?"

It would never have occurred to me to ask the question. If there is a truth and it affects one's life directly, why would it ever be an option to purposely ignore it?

"You're not going to find that," Virginia reiterated.

"I understand. But hypothetically, if we did, do you want to be told?"

"No."

Again Ms. Washburn nodded in some kind of understanding I did not comprehend. "Okay. We'll start with following Brett and report back to you if he's somehow seeing a ghost. But how can you be sure he's involved with her physically? Is that even possible?"

Virginia fixed a cold stare on Ms. Washburn that approximated that of some villains in Hollywood films. "It doesn't matter if they're having sex," she said. "What matters is if he loves her more than he loves me."

"I'm not sure we can quantify that for you," Ms. Washburn said.

"You don't have to. Report back what he does and I'll decide."

I believe Ms. Washburn was not comfortable with that response, but she did not contest it as I would have. Interactions between and among women should not be different than those involving men, but my experience has been that they are. I do not try to understand such things when it is not directly involved with my own work. This question was Ms. Washburn's responsibility.

"One last question, Ginny," Ms. Washburn said after a pause.

"Yes?"

"What is your favorite Beatles song?"

I could not have been more proud. Ms. Washburn was using a tactic I have often employed in answering questions. An answer to that question can help interpret the subject's personality and state of mind. I was not certain Ms. Washburn would use it since the question goes to a special interest of mine, the music of the Beatles.

"Excuse me?" People often find the Beatles question unexpected and need extra time to organize their thoughts. Ms. Washburn knew it was not necessary to repeat it and waited a moment.

"Please," she said. That is a way to get the other person to focus and to impress upon her that you are sincere in your request.

In this case, it worked as intended. " 'Drive My Car,' " she said.

I immediately analyzed Virginia's response. *Sees other people as staff. Probably a liar.*

Ms. Washburn wrote the information on her pad. "Thank you," she said. "Now I'll get to work on your question. I will call you whenever progress is being made, so there's no need to check with me unless there's some new piece of information you might think of that could help with answering your question." She looked toward the door, but Virginia did not get up from the client chair.

"That's it?" she asked.

Ms. Washburn, understandably, looked puzzled. "Yes," she said after recovering with a smile. "We'll get in touch with updates as soon as we have anything to tell you, I promise. We don't want to keep calling and say there isn't any news yet. You understand."

It's always a little risky, I have found, to assume that another person understands. I often do not understand when others clearly believe I should.

"I understand, but I do not approve," Virginia Fontaine said. "How do I know what you'll be doing?"

"Because I just explained to you what I'll be doing," Ms. Washburn said slowly. "If the plans change, I'll be sure to let you know."

Virginia sat up straighter and shook her head. "I want to go with you," she said.

I'm sure Ms. Washburn was as stunned as I was but she did not register her emotion facially, which was wise and impressive. I find Ms. Washburn more impressive every day. "Why would you want to do that?" she asked.

"Because I need to be able to verify your actions," Virginia responded.

Ms. Washburn did exactly what I would do under those circumstances. She removed the client intake form from her clipboard and held it out to Virginia to take. "If those are your terms, I'm afraid we can't help you." I could hear the regret in Ms. Washburn's voice; this had been her first opportunity to handle a question on her own and she was being forced to refuse it.

But Virginia did not accept the form. "Are you going to be using tactics you prefer I don't see?" she asked.

Ms. Washburn did not withdraw the form. "Ms. Fontaine," she began.

"Ginny, please."

"*Ms. Fontaine.*" The stress was evident in Ms. Washburn's voice. "We operate Questions Answered on a very simple basis—you ask the question and we answer it as accurately and completely as possible. It's a service business relying almost entirely on trust. If you don't trust me well enough to let me research and answer your question for you, there is no point to our continuing to discuss this matter. I am not going to invite you along on surveillance of your own husband, particularly if you don't want to be told what might be pertinent information. Quite frankly, if you want to be there when we follow your husband, follow him yourself. Now are you going to trust me or not?" She continued to hold the form out for Virginia to take with her.

Virginia held up her hands, palms forward, as if surrendering to someone holding a gun and pointing it at her. "I give up," she said. "It was just a suggestion."

What she'd said had not at all sounded like a suggestion, but Ms. Washburn was not about to contest the point. She put the intake form back onto her clipboard and resumed the welcoming smile she had affected for most of the conversation.

"Great," she said, as if Virginia had suggested they have lunch together at some later date. People often say such things and then fail to follow through on the appointment being discussed; it is a little confusing. "Go home and just go through your normal routine. I assure you we'll get in touch immediately when there's something to tell you."

Virginia left without further protest and I actually did resume my research on the question of the orangutan. But Ms. Washburn said, "Samuel," and I faced her. She was sitting at her desk but not looking at her computer screen. Instead she was looking rather deeply into my face, something I usually find extremely uncomfortable but welcome when Ms. Washburn is the other person. For a moment I thought she might walk over and kiss me again, which would not be at all unwelcome.

But she did not move. "Yes?" I said.

"How do you think I did?"

I could have protested and said I had not been listening but Ms. Washburn knew me too well.

"I think you did exactly as I would have done," I said. "I am very impressed but not at all surprised."

Ms. Washburn smiled. "Thank you," she said.

Then she came over and kissed me. We had to agree later that we should never kiss in the Questions Answered office again. It could be seen as unprofessional.

SIX

I DID NOT ACCOMPANY Ms. Washburn when she followed Brett Fontaine the next day. In fact, Ms. Washburn insisted on being at the Fontaine home very early in the morning and did not come to the Questions Answered office at all that day. My friend Mike the taxicab driver was available and he drove me to the office at eight forty-five that morning.

I do have an operative driver's license. I choose not to use it except when absolutely necessary. The last time had been when we had recovered Reuben in Los Angeles, and that experience had not made driving any more attractive to me than it had been previously.

That day was spent working on a new question, one that involved the amount of time it might take to circle the globe without flying in an airplane or helicopter. The answer would require a great deal of simple research and even more arithmetic.

I was, therefore, working on a complex series of computations involving steamship departure schedules and the wind speed in Madagascar in January when my cellular telephone rang. Ms. Washburn had been suggesting fairly frequently that I customize the ring tones on my device to better identify certain callers with whom I communicate frequently, like herself, but since the only others are my mother and Mike the taxicab driver, I have not seen any potential efficiency in doing so and have refrained.

The current call was from Reuben Hoenig. I had given him the number for my cellular phone while we were in Los Angeles in the hopes he would call then, but he did not for reasons that became evident before we left. Now I had to decide whether to accept his call and I found myself wondering why I hesitated to do so. It was complicated and emotionally charged, and probably something I should be discussing with Dr. Mancuso. There was no time to do that before deciding about the call from Reuben. The easy thing to do would be to ignore it, but in the moment I felt that would be cowardly so I hit the accept button.

"Samuel!" My father sounded as if it were a surprise that he had called me. I did not understand his tone and had not known him very long. "What are you doing for lunch?"

I did not know how to answer his question. "All I am doing for lunch is to come home and eat with you and Mother, like I do every day," I finally said. His asking was odd on the surface, but I was sure Reuben had some secondary reason for asking, or an alternative plan he had not yet introduced into the conversation.

"Well, suppose I come over and pick you up and the two of us go somewhere to have a sandwich and talk," he said. That was clearly the alternative plan I'd anticipated.

"Why would we not talk if I came home for lunch?" I asked. It wasn't as if we sat and ate in silence very often. It had only happened once or twice since Reuben had re-entered the house.

"I want to get to know you better," he answered. "Sometimes it's easier to do that when it's just us two guys." He meant he did not wish to include Mother in whatever conversation he had planned. I considered that rude.

"With whom will Mother have lunch if we are not there?" I said.

"Believe it or not, Sam…uel, your mom doesn't mind having lunch by herself every once in a while." Reuben had called me *Sam* before he left when I was four and had undoubtedly been thinking of me with that nickname all the years he'd been a mysterious presence in my mother's life from various places in the United States. He was still not comfortable with my name as I use it and hesitates when he says it. I am not sure if the momentary pause is intentional or not and Dr. Mancuso has told me it doesn't matter. What does matter, he says, is whether I *believe* Reuben is trying to co-opt my name. Dr. Mancuso tends to say things like that. I usually have to ruminate on them for weeks before I can decipher their meanings.

"I have lunch with Mother every day," I reminded him. The order of things and their predictability is more important to those of us identified as on the autism spectrum than it is to neurotypicals. Doing something other than what I am accustomed to doing on a daily basis is upsetting and would normally require a period of days to anticipate before I could accept it without protest.

"I know, and I'm aware that you don't like to change the way you do things." That was an inaccurate interpretation of the situation but I understood that Reuben was trying to comprehend. "But I promise we can go anywhere you like and order any food you want. I just want to talk to my son alone for a little while. That's fair, isn't it?"

It occurred to me that it would have been more fair if Reuben had mentioned this desire, for example, a week earlier and set a specific time and date for our father/son meeting but he clearly had a rather inadequate grasp of the way my mind works. In such cases, Mother says, it sometimes helps to be a little more flexible than usual. I do not like doing so and Mother knows it, but I have found her judgment and Ms. Washburn's to be impeccable in these circumstances.

"Very well," I said to Reuben. "We will go to the Applebee's restaurant on Centennial Avenue in Piscataway." I had been there a number of times before and found the fare to be absolutely predictable.

"Great." Reuben was apparently given to hyperbole. "I'll be there to pick you up at noon."

That left approximately sixty-three minutes before he would arrive. It was past my time to exercise, which I do every twenty minutes while working at Questions Answered. This allows for the proper number of calories to be burned at an efficient rate and keeps my cardiovascular system healthy. I stood and began to walk the perimeter of the office, raising my hands over my head and increasing my speed as I progressed. I would make thirteen such circuits and then allow myself to purchase a bottle of spring water from the vending machine we keep in the far corner.

While I walked I tried to imagine what Reuben might want to discuss. Having an idea of the topic before the conversation began would be one way to avoid surprises, which is always a desirable goal in my mind. But never having been a father who had abandoned his family for twenty-eight years, it was difficult to project.

Reuben arrived three minutes earlier than he had suggested. This was better than arriving three minutes late but was still not the time I had anticipated. I was in the midst of determining exactly how fast the Venice Simplon-Orient-Express might be expected to travel through a particularly mountainous region of Romania when the bells left by the pizzeria owners rang and Reuben arrived.

He was dressed somewhat less casually than I had become accustomed to seeing. He had not worn a necktie but he was dressed in what was clearly a business suit and a white shirt with a collar and long sleeves.

"Do you have another appointment after our lunch?" I asked him.

"No. Why?" Reuben walked toward my desk and for reasons I cannot identify I felt the need to shut down the screen with my research on it and activate my screensaver.

"You are wearing a suit," I pointed out.

"This is for us," he said, standing more straight in a proud pose no doubt meant to accentuate the clothing. "For *you.*"

It occurred to me that I was three inches taller than Reuben and approximately fifteen pounds heavier so I would not fit into the suit he was wearing. He certainly must have known that. Then I realized he meant he had worn the suit in order to somehow impress me. That seemed odd.

"I don't understand," I said. It seemed the only response that could not offend Reuben.

He waved a hand lightly. "Don't worry about it." I had not been worried about it but chose not to point that out.

I stood and walked to the door, bypassing Reuben, who held his arms out as if to embrace me. That sort of contact, particularly involving someone I know as little as I know him, is not appealing to me and I avoid it whenever possible. I did not note his facial expression as I walked.

It was a six-minute drive to the Applebee's restaurant and during the trip I said very little. Reuben went on about his search for employment. He was adept at some aspects of chemistry and technology in which I have little expertise and was attempting to market himself both to local businesses, chiefly Johnson & Johnson, and to Rutgers University, which employs thousands of people in the area.

I will confess that I was not paying close attention to Reuben's tale. I was instead wondering how Ms. Washburn was progressing with the surveillance of Brett Fontaine. She had not checked in at all with me. I considered making that a requirement for work outside the Questions Answered office in the future. But as Ms. Washburn's employer, I felt it best to allow her freedom on her first independent work. As the man who kissed Ms. Washburn on a regular basis, the emotion was somewhat more complicated.

Once seated at the Applebee's we scanned the menus offered to us by Nelson, the young man who was assigned to our table. I knew the offerings on the menu by heart but Reuben requested extra time to consider them so Nelson smiled, nodded, and walked away. The added wait would no doubt make me later in returning to my office than I would have wanted, but the fact was I would have preferred to have lunch at the house with my mother as I usually did.

After some consideration and another visit from Nelson we had ordered our meals and received beverages, which in my case was a glass of water and in Reuben's a beer. I wondered if drinking during the day was a standard routine for him. I would have to ask my mother when I saw her.

"You're probably wondering why I insisted on having this lunch," Reuben said once we were alone again.

I assumed he was having the lunch he ordered because that was the food he most desired from the available choices at the moment. "It had not occurred to me to ask," I said.

"I wanted to talk to you because I think you resent me," Reuben said. So his point had been about making the appointment for to-day's lunch and not the selection of meal itself. But I did not have time to respond before he continued talking. "I don't blame you. I know you were a little boy when I left and you grew up without a fa-ther. You're a full-grown man now and you have a business and a girl-friend, and I think that's great. But I wanted to see if there was a way we could maybe get beyond what happened in the past and start fresh. So I decided to talk to you alone." He took a long drink from his beer as if to fortify himself and then looked expectantly—I thought—into my face.

"I am not sure what sort of response you are expecting," I said. This kind of conversation was something I usually had with Dr. Mancuso, and it was always about people who were not in the room. If I ever had issues with Dr. Mancuso, I'm not certain who might be the right person to share them with. Luckily I had no issues with Dr. Mancuso. But I was somewhat irritated by Reuben's characterization of Ms. Washburn as my "girlfriend."

"An honest one," Reuben answered. "You don't have to hold back with me. No matter how long I was away, I am your father."

"I have no difficulty being honest," I assured him. "I don't know what question is being asked."

"I'm asking you if we can turn the page and start dealing with each other as father and son," Reuben said. "I need to know what it is you expect of me so I can try to give it to you."

The issues he raised were so vague and general that I had no idea how to answer. "I expect nothing of you," I told him. "I have never been in a position to expect anything of you and I don't know you well enough to predict your behavior."

Reuben took a moment to absorb that while a young woman, not Nelson, brought our orders. Mine was exactly as I'd expected and so required no further communication with the waitstaff. Reuben did not really look at his lunch at all because he seemed to be trying to decipher something I had said and was looking very carefully at me. That prompted me to look very closely at my six-ounce USDA sirloin steak, medium well.

Once the young woman, who wore no nametag, had left our table, Reuben coughed in a somewhat theatrical fashion, presumably as a way of restarting the conversation. I did not take my gaze off the steak, which was prepared as I'd requested.

"You're angry with me," Reuben said. "I get that."

"I am not angry with you," I answered. "I have no emotions at all regarding you. Until very recently you were not a presence in my life at all. What I am concerned about is your treatment of my mother."

Reuben drew in a breath. I was not looking at him but I did not hear his cutlery making an impact on his plate at all. He wasn't eating what he'd ordered. That was not a normal response.

"I realize I caused Vivian a lot of pain when I left and stayed away, but she understood," he said slowly. "After a while I just didn't know how to come back and have a life with her and with you. But she never complained and we stayed in touch all those years. Now I'm happy to be back and she seems happy to have me. I'll never make up the time I was away and the way that made her feel, but I'm glad we've managed to get to where we are now."

My steak was not large and it was half gone already. I stopped for a moment and reached into my jacket pocket for the bottle of spring water I'd brought with me. Nelson had brought me a glass of water but it was undoubtedly from the tap in the kitchen and therefore not predictable. I took a sip and put the bottle on the table.

At that moment, thinking about Ms. Washburn and the question she was researching, I looked at Reuben. "Did you cheat on my mother?" I asked him.

His eyes widened in surprise or offense; I could not be certain which. "I'm sorry?" he said.

"While you were away for twenty-seven years but still married to my mother," I explained. "During that time, were you involved with other women?" If he had cheated on Mother, it would be useful to ask him how that felt and what his motivation was, perhaps to better understand Brett Fontaine. I could give the information to Ms. Washburn when I saw her again, which might not be until the next day. I hoped she would accept my phone call tonight.

"Why are you asking me this?" Reuben said. I glanced at his plate. His food was untouched. He had ordered a turkey club sandwich, something that has far too many foods together for my taste. But he had asked for it and was now ignoring it.

"It is a simple question," I told him. "Did you cheat on my mother in the years you were living away from us?"

Reuben bit his lower lip lightly and for the first time averted his gaze. "Yes," he said.

I was not expecting my immediate response. It is very rare that I say something I have not thought carefully about ahead of time. "Mother did not," I said.

Reuben closed his eyes briefly and nodded. My question appeared to be causing him some sort of emotional distress. "I know."

"Why did you?" I asked. "You had made a promise to my mother when you chose to marry her. Why did you break it?" I paid careful attention so I could report my findings to Ms. Washburn.

"It was twenty-seven years, Samuel," Reuben said. "You can't expect a man to be perfect for that long a time."

The fact that he seemed to be making a gender distinction was important, I thought. I chewed the piece of steak I'd cut and waited until my mouth was clear. One doesn't speak with food in one's mouth. "So it is acceptable to expect a woman to remain chaste for a period of time that long but not a man?" Was there that difference between the genders? I'd seen no research indicating so.

"You're not making this easy on me, Samuel."

It had not been my intention to make things simple or difficult for Reuben, so his comment seemed random. "This lunch was not my idea," I pointed out. "You said I should be honest." He still had not answered my question about women and whether the expectations should be the same for both sexes.

"I guess I wasn't as ready to start being a father as I had thought," Reuben said. He looked at my plate. "Your steak is just about gone. Should I get the check? I imagine you want to be back in your office."

We were at the door of Questions Answered fourteen minutes later. Reuben did not come inside; he merely dropped me off at the door and drove away. I was not sure if he'd gotten what he wanted from the conversation he'd initiated. I had never heard the answer to my question and was now thinking about how to research it to provide an empirical answer.

I unlocked the door and walked to my desk. There is a light that flashes on the office landline to indicate a message has been left, and it was operating. I was about to press the button when my cellular telephone rang. I reached into my pocket and retrieved it. I was pleased to see the call was coming from Ms. Washburn.

"I am very glad to hear from you," I said as soon as I had accepted the call. "I was anxious to find out about your progress." I did not mention my failure to add to her available information. I knew she had not expected the assistance and had been somewhat reluctant to appear to be looking over her shoulder, an expression I can actually understand.

Ms. Washburn's voice sounded slightly hoarse, as if she had been shouting at length. She was not shouting now. "Samuel," she said. "You have to come here as fast as you can. Call Mike." That would be difficult as I did not know where Ms. Washburn was at the moment. But her tone indicated the matter was of paramount importance.

"What is wrong, Ms. Washburn?" I felt I knew her well enough to infer that there was a problem.

"Brett Fontaine is dead," Ms. Washburn answered. "Someone hit him over the head at least eight times with a tire iron. I need you to come and help me."

"Tell me where you are and I will be on my way."

SEVEN

"Somebody really didn't like that guy." Mike the taxicab driver was standing to my left on the sidewalk of High Street in New Brunswick, New Jersey. It had been necessary to explain to the officer guarding the scene that Ms. Washburn, who was standing inside the police line, had requested we come to this place. He had checked with the detective on the scene and been told it was acceptable for the two of us to enter the perimeter.

He was understating the obvious: Brett Fontaine's body had not yet been removed from the scene, but it had been covered with a tarpaulin despite there being no evident threat of rain. There was a good deal of blood on the sidewalk and on the tarpaulin.

"I would say that is fairly clear," I told Mike.

Ms. Washburn, whom I knew had seen a dead body before, stood to my right. She had embraced me when we'd arrived and held the clench for eleven seconds, which is a very long time for such a thing. She was obviously upset although there were no signs of tears on her face. But she was not speaking very much and held my right arm as we watched.

A very tall African-American man wearing a gray suit showing creases in the knees and elbows, which indicated he spent a considerable percentage of his day in a car, approached and spoke to Ms. Washburn. He showed her a police badge—they call it a shield—indicating he was a detective in the New Brunswick Police Department.

"Jack Monroe," he said. It took me a moment to realize he was telling us his name and not simply reciting one for an as-yet-undetermined reason. "I need to ask you a few questions." Monroe looked toward me. "If you'll excuse us, gentlemen."

"I want Samuel to stay," Ms. Washburn said, more rapidly than she usually spoke. "I promise he won't do anything to keep me from answering. Right, Samuel?"

I could not begin to imagine a situation in which I would impede a police investigation, so I simply said, "Yes."

"That's against policy. Is he your lawyer?" Monroe looked me up and down. Clearly he saw that I was not dressed in clothing an attorney would be likely to wear.

"I am not," I said. "I am Ms. Washburn's employer and the proprietor of Questions Answered." I considered giving him one of my business cards but chose not to make any gesture that Monroe could see as intrusive or inappropriate.

Monroe did not ask what Questions Answered might be, which was unusual in my experience. Most people, even those who are not police detectives, are curious about the nature of my business when hearing the name. I had thought the name Questions Answered would speak for itself but apparently most people believed otherwise.

"If he's not your lawyer, I really shouldn't let him be present when I'm questioning you," Monroe told Ms. Washburn.

"It's only for emotional support," she answered. "If you like, he won't say a word at all. I'm sure you can do that, can't you, Samuel?"

I preferred to watch and listen under these circumstances. "If necessary," I said.

Mike the taxicab driver, who had military experience he preferred not to discuss in detail, had already sat back on the front stairs of the home in front of which we were standing. He is a master observer and would be very helpful to the police if they had asked and to me later. He misses nothing.

Detective Monroe let out a long breath and pointed a finger at me. "You're going to agree to that, then," he said. "Not a word out of you, all right?"

I had already said I would adhere to his rule and wanted to prove I understood his instructions so I nodded rather than responding verbally.

"Don't be a wise guy," Monroe said. I hadn't thought that was what I was doing so I looked at Ms. Washburn, who shook her head slightly. I said nothing and walked with Monroe and Ms. Washburn to a less-populated area about ten yards to the left.

"Tell me what you saw," he said to Ms. Washburn.

"I had just turned the corner and I was looking for a parking space," she answered. "That's my car over there." She pointed toward her blue Kia Spectra, which was parked on an angle next to a fire hydrant on the other side of the street. "I put it there when I saw him lying on the sidewalk. That's his car next to him. He must have gotten here right ahead of me."

"And what was he doing when you first saw him?" Monroe asked.

"You're looking at it. He was already down by the time I got here. I called 911 as soon as I saw him."

Monroe nodded, but I did not believe it was a gesture of acceptance. He looked at a small tablet computer he had brought with him on which he was clearly taking notes. "Did you see anyone else?" he asked.

Ms. Washburn shook her head. "Nobody. The street was empty, or at least the part I was looking at. I focused on Brett initially because I was looking for him and then because I saw him on the ground bleeding."

Detective Monroe's head jerked up when Ms. Washburn spoke. "Brett?" he said. "You knew the victim's name?"

I wanted to answer but had promised not to speak a word and I would hold to that vow. Ms. Washburn said, "Yes. I was following him."

Monroe blinked twice. "Why?"

"It's my job. I work with Samuel at Questions Answered and we had a question from a client about Mr. Fontaine. I was following him from his office in Somerset when he turned here onto High Street and as soon as I got here I found him like this."

"Questions Answered?" Monroe asked.

Now that the issue had become relevant Monroe was asking about my business. I understood that; it had not been important to him until it directly affected his work. I wondered if Detective Monroe might be classified as having an autism spectrum disorder of some type but decided he probably did not.

"It's our business," Ms. Washburn said, despite the fact that she did not own any percentage of Questions Answered. She is an integral part of the firm and I was not supposed to speak, so I ignored the slight inaccuracy. "When people have a question they can't answer themselves they come to us and we find the right answer for them."

Monroe, to his credit, did not respond with the kind of skepticism I often encounter; he simply nodded his head. But his eyes were indicating he had not completely accepted Ms. Washburn's explanation.

"It's not a detective agency," Ms. Washburn added as a way to clarify. "We don't solve problems. We answer questions of any kind." In fact, we answer questions only when I find them interesting, but again there was no need to add to Ms. Washburn's account.

"What was the question?" Monroe asked.

This is always a difficult area when Questions Answered has taken on a client. We have no legal standing as a physician or an attorney might in such cases, but we do like to maintain our clients' privacy when we can. Ms. Washburn looked at Monroe as a stalling tactic, I believe, and said, "Excuse me?"

That was a way to find more time during which to formulate a response. I had seen the tactic used more than once and had probably done so myself at some point, although I prefer to answer truthfully when possible. Mother always says it is easier to tell the truth because then you don't have to remember the lie.

"The question you were trying to answer. What was it?" Monroe shifted his weight from one foot to the other. I guessed it was a sign of impatience.

Ms. Washburn had used her extra time well. "We were being asked whether Mr. Fontaine was having an extramarital affair with his college girlfriend," she said. I thought it wise to omit the notion that Brett Fontaine's lover was deceased.

Monroe's voice had an edge to it that suggested he already knew the answer to his next question. "Who is your client?"

Ms. Washburn looked at me, which put me in a delicate position. Clearly she was requesting my assistance with the detective, but I was bound to remain silent. I felt it was not necessary to protect our client's identity if she might be a suspect in a murder. That could leave my business open to charges of obstruction of justice and Ms. Washburn and me subject to other legal entanglements. I nodded to her.

"His wife," she said. "Virginia Fontaine."

Predictably, Monroe did not look surprised. "The wife," he echoed. I think he was speaking more to himself than to Ms. Washburn.

I noticed Mike the taxicab driver paying closer attention to us than he had appeared to be doing only moments earlier. I doubted he could hear the conversation from where he was sitting, so I could only assume there was some visual information he'd be able to impart when we spoke. I had seen nothing out of the ordinary.

Then I realized Mike had been watching the street and saw an ambulance approach. The county medical examiner's office had sent someone to see about Brett Fontaine. I was surprised they hadn't arrived before Mike and me.

"So you're not private detectives," Monroe said to Ms. Washburn, "but you were following a husband because his wife thought he was playing around? Why didn't she go to a detective agency instead of whatever it is you are?"

Ms. Washburn's lip twitched a bit on the left side but I doubt Monroe noticed. "You would have to ask her," she said. It was a very good answer. I wondered if it was motivated by a desire to keep the supernatural element out of the conversation or because Monroe had seemed to disparage Questions Answered. Ms. Washburn is very protective of me and the firm.

"I intend to," the detective said. "Were you going to take pictures and show them to the wife?"

Ms. Washburn is a former photojournalist for a local newspaper so the question was not unreasonable, although Monroe had no way of knowing about her former profession. "I might have if I'd seen him doing anything she would have wanted to know about," Ms. Washburn said.

"So your camera is in your car, or were you going to use your phone?"

It was becoming clear that Ms. Washburn was not pleased with the tone Monroe was using in his questioning. She was not faced toward the street and did not react as the medical examiner left her transport and walked to Brett Fontaine's body.

"I don't use my phone to take pictures," Ms. Washburn told Monroe. "The definition isn't as good and you can't change lenses. I didn't take my camera out of the glove compartment of my car, where you'll find it if you look, because the client specifically asked not to show her anything that might get her upset."

"Okay." Detective Monroe's voice was indicating his skepticism if I was reading the tone correctly—and I have heard enough sarcasm to recognize it after years of study. "So you have a client, the victim's wife, who asked you to follow her husband because she thought he was fooling around. But she didn't want you to take pictures. She came to you instead of a detective agency because she wanted you to answer her question about the affair and not…follow him and find out if he was getting some on the side?"

Ms. Washburn touched me on the arm. Normally I am not fond of physical contact but I don't seem to mind it coming from her. I moved slightly closer to her instinctively.

"I can't speak to my client's thinking," Ms. Washburn said, the defiant edge in her voice a bit muted. "I was only doing as she asked."

"Did you call your client after you found her husband with his brains all over the sidewalk?" Monroe said. "Or did you walk back to your car and put your tire iron back in the trunk after you wiped it off?"

Now Ms. Washburn gripped my arm tightly. I was fighting the urge to speak and it was becoming increasingly difficult.

Ms. Washburn's voice was now small and sounded more like an exhalation than speech. "You think I killed Brett Fontaine and then called 911 and stuck around waiting for you to show up and catch me?"

"I've seen it happen. But I don't think anything yet. At the moment all I know is that you seem to have been the only person on a street in New Brunswick who saw this guy on the ground. And during the Rutgers school year, that's really unusual. Things that are unusual are a problem or a clue. I haven't figured out which this one is yet."

"If you're going to arrest me, I'm going to need a lawyer," Ms. Washburn said. I didn't know any criminal attorneys but I was sure I could find one. It was a question that would be simple to answer.

"Relax," Monroe said. "You're not getting arrested here today. I don't have anywhere near enough evidence to even suspect you yet." Coming as an expression of comfort, that sounded oddly ominous. I would have to remember the exchange to better analyze it when I returned to the Questions Answered office. I thought it was mostly the word *yet*.

"If you're still asking, no, I didn't call Virginia Fontaine after I called the police," Ms. Washburn said, still slightly glaring at the detective despite his nominal attempt to be more civil in his discourse. "I waited for you. I didn't want to be the one to tell her."

"All right," Monroe said. But he did not put down his tablet computer. "I'm just trying to figure it. It seems pretty clear that the wife would have a motive to kill a husband she thought was cheating on her. But why not wait until she had the proof she asked for? Why kill him now, knowing someone was following him around?"

Ms. Washburn put her hands up palms out and spread them in a gesture of uncertainty. "No idea. Maybe it means that Virginia isn't the one who killed him."

"And I imagine you'll say it wasn't you." I believe Detective Monroe was trying to exhibit a sense of humor at that moment but it was difficult to determine definitely.

"It wasn't me." Ms. Washburn did not sound amused either.

Monroe cocked his left eyebrow. "The girlfriend?" he asked.

Ms. Washburn looked at me. I was careful not to gesture or change my expression because I did not have a response to the question her face was asking. This was Ms. Washburn's job to do and I did not wish to influence her in any way.

"It seems unlikely," she said finally.

But Monroe would not accept that as a definitive answer. "Why?"

Ms. Washburn let out a breath, no doubt knowing how what she was going to say would sound to the detective. "Because she's dead."

Monroe's eyes widened. I could only speculate that he was now seeing a possible career advancement opportunity in this case. "They both got killed? On the same day?" he asked.

"No. Brett Fontaine's supposed lover has been dead for three years." Ms. Washburn, in an attempt to avoid the incredulous gaze Monroe was about to aim at her, turned toward the street just in time to see the medical examiner walking toward us wearing latex gloves and carrying a small evidence bag.

She approached Detective Monroe before he could express his disbelief or confusion at what Ms. Washburn had just told him. "Detective?" the woman said.

Monroe pivoted to see the woman, who I'd say was in her early thirties and fairly small, standing next to him. They made an interesting tableau as Monroe was unusually tall. "What?" he said. He was still obviously trying to understand Ms. Washburn's claim.

"I wanted to let you know I'm releasing the scene," the medical examiner said. "But there's something I found on preliminary examination that you ought to know. According to the body temperature I took just now, this man was not killed here on the street."

Monroe, already reeling, was not prepared for another assault on what he believed he already knew. "What do you mean?" he said.

"There he is on the sidewalk with his head beaten in. Where do you think he got killed?"

"I don't know, but it wasn't here. This man's been dead at least four hours."

Monroe turned to face Ms. Washburn. "She'd been dead three years?" he said.

EIGHT

"THIS IS A LOT to unpack." Mike the taxicab driver knows I am uncomfortable with conversation when he is driving, but at the moment we were stopped at a red traffic light and at those times I am less anxious about the distraction. However I did not understand his reference, as I had certainly not brought any luggage with me to High Street in New Brunswick. We were on our way back to the Questions Answered office. Ms. Washburn had been clear that she'd prefer to spend a little time alone to think so she was driving back independently.

"Unpack?" I asked. People like Mike who know me fairly well will understand my difficulty with what they consider to be typical conversation.

"Sorry, Samuel. What I mean is that there is a lot of information for us to figure out here." Mike, particularly since he had been integral in the trip to Los Angeles to find Reuben, had taken to speaking of himself as part of the Questions Answered team. I did not see any utility in dissuading him from doing so.

The traffic light switched from red to green at that moment so we did not speak again for three minutes until we found ourselves stopped at a similar intersection. "We do indeed have a great deal to discuss," I said. "I thought you noticed something while Ms. Washburn was being questioned. Was there a detail I missed that you think is relevant?"

"It was the coroner who came to look at the body," he said. He was misusing the word. Coroners are often appointed officials who are funeral directors or involved in some related service. Medical examiners are doctors who are trained in the specialty of forensic science. But I did not correct Mike at the time because I was more interested in hearing what he had to say. He can be a very helpful person to have around.

"What about her?" I asked.

The timing on this traffic light appeared to be especially leisurely. "She was really attractive," Mike said.

We did not speak until he pulled the taxicab into the parking lot of the Questions Answered office in the Stelton Road strip mall.

That gave me time to think about the things Mike might miss because he was busy looking at an attractive woman. It seemed an unusually inefficient trait of his. I understood the impulse because I have had it myself, but did not see how it would interfere in the observation of a crime scene when that was necessary. Sometimes I think having Asperger's Syndrome is an advantage that others see as a disability. It is odd.

"I think it is more significant that Mr. Fontaine's body was cold and that the medical examiner believed that meant he had not been beaten to death on the spot where he was found," I said when the taxicab was safely parked. "It would seem to contradict Ms. Washburn's account of following Brett Fontaine to that spot only seconds before she discovered his body. And since we know Ms. Washburn was telling the truth, there is a fairly large discrepancy between what happened and what she saw."

"Maybe she was following his ghost all day," Mike said. I believe he was attempting to be humorous. "There's already one ghost involved in this business."

"Clearly that is impossible," I reminded him. "Another explanation will have to be found."

Mike chuckled. "I know, Samuel. Now go to your office. I need to find a paying customer before I go home tonight." Mike refuses to let me compensate him for the rides he gives me. I have learned not to argue the point with him because I always end up on the losing end of the conflict.

I got out of the taxicab, thanked Mike for his help, and got out the key to open the front door to my business as Mike pulled the cab out of the parking space and drove away. Once inside I turned on the lights and went to the vending machine for a bottle of water. I had not done the requisite exercise to earn the water but the day had taken an unexpected turn. I would do my walking the perimeter again in fifteen minutes to do my best about staying on schedule.

The telephone answering machine's button was flashing red to indicate someone had left a message. I walked over and pushed the playback button, but the message was from a company asking to place solar panels on the roof of my business. I do not own the property but such telephone solicitors never seem to care about such things.

I heard the bells over the front door ring and turned to face it. I expected to see Ms. Washburn walk in but instead saw my mother. Her knee surgery has slowed her gait a bit but made it smoother and she walked from the door to my desk without showing any sign of discomfort, which I found reassuring.

"Samuel," she said before I could ask the reason for her visit. "What did you say to your father?"

Although Reuben had been absent for most of my life, I had said many things to him in the short time he'd been back. Before he left when I was four years old I had no doubt conversed with him a large number of times. Mother was going to have to be more specific. "What did I say to Reuben on what subject?" I asked as Mother settled into the chair I have reserved for her in front of my desk.

"You told him that he didn't matter to you," she said. Mother's voice was unusually strained, almost harsh. I could not think of any concern that would make her feel that way.

"I did not," I said. "I never used those words. If he had asked me, I might have said that he is not a very high priority in my life, but he did not ask."

"You told him you have no feelings at all toward him." Clearly Reuben had gone home and related our conversation to Mother, which I thought was odd considering he had wanted it to be held without her to begin with. Once again I could conclude only that neurotypical people act strangely and one must make allowances.

"That is true. Should I have told him otherwise?" I was beginning to type in a search for the recorded reliability of estimated times of departure for trains out of Nepal, but I felt it would be rude to do so without looking at Mother so I turned my gaze toward her.

She looked shocked. I have not often seen my mother with that expression since I was a young boy. It surprised me and I stopped what I was doing. "How can you have no feelings at all about your father?" she said after a long pause.

"I barely know the man," I said, stating what I considered to be obvious. "I have had almost no contact with him since I was four years old. Why would I have strong emotions about him when he was not a factor in my existence for twenty-seven years? What information would I have on which to base an emotional foundation?"

Mother's eyes seemed to age as I spoke. She looked very tired and I was concerned there might be a problem with her health as there had been some years earlier. "Are you all right?" I asked.

"No. I'm not all right. I am hurt and I am stunned and I am very disappointed. Samuel. Emotions are not based on gathered data. They're something you feel. Like it or not, that man you brought back from Los Angeles is your father. I don't understand, even given the way you are, how you can not care about that at all."

"Mother, you of all people know that I am not a computer. I am not devoid of emotions. You taught me that and you have been teaching people we've met that very point for as long as I can remember." I put my hands on my desk to better show I was no longer working while we spoke. I did give a very quick glance to the screen, which was making a differentiation among various railroads flying out of Nepal. "But I need something on which to base a feeling other than a biological relationship. You have a cousin by blood in Illinois and I would wager you have very little invested emotionally in her."

Mother's head dropped forward a little. I had a brief moment of concern and then realized she was simply showing some disappointment. "My cousin Sheila is not what we're talking about," she said softly. "We're talking about your father."

"We are talking about a man who, for all intents and purposes, I met a very short time ago. Whatever will develop between us must do so naturally. I need more information." I thought that was fair.

Apparently Mother disagreed. "Do you need more information to know how you feel about Janet?" she asked.

I did not see how Ms. Washburn was relevant to this discussion. "What do you mean?" I asked.

But Mother did not have time to answer before the bells over the front door rang again and Ms. Washburn walked in, looking slightly distracted but determined not to show it. She looked toward my desk. "Vivian," she said. "It's nice to see you."

Ms. Washburn reached over and gave my mother a kiss on the cheek. Mother had not attempted to rise out of the chair. The new knee was helping but it wasn't going to make her leg perfect again, she had told me. "Always a pleasure, Janet," she said. But she was looking in my direction, not Ms. Washburn's, as she spoke.

"Was Samuel telling you what happened?" Ms. Washburn asked.

Mother looked at me, then at my associate. "No. Is something wrong?"

Ms. Washburn sat behind her desk as she told Mother about Brett Fontaine's murder and how Detective Monroe had questioned her on the matter. I had not been interrogated, as it was quite clear I was not in the area when Mr. Fontaine was found in the street.

As I would have expected, Mother looked very surprised when Ms. Washburn told her the story and then she looked at me. "Why didn't you tell me any of this, Samuel?" she asked.

"I had no time. You came in and immediately began asking me questions." I was going to continue but Mother turned her attention toward Ms. Washburn.

"Are you all right, dear?" she asked. "That must have been terrifying."

Ms. Washburn smiled but her demeanor was not consistent with her facial expression. "I'm okay," she told Mother. "I've sort of gotten used to this sort of thing since I started working here." We had encountered three previous incidents of people being murdered, but it was hardly a normal part of the Questions Answered routine. Ms. Washburn was probably exaggerating.

Mother took a moment to stand up. "Well, I won't take up your time when you have something that important to discuss," she said. "I have to get home anyway. I'll see you at six for dinner, Samuel." Her voice did not have its usual encouraging lilt as she spoke. She headed for the door.

"You're not at all a distraction," I said. "You may stay if you prefer."

But Mother continued to walk to the door and reached it. "Not this time," she said and left.

Ms. Washburn looked over at me with a quizzical expression on her face. "What was that about?"

"I don't understand."

"Your mother seemed upset. Is something wrong?" Ms. Washburn put her hand, fisted, to her lips. This can be a gesture meant to show concern.

"I don't know," I said honestly. "She asked me about a conversation I had with Reuben Hoenig today."

"You spoke to your father today?" Ms. Washburn asked. She believes that my referring to Reuben by his first name rather than acknowledging his biological role in my life is somehow a sign of hostility. I consider it appropriate to the level of intimacy he and I have established.

I told her of Reuben's invitation to lunch and the conversation that followed. Ms. Washburn listened carefully, as she always does. When I had completed my recount she nodded thoughtfully. "I think your mother is concerned that you're not giving your father a chance," she said.

"A chance for what?"

Ms. Washburn looked at me for a moment. I recognized the look: She was trying to decide how to respond to me because apparently I had said something unexpected or inappropriate. She waved her right hand. "Samuel, I think we need to concentrate on Brett Fontaine."

We? "I would think the question Virginia Fontaine asked is your own assignment," I said. "I would not want to intrude on your thinking in that matter, but it seems to me the answer is moot now that Mr. Fontaine is dead."

Ms. Washburn started as if prodded. "You mean you won't help me?" she asked.

I stood and walked to her desk and leaned on it with my hands gripping the edge. "I am happy to do anything I can to help," I told her. "But I do not want you to think I have anything but the highest regard for your judgment. I do not wish to be seen as helping on something you could not do, because I believe you are more than capable of handling this question."

Ms. Washburn put her hand on mine. "That's possibly the nicest thing you've ever said to me, Samuel."

"I meant every word." Of course, I mean every word whenever I speak, so the iteration was probably unnecessary.

"Thank you. But even you ask for my help on some of the more difficult questions. I think it would be best if we worked together on this one going forward." Ms. Washburn smiled sincerely at me.

But her request was baffling. "I do not understand the problem. Ms. Fontaine asked if her husband was having an affair with a dead woman. You and I had some disagreement on whether that might be possible, but now that he is deceased himself, I see no reason to pursue the question. Even if one believes in a physical afterlife, Mr. Fontaine is no longer capable of being Ms. Fontaine's husband. Whether or not he is now involved with his dead college girlfriend is no longer relevant, in my view. Tell Ms. Fontaine the answer is no and close the file."

But Ms. Washburn had withdrawn her hand and begun shaking her head some eight seconds earlier. "But what about Brett Fontaine's murder?" she said.

"That is Detective Monroe's business now. We have not been engaged to answer a question about it." I walked back to my desk. "You would know better than I if enough time has passed to call Ms. Fontaine and conclude our business with her. We should do so whenever it is appropriate." I walked back to my desk and sat down. Surely the Nepalese computations had been completed and were waiting for my perusal.

"I don't think I can do that, Samuel." Ms. Washburn looked worried. "Ginny Fontaine asked us to find out if her husband was cheating on her and now he's been killed. She's a logical suspect in the murder. Don't you think we need to follow through on the question she asked to try and clear her name?"

I diverted my attention again from my screen and swiveled my office chair to face Ms. Washburn. Three minutes until I would exercise for the first time in four hours. "We have not been asked the question, and even if we had been it is always a mistake to research a question with a particular answer in mind. It prejudices the process."

It took Ms. Washburn a moment to absorb what I had said. "You think Ginny killed her husband?"

"I have no opinion on that question at all," I answered. "I have not done any research on it and have left Detective Monroe to do his own investigation. Ms. Washburn, you know how we operate. No one has asked us who killed Brett Monroe."

Ms. Washburn reached into the top drawer of her desk and retrieved a client intake form. She put it on her desk and began to fill it out. "I'm going to ask you the question, Samuel, and I will pay your fee. So let's get to work on this right away."

I stood up and walked past Ms. Washburn's desk. It was time for me to raise my heart rate and exercise my legs and arms as well as my cardiovascular system. In the early stages, perhaps until the fourth lap around the office perimeter, I can still speak without sounding like I am gasping for air. (I have in the past alarmed my mother with the sound, although it is simply the result of normal exercise and making one's pulmonary system work harder than usual.)

"I will not accept your question, Ms. Washburn. I don't want your money and I do not think this is an area we should explore as a business." The first lap is not very difficult but I do have to keep a clear head or I will begin at too rapid a pace and find it more taxing to continue when I am in the later stages of the program.

Ms. Washburn, I saw as I turned in her direction, had stopped filling out the intake form. She said nothing but was quite clearly in thought as I passed. After a moment her voice lowered in volume but was still audible. "But you can't object if I take the question on myself, can you?"

The question was badly phrased. Of course it was within my ability to express my objections to Ms. Washburn taking on the issue of Brett Fontaine's death. But I sensed she was asking whether I was within my rights as her employer to forbid her from doing so. That was an entirely different thing to consider. Legally I could not stop Ms. Washburn from taking on any project she wished to explore. Whether I could insist research on a question not be done on company time would eventually hinge on my willingness to dismiss her as an employee of Questions Answered if she did not obey the firm's rule, which would be one I would have to create on the spot because the issue had never been raised before.

"If you are asking what I believe you are, I would ask you a question in response," I said as I began my third circumnavigation of the office space. My voice would have to increase in volume as I moved away from Ms. Washburn, but I did not wish to sound like I was angry with her. "Whose question are you answering? Virginia Fontaine's question is about her husband carrying on with a dead woman. No one has asked this firm who killed Brett Fontaine, or why."

I was not in a position to see Ms. Washburn at that moment. I did hear her say, "Give me a minute," and believed that meant she needed some time to formulate a response, which would indicate that my logic had indeed stumped her and perhaps lead to the conclusion that this discussion could be ended.

Forty-three seconds later it became clear that I had been incorrect in my deductions.

"Virginia has asked who killed Brett," Ms. Washburn said. "She asked me directly, and since you suggested I should work on her question myself, I've already told her I would accept."

I turned the corner, feeling a bead of sweat at my hairline that was a little premature for this stage of my exercise program. "How did she ask you?" I said. "I heard no conversation on the phone, and surely you didn't call a woman who just discovered her husband had been murdered to solicit business for the firm."

Ms. Washburn's arms were folded in front of her in a gesture of determination. "I texted Detective Monroe. I figured he was with Virginia, and he was. I suggested he ask whether Virginia wanted us to look into her husband's death and he texted me back saying she did. I can show you the texts if you don't believe me."

That last sentence was unnecessary; I had no reason to disbelieve Ms. Washburn now or ever before. "I can refuse the question," I said. "I don't find it interesting."

"But I do." I turned past her desk and Ms. Washburn's eyes were clear and certain.

I found myself increasing my pace and made no effort to correct myself. The sooner I could sit down with a bottle of spring water, the better things would be. "Very well," I said to Ms. Washburn. "We will answer the question."

"We?" she asked.

I had not misspoken. The idea of Ms. Washburn researching a homicide with no idea of the killer's motive led to the probability of antagonizing a violent person and putting Ms. Washburn in harm's way. I could not abide that.

"If you don't mind," I said, walking faster still.

NINE

"Is it possible that this was just a robbery that went wrong?" Ms. Washburn asked.

After I had called my mother to ask if Ms. Washburn might join us for dinner and been told she was welcome without asking any evening, my associate had indeed accompanied me home and eaten with my parents and myself. Once the meal had been completed and we had helped Mother by cleaning up afterward, Ms. Washburn and I had gone to my attic apartment to consider the question of Brett Fontaine's death.

"It is unlikely," I answered, "although not impossible. Mr. Fontaine's wallet was still in his pocket with no apparent missing items and a package containing a vase worth a few hundred dollars was discovered in his car. If someone robbed Mr. Fontaine, that person did a very poor job of it." I had asked Detective Monroe for any help he could offer and was emailed a copy of the police report on the incident, which was a matter of public record.

"Besides, the medical examiner said the body had been moved. If someone robbed him, they would have done it wherever they killed

Brett. Why bother to drive him all the way to High Street for a robbery?"

"There has not yet been a medical examiner's report issued," I answered, "but from what I overheard at the scene it would seem the technician based her statement on the conclusion that there was not enough blood on the sidewalk for the crime to have happened there. She suggested no explanation for moving the body other than to confuse the police."

Ms. Washburn sat down on my bed while I stayed in the desk chair. I was already noticing the urge to kiss her again and wondered if I could focus on the question at hand. So far the intellectual puzzle was foremost in my mind. I did not make any internal predictions as to how long I could maintain that discipline.

"And to confuse *me*," Ms. Washburn said. "I can't shake the feeling that whoever did this knew I was following Brett and wanted me to think what I thought. Why would somebody do something like that? *How* would they do it?"

Both were intriguing questions, but the foundation upon which they were built was not yet verified with facts. "I do not discount the importance of your feelings, but we don't know that what you are describing was the case," I reminded Ms. Washburn, using language I thought was sensitive to her emotions. "We need to gather information we know to be factual."

Ms. Washburn's eyes narrowed a bit but she did not look angry, as is often the case with that facial gesture. She was thinking. "All we know so far for sure is that Brett Fontaine was killed with a tire iron on High Street in New Brunswick. Or more to the point, that he was *left* on High Street after he was apparently beaten to death somewhere else. That's the thing that keeps getting me crazy." Ms. Washburn did not mean to imply that she had a mental illness; this was an expression indicating some irritation with the circumstances she described. "I don't understand why they moved the body, and specifically why they moved it there of all places."

The urge to kiss Ms. Washburn was very strong now and threatened to cloud my judgment. I swiveled the desk chair to turn away from her and toward my three computer displays to distract myself from the temptation.

Part of the problem, of course, was that I have some difficulty with the social cues involved in romantic gestures. Kissing Ms. Washburn was something I would happily do to fill an entire day, every day. But there were times when it was appropriate and times when the action would be seen as wrong. Also, it was imperative to be sure Ms. Washburn wanted me to kiss her at any given moment. That was especially problematic for me because I could not always tell if she was open to the gesture or not. This relationship was very nuanced and therefore confusing.

I centered my attention on the center computer display and began a search for Brett Fontaine generally. Since this had been Ms. Washburn's question to answer on her own, I had done very little to understand the parties involved and therefore was at a disadvantage to Ms. Washburn, whom I was sure had become very well versed in their histories. I could ask her questions, but this would be faster and I could avert my gaze for a while.

"What do you know about Brett Fontaine's business dealings?" I said without turning my head toward Ms. Washburn.

"Ginny listed his profession as 'real estate entrepreneur' on her client intake form," she answered. "I figured that meant he was a landlord and I was right. Brett owned six buildings in New Brunswick that Rutgers students would rent, trash, and then leave. He did a lot of the repairs—they always needed repairs—and maintenance himself because he didn't want to pay someone else to do it. The building he was *staged* in front of today was near one of his. It's possible someone thought he was a really bad landlord, I guess."

"Let's not form opinions until we have the facts," I reminded her, although her research seemed thorough and accurate, in line with the information I was getting in my internet search. "Brett Fontaine was the owner of several buildings used by students but his reputation as a landlord is not verifiable. It would be a serious breach of protocol to leap to a conclusion about the motive in this killing. That is particularly true in that the police obviously believe his widow is the prime suspect in the murder."

"*Ginny?*" she said. I did not see Ms. Washburn's expression but I could hear the surprise and something approaching outrage in her voice.

"Certainly. All the circumstantial evidence we have gathered or seen so far would appear to point directly to her."

"Like what?" Ms. Washburn was obviously being somewhat protective of her first personal client. In my judgment, that was blinding her to some of the facts involved in the question.

I began a search concerning the name of William Klein. "Ms. Fontaine believed her husband was having a romantic relationship with a woman from his past. She thought that woman to be deceased, which was unusual, but the fact is in such cases the logical assumption is that a jealous wife would be quite angry with the cheating husband."

"Ginny was calm and came to us for help," Ms. Washburn pointed out behind me. "She didn't present as angry or vengeful, but confused and hurt."

"Either of those emotions can lead to rash acts," I answered. Now the urge to turn around and look at Ms. Washburn, which would undoubtedly lead to an urge to kiss her, was becoming impossible to ignore.

"This was anything but a rash act," she countered. "Brett was bludgeoned to death and then put in a car and moved to High Street. That doesn't sound like a crime of passion to me."

The word *passion* reverberated in my mind. That was a distraction as well. "The time of death was hours before you discovered the body," I said. "Ms. Fontaine's alibi for that time, according to Detective Monroe at the scene, was that she was shopping at the Menlo Park Mall. Until security footage can be found and viewed it will be impossible to verify her whereabouts when her husband died. And there is also the possibility that she hired someone to do the killing. The fact that she wanted to come along with you when you were doing surveillance on Mr. Fontaine would seem to point to that conclusion."

"How?" Now Ms. Washburn's voice was enough to distract me. I had to find a way to normalize my thinking. I concentrated more directly on my computer display.

"It would establish an airtight alibi if she were in the car with you when the body was found," I suggested. "But that is pure speculation."

Then something on the screen actually did demand my attention to the point that I briefly abandoned any thought of physical contact with Ms. Washburn. She noticed that I leaned forward to read the text on the display, and I imagine my facial expression betrayed a sudden increase in interest. "What is it?" she asked.

"I believe I have found another piece of circumstantial evidence that has a connection to our client," I told her.

I scanned the article dated fourteen years earlier, a routine newspaper report on the accidental death of a man who fell from his fire escape. "It's about William Klein, Virginia Fontaine's first husband," I said to Ms. Washburn.

"What about him? Is he a ghost too?" She stood up and leaned over my shoulder. Her presence was not lost on me, but I had found a significant piece of information and that provided a more immediate priority.

"Perhaps," I said. I did not literally mean that I thought William Klein had become a vengeful spirit who was haunting his widow. I was being figurative. "Ms. Fontaine failed to tell us an important detail about her husband's death."

"Which husband?" Ms. Washburn asked.

Of course; I had not taken the circumstances of the conversation into account. Ms. Washburn is invaluable at keeping my focus on the subject. "Brett Fontaine," I answered. "We might have an answer as to why his body was left in front of that house on High Street, even if we don't know where he was killed."

Ms. Washburn leaned over farther so that when she spoke her voice sounded louder than it should. "Don't make me play guessing games, Samuel," she said. "What's the big clue?"

I indicated a point on the screen. "It's the house in front of which you found Brett Fontaine's body," I said. "It's the same house in which Virginia and William Klein were living when he fell off the fire escape to his death."

"That's crazy," Ms. Washburn said, I believe mostly to herself.

"That is only half of it," I said. "The police report indicates there were three bolts missing from a coupling on the fire escape. In short, it appears that someone wanted Mr. Klein—or someone—to fall three stories."

TEN

"Yes, I am aware that Brett was found...in front of...that house." Virginia Fontaine dabbed at her right eye with a facial tissue. She was a very skilled liar, I had decided, and therefore it was difficult to know when she was telling the truth. In this case, the deception might not have been in her words as much as her demeanor. She was very much the grieving widow right now, but that might have simply been for our benefit. "It sends a shiver up my spine to think about it." That part was definitely a lie.

"And the missing bolts on the fire escape?" I asked. Ms. Washburn looked at me, indicating I had been too abrupt.

"I don't know anything about that," Virginia said. "I was at work when William fell and the police told me it was an accident. Maybe the bolts just fell out."

Ms. Washburn and I had not suggested a visit to Virginia's home one day after her husband had been found dead on a street in New Brunswick. In fact, I had thought we should simply confront her with the growing cache of circumstantial evidence in a phone call, but Ms.

Washburn had suggested we email Virginia and ask when she might be available.

Virginia had said she wasn't doing anything and we should come over immediately.

For a new second-time widow it seemed strange that Virginia would have so little on her agenda. Once we'd arrived at her Highland Park home—a newly built "McMansion" as the ruder real estate agents might say—she had explained that relatives of her late husband were flying in from California and the funeral home would be handling all the arrangements for a final service the next day, assuming the medical examiner's office had completed an autopsy by then.

"What connection is there between your second husband and that house?" I asked. "Did he own the property?"

Virginia shook her head. "He owned one up the street, but not that one. I wouldn't even let him bid on it. But leaving his body there? It seems cruel. As if there were any question what he died from. They found the tire iron in the street next to him. What do they think happened? That Brett had a heart attack and the welts on his head were an accident?"

"A great deal of information can be uncovered in an autopsy," I assured her. "Much of it might very well help in determining who killed your husband and why." I trained my eyes on her face against my natural impulse. I wanted to see her expression, but she continued to have a neutral look in her eyes and on her face.

"I don't care who killed my husband, or why they did it," she said after a long exhalation. "He's dead. What difference does it make?"

"You hired us to answer those very questions," Ms. Washburn reminded Virginia.

"I probably shouldn't have done that. It seemed like a good thing to do in front of that detective. He thinks *I* had something to do with Brett's…with what happened to Brett."

I looked up, just then realizing I had trained my gaze on the floor, no doubt in reaction to having to search our client's face for so long. "Does that mean you wish to terminate our agreement?" I said. Ms. Washburn glanced at me with a somewhat disapproving look in her eye. Perhaps my tone had been too hopeful.

Virginia made quite the display of thinking about what I'd asked. "No," she said. "I didn't mean it when I said I don't care. I do care. I care because the police think I did it and I need you to prove I didn't."

Clearly the veneer of the grieving widow had been removed.

"We don't actually do that," Ms. Washburn told Virginia. "We can't answer a question if you already have an answer you want us to find. We go where the facts lead us."

Virginia Fontaine's eyes reminded me of a woman in a film I'd seen as a child. That character had wanted to skin Dalmatian puppies to make a coat, as I recalled. I had been very disturbed by her when I was four and my mother never showed me that film again.

"You think I killed Brett too?" she growled at Ms. Washburn.

I do not respond well when people show my associate hostility, but in this case Ms. Washburn spoke before I could. "We don't think anything yet," she answered. Her statement was not technically true; both of us had a great many thoughts, but our opinions on the outcome of her question were not yet formed, and that was what Ms. Washburn was attempting to communicate. "But I can't guarantee for you that you'll get the answer you want. We tell that to every client we take on." She smiled at Virginia.

I noticed that Virginia did not smile in return. "But you *do* think I killed Brett," she repeated.

This time I felt it was my responsibility as the proprietor of Questions Answered to state the business's philosophy. "We have not yet formed a theory about the way your husband died," I told Virginia. "We have the question to answer and we will do so based strictly on empirical evidence and not emotional prejudices. At the moment all the circumstantial evidence points in one direction, but the research is in a very early stage. I have answered many questions that seemed certain to have one possible solution and found they were in fact based in another one completely. The facts will lead us to a conclusion. We make no judgments."

That was a very clear statement in my opinion. Virginia did not seem to share that view, however. She looked toward Ms. Washburn. "What did he just say?"

"The same thing I just said. We don't have an opinion. We won't answer the question in any way except accurately." Succinct, but true.

Virginia Fontaine, if I understand the expression, heaved a sigh and put up her hands palms out. "Fine," she said. "Do what you do. But I didn't kill Brett."

Having been adequately informed of our client's declared innocence, Ms. Washburn wisely decided to move the conversation in another direction. "Why would someone leave your husband's body in front of the house where your first husband died?" she asked. "Was there some sort of question about what happened to William that might make a person you know feel justice had not been served?" Revenge is not an uncommon motive for violence.

"I don't know," Virginia said, looking at something on her leg rather than Ms. Washburn's face. "There was an investigation by the police after William fell but it was determined that his death was accidental. I wasn't there when it happened so I didn't have much to tell them."

I had in fact found the police report of the incident when I was researching William Klein's death the night before. The conclusion had been reached that there was no evidence of foul play but did not specify the fall could definitively be classified as an accident. There was some question about missing hardware on the fire escape, but it had never been revisited as far as I could tell.

I felt it would be unwise to point that out to Virginia at the moment, however. Her mood was so defensive that we could receive no useful information from a woman who might react as I would anticipate she would if I suggested she had been even slightly evasive regarding her first husband's death.

"Your husband, Brett, was involved in real estate," Ms. Washburn said. I thought it odd that she would give Virginia a piece of information the woman clearly knew, but I said nothing. "Was there anything in his business that might have made him some enemies?"

"What are you suggesting?" Virginia Fontaine's immediate reactions to all our questions seemed to be defensive.

"I'm not suggesting anything," Ms. Washburn assured her. "I'm asking a question. I need some direction in researching your question and thought as his closest confidante he might have mentioned something to you."

Virginia, apparently remembering she was a new widow for the second time, sniffed rather obviously. "No. He didn't say anything about enemies at work."

"What were his business practices like?" I asked. "Was he a decent landlord, or did he raise the rent without providing basic services?" I had seen a news report about such a property owner only three nights previous.

Virginia's back straightened. "He was a great landlord. Brett would come out in the middle of the night if one of those kids needed something. They don't know how to change the battery on a smoke detector, I swear. Can you imagine calling the landlord for something like that?"

I could imagine literally anything. Imagination is limitless. But I doubted if that was what she was truly asking. "Did your husband— Mr. Fontaine—have *any* people who disliked him enough to do this to him?" I asked. I believed that *do this* was a more sensitive phrase than *hit him repeatedly with a tire iron until he died.*

"Brett had no enemies," Virginia Fontaine said with an air of superiority in her voice. "None. Everybody loved him."

"Clearly not everyone," I pointed out.

Virginia's head swiveled in my direction, but Ms. Washburn was quick enough to prevent what was clearly about to be an unexpectedly emotional response. "If no one was especially angry with Brett, maybe we need to look at this from another angle," she said. "Who would benefit from his being…out of the picture?"

I was unsure which picture Ms. Washburn meant, but I had read enough crime fiction to understand after a moment that she meant to ask if there were those who would do well financially or in some other way because Brett Fontaine was dead. Someone might indeed have decided to accelerate the moment when that would have occurred naturally. People can be extremely impatient when something they want is being withheld from them.

"Nobody," Virginia said. "Not even me. I mean, I was already his wife, so all his money was partially mine anyway. We never worried about whose bank account something came from. If we needed to buy something, we just bought it."

This meeting had proven especially fruitless. "So if you had to guess," Ms. Washburn said, "who would you think might have done this to your husband? Brett."

"I know exactly who killed him," Virginia said. "It was that bitch he was cheating with."

Some people use the term for a female dog as a pejorative. It is also considered an inappropriate word to many, but I am not certain why. Still, that did not seem to be the most pertinent issue here.

"But Melanie Mason has been dead for years," Ms. Washburn reminded Virginia. Ms. Washburn looked as if she was afraid her client was having some sort of health-related episode.

"Her ghost did it," Virginia said with a confident tone. "She wanted Brett all to herself."

ELEVEN

"THE WIFE IS CRAZY," Detective Monroe said. "Plain and simple. She bashed her husband's head in and now she's blaming it on a ghost. Either she's really nuts or she's pretending to be so she can plead unable to stand trial. Doesn't matter. She did it."

Ms. Washburn and I had called the detective after meeting with Virginia Fontaine with two purposes in mind: I wanted to hear Monroe's thinking on Brett Fontaine's death in relation to that of Virginia's first husband William Klein. Ms. Washburn appeared to be on a mission to convince the detective that there should be more suspects in the case, despite the fact that we had no information to which we could refer and no names we might offer as possible killers besides that of Virginia Fontaine. I was not trying to impede Ms. Washburn so much as I wanted to speak only about empirical evidence.

"Isn't it a little early to come to that conclusion?" Ms. Washburn asserted.

I had to admit she had a valid point. Monroe had been investigating Brett Fontaine's death for less than a full day and seemed to have decided the outcome of his research in a very short time.

"Just because the solution is easy doesn't make it wrong." Monroe was sitting behind a rather battered wooden desk that was separate from the rows of desks the uniformed officers used. Here in the Major Crimes unit, there were fewer investigators and less hectic quarters. I found that beneficial since loud noises and cacophony of sounds tend to distract or disturb me. "In a case like this, you look at the wife first. Did she think he was cheating on her? Yes, she did. Does she think he was cheating on her with a *ghost*, which makes her crazy? As a matter of fact, she does, and it does. Did she have access to a tire iron? Pretty much anybody who owns a car has one. Could she have bashed her husband over the head a bunch of times? You bet. Are there any other suspects who seem obvious? There are not. So you tell me: Why shouldn't I think the crazy lady killed her husband?"

"A few reasons," I said. "Ms. Fontaine would have had to assault her husband with a heavy tire iron numerous times until he was dead. Based on the evidence from the medical examiner's office, she then would have had to lift Mr. Fontaine's body, place it in a car or trunk, drive it to the scene where it was found and pull it out to arrange it, with fresh bloodstains, in the time between when her car turned the corner and when Ms. Washburn, who was following the car and probably would have seen her dragging the body into it, turned onto High Street only seconds later. I have met Ms. Fontaine and believe she does not possess the upper body strength necessary to perform those tasks."

Monroe looked at a file on his desk. I felt he was trying to avoid eye contact. "I don't believe the theory the ME is using about him being killed somewhere else," he said. "There was plenty of blood at the scene. How'd it get there if he wasn't killed there?"

It was a fair point and one for which I had no answer yet.

"What about Virginia's alibi?" Ms. Washburn asked.

"She said she was at the mall. She didn't buy anything so there are no credit card records. She said she bought a soft pretzel but she paid cash. She didn't keep the receipt; go figure. And I don't have the security records from the mall yet, but I'm willing to bet she won't show up on those video files." Monroe redirected his attention from the file to Ms. Washburn, no doubt to reassert his authority. "She's crazy. She believes in ghosts. She killed him."

There was no point in trying to change Monroe's mind and that was not why I had come here anyway. "Have you looked into Mr. Fontaine's business dealings?" I asked.

"It's been less than a day and I have other open cases. No, I haven't actually found out much about how he rents houses to college kids who trash them on a regular basis. Not yet. But who's your suspect there? Some sorority girl who saw a roach and decided to take revenge on her landlord?"

"I was thinking it might be a rival who wanted one or more of his properties or believed Mr. Fontaine had somehow did him or her wrong in a business deal," I told him. The idea of a frightened student had not occurred to me and seemed implausible. That was the impetus for a phone call to the landlord, not a murder. Perhaps Monroe had been joking.

"There's no evidence other than what we have on the wife," Monroe reiterated. "So why am I talking to you, again?"

"I am wondering about the fact that the body was found in front of the very house from which Ms. Fontaine's first husband, William Klein, fell to his death some fourteen years ago," I said. "Surely you must admit the coincidence is too severe to ignore."

Ms. Washburn's face looked slightly tense. I wondered if she believed I should not have mentioned that aspect of the question we were researching.

"That just proves my point," the detective said. "She probably killed the first husband too. Who else would go to the trouble of killing the second husband in exactly the same spot?"

"Did you look into the death of William Klein?" Ms. Washburn asked. "Was there any evidence that someone killed him?"

"I have a cop researching that now," Monroe answered. "But I'm willing to bet you someone pushed him off that fire escape. A woman doesn't lose two whole husbands this way with no connection whatsoever." He seemed to find some pleasure in what he'd said and leaned back in his chair in a pose of relaxation. I decided not to bring up the missing bolts because that would only have fueled Monroe's suspicions about Virginia Fontaine, and he obviously had not researched the incident energetically.

"One last thing," I said. "The angle of the blows to Mr. Fontaine's head. Has there been any analysis of the height of the assailant, and how tall he or she might be?"

Monroe's relaxed disposition evaporated in a blink. He leaned forward. "We haven't done the math yet," he said. He sounded oddly defensive, as if I were accusing him of something. I was simply asking a question that might have aided in the answering of Ms. Fontaine's question. "I can tell you that Fontaine was about six feet but pretty light for a guy that size. So she might have been able to drag him around the way you said, but I don't think that's what happened."

"What do you think happened?" Ms. Washburn asked the question I felt Monroe had been quite clear, if baseless, in answering more than once before.

But his answer was not the one I'd expected. "I think that if the ME's report comes back that Fontaine *was* killed somewhere else and moved to High Street, it doesn't rule out his wife as the killer. It just means she had help."

I had considered this previously but had no expected response to the question I asked. "Who do you think was abetting her?"

Monroe's eyes narrowed. I believe it was possible he was trying to conjure up the correct definition of the word *abetting*. "The guy who's been *abetting* her for two years," he said with an edge of triumph in his tone. "Her lover, Leon Rabinski."

———

"Leon Rabinski is vice president for development at Fontaine and Fontaine Real Estate. He's essentially the second-in-command," Ms. Washburn said. She was looking at her computer display in the Questions Answered office and reading from the company's website. Still feeling that Ms. Fontaine's question was chiefly her responsibility, she had walked directly into the office and begun her work. I had the utmost confidence in Ms. Washburn's abilities and saw no reason to step in ahead of her. I was looking into some other aspects of the question, including the death of Melanie Mason and her connection to Brett Fontaine. Just to be certain, I was also trying to discern if Melanie had somehow intersected with William Klein as well, but my research was in its very earliest stage at the moment.

"Development?" I asked. "As I understood it, Mr. Fontaine owned a few apartment buildings and rented them out to Rutgers students. What does the vice president of development do?"

"According to the *About Us* page on the website, he is responsible for finding appropriate properties for the company to acquire," Ms. Washburn answered. "But Brett Fontaine appears to have been the face of the operation, because prospective tenants are directed to him by phone or email if they're interested in renting an apartment near campus."

I felt myself stroking my chin, which required shaving. "I doubt such information would be on the company's website, but have you found any indication that Leon Rabinski was somehow romantically involved with Virginia Fontaine?"

"It's not the kind of thing a person with a working brain posts on Facebook," Ms. Washburn noted. "There are no Instagram pictures of them together or Pinterest posts that even hint they ever met each other. I'm going to keep looking. Should we call Ginny and ask her about this?"

I shook my head, glad Ms. Washburn was still looking to me for advice. "I don't think there would be a point. If she were having an affair with Leon Rabinski, I believe Ms. Fontaine would surely lie about it. Besides, she is planning her husband's funeral."

"You're right," Ms. Washburn said. "That was kind of insensitive of me, wasn't it?"

The thought had not occurred to me. "I just meant she was probably quite busy and would not answer the phone," I told her.

"Either way." Ms. Washburn turned toward her screen and began working the mouse attached to her computer. She looked distressed. I did not know if I should do anything to relieve whatever feeling she was having, or what it was I would do if I were sure such a thing was appropriate. I chose to get back to my own research largely because it was the job I had agreed to do, but also because I decided Ms. Washburn would be more cheerful if we were showing some progress in answering Virginia Fontaine's question.

Without being excessively detailed about my process, I spent seventy-three minutes delving into two aspects of Brett Fontaine's murder: the idea that the body had been posed in front of the home on High Street and Mr. Fontaine's friends and business associates.

Since Virginia had mentioned the name, I began with a look at her late husband's friend Peter Belson. He was currently working for a chain of three car dealerships in Bergen County as director of advertising. Belson had graduated from Fairleigh Dickinson University at the same time as Brett Fontaine with a degree in communication and had worked as an advertising consultant on a freelance basis before starting his current job seven years earlier. He was married with three children and lived, if my information was correct, in Paramus.

It took only a few passes to find a telephone number for Belson, although I could not be certain if it was a landline at his home—which in the current climate would probably have been disconnected or fallen into disuse—or a cellular telephone. Once I had the number and had confirmed it was Belson's however, I was reluctant to use it. I do not like speaking to people I have not met and am especially reluctant to do so on the telephone. Even though I miss a good number of visual cues in a face-to-face conversation it is somewhat reassuring to know they are there. I might notice some of them. With a telephone that is not a possibility.

My dilemma was postponed but not solved when Ms. Washburn broke the relative silence (there had been the sound of computer keyboards being used and chairs being shifted). With no prior indication, she said, "Samuel, I think I've found something."

Normally I would have suggested that Ms. Washburn would know if she had found something or not, but I was relieved to stop thinking about calling Peter Belson and was trying to be especially sensitive to Ms. Washburn's feelings, which is not easy for a person like me. First I have to determine what those emotions are, then try to imagine how it feels to have them, and finally decide how best to deal with them. It can be mentally exhausting.

In this case I looked at Ms. Washburn. "What have you found?" I asked. It seemed she'd been waiting to be asked so I provided the stimulus for a response.

"I was looking for a connection between Virginia Fontaine and Leon Rabinski but I didn't find one," she said. That seemed to be the opposite statement to what I had asked. I decided, however, that Ms. Washburn surely must have more to reveal because I have noticed her judgment many times in the past and she is not the type of person who would make a declaration with no facts to support it. I waited and she continued. "But I stumbled over something that might give some weight to Virginia's original claim."

It took me a moment to consider that. "The idea that her husband was involved in an extramarital relationship with a ghost?" I asked. That hardly seemed possible. I have been clear about this subject: There are no ghosts.

"Exactly. I looked into Leon Rabinski's background and I found that he graduated from Fairleigh Dickinson the same year as Brett Fontaine." Ms. Washburn looked at me, but I was irritated with myself for not having found this piece of information when I was researching Peter Belson.

"I imagine there are several hundred people in the graduating class at that university," I said. (In fact, research has shown that more than 3,000 people are in a typical commencement at Fairleigh Dickinson University.) "Is that fact significant?"

"It is when I found that Leon Rabinski and Melanie Mason were married six years ago, three years before she died," Ms. Washburn said.

TWELVE

"MELANIE WAS THE MOST amazing woman I ever met." Leon Rabinski smiled softly at the memory of his late wife. "She was so alive, so energetic and enthusiastic, that for three weeks after she passed I was sure it was all a mistake and I waited for her to come walking through the door." Rabinski looked toward the entrance of Fontaine and Fontaine Real Estate, a rather disappointing office in a nondescript office building in New Brunswick, as if this were the door he had been discussing. I assumed it was not.

Ms. Washburn and I had intended to visit Brett Fontaine's place of business anyway, but the revelation about Rabinski's marriage to Mr. Fontaine's college girlfriend had accelerated our interest in the office. It was as plain and indistinct as such businesses usually are. Real estate agents do not often bring clients to their places of business, preferring to view properties in person and signing documents in the clients' homes. There is no reason to have an especially aesthetic workplace.

"Did you meet your wife at Fairleigh?" Ms. Washburn asked. New Jerseyans often abbreviate the name of Fairleigh Dickinson

University as a kind of insider shorthand. I have never heard it questioned.

"Actually, no," Rabinski answered. "I met her at a party at Pete Belson's apartment ten years ago. Fairleigh's a pretty big campus and you don't get to know everybody in the place or even everybody in your class."

"But when you met her at Mr. Belson's place, you hit it off right away?" Ms. Washburn said. I disagreed with her choice, giving the person being interviewed an answer instead of insisting on his own account of the event. But I was allowing her to do most of the questioning. I was finding it difficult to restrain myself but I did trust Ms. Washburn. To this point she had not made what I considered to be a major error.

"Sort of," Rabinski answered. "She was so beautiful I figured I didn't have a chance with her so I didn't really do much except stand around and talk to her. She told me later she liked that and thought I was funny. In a couple of weeks we were dating. Go figure."

"She died in an automobile accident?" I said. I had not agreed to remain entirely silent; Ms. Washburn had not asked me to do so. But her expression indicated some impatience. I later asked and she told me it was not about my asking a question but that she thought my manner would especially upset Rabinski.

Indeed, he almost winced at the memory. Then he nodded. "Yeah. She was driving on Route 22 in Union and a guy in a truck came around one of those crazy ramps they have there. I don't even think he'd been drinking; he just didn't look. Mel's car was pushed and hit by a BMW, then went up in flames. Everyone else walked out without a scratch." He shook his head at the idea. "Ruined my life and nothing happened to that truck driver at all."

Ms. Washburn's tone was certainly gentler than mine had been, I see in retrospect. "So you had a happy marriage." It was stated as a fact, not posed as a question, and Rabinski did not respond. He accepted the information and confirmed it by not challenging the speaker. Ms. Washburn did not lean forward, did not suggest through her body language that she was about to ask a more personal question than before. "Were you aware that your wife and the man you work with were involved years before you met her?" That was as sensitive a way to ask an insensitive question as I could imagine, so I took note of Ms. Washburn's style.

As fitting the tone, Rabinski did not seem at all offended. "Of course I knew. We laughed about it. Mel never told me much about that time but when she found out I worked with Brett she was kind of stunned for a minute." He meant she was stunned for a *moment*, but I thought it counterproductive to intrude on the conversation. "She said they stayed friends, sort of, but I noticed when they saw each other at business parties and such, she made sure to be on the other side of the room. They said hello and that was pretty much it."

I thought it would be time to ask Rabinski about the rumors Detective Monroe had alluded to, that he was having an affair with Virginia Fontaine. But Ms. Washburn obviously wanted to take the inquiry in another direction, one I would not have pursued on my own.

"Forgive me for asking," she began, "but sometimes when a loved one passes away so abruptly, there's the feeling of unfinished business, that things were left in the middle and not at the end." Despite her asking for forgiveness, she had not asked Rabinski anything.

"I know what that feels like," Rabinski said. "I spent months rehearsing the conversation I thought we were going to have when she got home. I kept thinking, I guess, that if I got it right Mel would come back and I could talk to her again."

That seemed to charge Ms. Washburn's interest. "Did you ever try to talk to her again?" she asked. "A lot of people in your situation do that. They seek out someone who says they can reach to those who have left us and pass messages. Did you do that?"

Rabinski's mouth turned to one side as if he were chewing on an especially tough piece of meat. "You mean like mediums and that?" he said. "People who take your money and pretend they can talk to the dead? No, ma'am. I was devastated, but I wasn't crazy."

"So you've seen no sign of your wife since that night," Ms. Washburn continued. This was the ghost theory she was trying to pursue and I thought it particularly pointless.

"Of course not," Rabinski said. "Now, if that's it, I have to lock up the office and take off. I have a couple of appointments before I go home tonight." He stood up to signal that our conversation had ended.

I saw no other choice. "Are you having an affair with Virginia Fontaine?" I asked. It seemed the most likely way to obtain a direct response.

Ms. Washburn's expression indicated I had been socially inappropriate. I did not see how. Rabinski and I were not friends or even acquaintances. I was here to ask questions and receive information. I was asking the most pertinent question to the matter we were researching. Sometimes even Ms. Washburn interprets things in ways I fail to understand.

"What?" Rabinski was not, it should be noted, asking me to repeat the question because he had been unable to hear it. He was expressing some level of outrage, assumedly at me for asking such a personal question, but I saw no reason to respond and simply waited for him to continue. "Get out of my office."

That was not an answer to the question. "It is an important point," I explained. "If you are seeing Ms. Fontaine that might shed some light on a possible motive for Mr. Fontaine's murder. If you are not, we will know there is a definite flaw in the thinking of someone involved in that question. Do you understand?"

"I said get out," Rabinski responded. "And don't come back. You're not cops and I don't have to talk to you." He pointed to the door, as if our continued presence was evidence that we did not know how to leave the office.

"Thank you for your time," Ms. Washburn said, standing up and walking toward the door. "Sorry if we upset you."

"Just get out," Rabinski repeated. He wiped his face with his left hand although it had not seemed especially damp with perspiration.

I rose from my chair and followed Ms. Washburn to the door. Then I turned and looked at Rabinski, who had now covered his eyes with his palms and was inhaling deeply.

"Now that Brett Fontaine is dead, are you president of the company?" I asked.

Ms. Washburn led me out of the office before Rabinski could answer.

THIRTEEN

Ms. Washburn spoke very little during the drive back to the Questions Answered office, which took twelve minutes. This was not unusual, but she continued her relative silence even after we resumed our workstations, and that was not what I had expected. I decided she was deep in thought. I am often fairly uncommunicative when a question is consuming my interest.

She worked at her desk for thirty-two minutes while I attempted to make some sense of the succession of ownership at Fontaine and Fontaine Real Estate. The business listing with Middlesex County filed at its inception indicated that it had been owned jointly by Brett and Virginia Fontaine, but there were additional papers filed only six months ago redistributing the ownership equally to Brett Fontaine and Leon Rabinski with no mention of Virginia. There was no need at that time to explain the change in ownership and none was offered.

I had struggled to find additional documentation when Ms. Washburn broke the silence in the room by saying simply, "Samuel." My natural response was to look in her direction and I saw that Ms.

Washburn was walking toward my desk. "I have a thought about the way we're looking into Ginny Fontaine's question."

Since Ms. Washburn had been the lead researcher on the question and since I have always held her intelligence to be very high, it occurred to me that she was placing more emphasis on her current notion than usual. I nodded for her to continue because I wanted to communicate my interest in hearing more.

"I think maybe we should start interviewing people involved separately," she said. "It could make more efficient use of our time and we could choose our subjects based on our strengths. There's no reason for both of us to be there every time we talk to someone about this question."

To split up the work would be a break in protocol. For one thing, I do not drive very often so any interviews I conducted would require a ride to and from the venue assuming it was not within walking distance. But more interesting to me was Ms. Washburn's impetus for suggesting her strategy precisely at this moment.

"Surely that has always been the case," I answered. "What has raised this issue now?"

One thing Ms. Washburn has never done is to lie to me. But I could tell when she suddenly found a pen on my desk fascinating enough to watch it intensely that she was uncomfortable answering my question. "I've been thinking about it for a while," she said.

That was not an adequate response. "But you did not say anything to me," I answered. "Is there a reason on this question that it is better we split the interviews?"

Ms. Washburn squinted for a moment, almost as if wincing in pain. "I don't want to say this the wrong way, Samuel, because I don't think it will sound the way I mean it and I really don't want to hurt your feelings."

My feelings? There was something about this issue that would in some way embarrass or wound me and Ms. Washburn was attempting to shield me from the pain. What could that point be?

It came to me in a moment, all at once. "You felt that I was a liability at the interview with Leon Rabinski," I said, almost forgetting I was talking to Ms. Washburn. Neurotypicals tend to call this *thinking out loud*, as if such a thing were possible.

Ms. Washburn shook her head but continued looking at the pen. "Oh no, Samuel," she said. "I wouldn't say a *liability*."

The ideas came flooding into my brain. I had been blunt and socially awkward in the interview with Rabinski, asking him questions he found upsetting and interrupting Ms. Washburn. I had gotten us thrown out of his office. We might have gotten more information, as she was suggesting, if Ms. Washburn had been sent to talk to Rabinski alone.

Without me.

I stood up and began circumnavigating the room, raising my arms and increasing my speed. I barely heard Ms. Washburn say, "Samuel, it's not time for you to exercise yet. Samuel!"

But my momentum, fueled by the recriminations I was hurling at myself mentally (that is a metaphor), would not abate. I walked faster and faster and flung my arms into the air with increasing levels of force as I walked. I knew I was muttering aloud but was not able to control my thoughts or my speech.

"I *am* a liability, a drag on the business…It is my fault we have no strong information on this question…Ms. Washburn would be better off alone…If I could empathize with others I could find the answer…"

My mind was so cluttered with words and emotional thoughts that I had not even managed to count the number of laps I had completed around the office. I stopped only when I became aware of Ms. Washburn standing directly in my path at an especially narrow junction between the drink machine and one of the pizza ovens. She had a determined look on her face and was holding her arms out, palms extended, to halt my progress as I walked. Her strategy was successful, as I stopped directly in front of her. It is possible I even stopped talking to myself.

"Listen to me," Ms. Washburn said. "Nobody is suggesting that you aren't really good at what you do. The last person on this planet who would say such a thing is me. You've taught me so much I can't even begin to measure it. But in some cases the key is establishing a bond with the person you're talking to, and as it happens I might be better than you at that one thing. It's not a failure and you're anything but a liability. Samuel, you know you have a special mind and that's one of the reasons I love you. So stop blaming yourself for not being perfect and understand that maybe if we manage to split things up we can *both* do better."

I was breathing heavily and I felt a ring of perspiration at my hairline. My arms felt heavy. My head was hanging a little low. I found myself looking at Ms. Washburn's feet rather than into her eyes and corrected my posture.

"Yes," I said. "Yes, you are correct about that. All of that. We should separate the work. I can ask Mike the taxicab driver to take me to my appointments. It would be more efficient and you can do better on your own without me to irritate some of the subjects. I see that you are right. But I think perhaps it would be best if I sat down now."

Ms. Washburn reached over to take my arm but I walked to my chair unassisted, feeling the cling of my shirt and wondering if I should consider bringing an extra set of clothing to the office for just such occasions.

She knelt down by the chair as I caught my breath, an expression that would indicate breath could try to elude someone. "Are you all right?" she asked.

I realized then I had sent an improper signal. "Of course," I assured Ms. Washburn. "I simply tried to do the laps around the office too quickly."

"Good." She took eight seconds to be certain I was not having a medical issue and saw my breathing was normalizing. "So you agree that we should split up the interviews?"

I had already said that was the case, but I nodded. "It seems logical to do so."

Another six seconds. "Is there anything you want to say to me, Samuel?" Ms. Washburn asked.

It would be possible to store an extra shirt and other items of clothing in the men's restroom in the office, but Ms. Washburn's question penetrated my thoughts and puzzled me. Clearly there was some response she was expecting. I did not know what it might be and that created some anxiety for me. If I said something that was not what Ms. Washburn was expecting, she would think me rude or insensitive. I am especially careful about this when talking to Ms. Washburn because by contrast I usually don't care whether other people consider me rude or insensitive.

"Thank you," I said finally. It seemed the safest choice, and I was grateful to Ms. Washburn for clarifying the issue and disillusioning me of the notion that I was a useless member of the Questions Answered organization. I hoped that was the issue to which she was alluding.

Her mouth twitched a tiny bit on the left side and she studied my face for four seconds. "You're welcome," she said. She stood and walked back to her desk and resumed her workstation.

I was not certain, but I thought I might have given her the wrong response.

Even as I continued to research the ownership of Fontaine and Fontaine—and became more convinced that Leon Rabinski and not

Virginia Fontaine was now sole owner of the business—I mused over the most recent exchange with Ms. Washburn. Should I ask her what response she had been expecting? Should I consult Mike the taxicab driver (who often explains some human interactions to me) when he drove me home this evening? Would it make sense to ask my mother over dinner, or would I be inhibited by the presence of Reuben Hoenig?

The interaction had dominated my thinking for twenty-six minutes when Ms. Washburn stood and said she was going to leave for the day. She asked if I'd like a ride home and I declined. Tonight it was probably best to contact Mike the taxicab driver.

───────

"So Janet told you that you weren't a drag on the company and you said thank you." Mike the taxicab driver knew better than to converse with me while operating the Toyota Prius he drives professionally. He was speaking as we waited for a red traffic light. "I don't see anything wrong about that, Samuel."

I will admit to a sense of relief. "I am glad to hear it. I would not want to hurt Ms. Washburn's feelings."

"Especially now that she's your main squeeze," Mike said. I could see the side of his mouth widen to a grin even from the back seat of the taxicab. Mike likes to use such terms just to see if I will react to them, but with an iPhone I have been able to look up definitions even as we travel so I can respond appropriately. He had used this one four times previously.

"I do not think you are analyzing our relationship accurately," I said, most likely for the fourth time. "But I am glad you don't see a serious mistake in what I said."

We were silent as Mike began to drive again and waited until he had parked the car in my mother's driveway. Mike secured the parking brake and turned to face me before I could make my way out of the taxicab.

"I know Janet," he said. "If she reacted the way you said she did, something was bothering her maybe just a little. Are you sure you didn't leave anything out of the story?"

I did not believe there had been an omission but tried to remember everything that had been said. I recited as much of our conversation as I could recall verbatim to Mike, but it was not complete. I do not remember everything people say to me. Even when I care about the other person's emotions and the topic being discussed, my mind tends to focus on certain areas at the expense of others. It was something I had been attempting to work on in sessions with Dr. Mancuso.

When I had finished my recitation Mike tilted his head slightly to one side and pursed his lips. "I'm not hearing anything that would get somebody upset," he said. "Maybe Janet's just in a mood."

"Everyone is in a mood," I told him. "They vary in tone and intensity."

Mike laughed. "That's true, Samuel. You need me in the morning?"

I got out of the cab and walked to the side of Mike's open window. "I will text you if I do," I said. "Is the usual time agreeable?"

"That's why it's the usual time," he answered and nodded as he backed the taxicab out of the driveway. Mike does not allow me to pay him for the rides he gives me and I have, after many attempts, stopped offering because he told me to do so.

It was, as had often been the case, comforting to talk to Mike about my conversation with Ms. Washburn and more so to hear him speak on the subject. Mike says he has had many interactions with women and understands such relationships much more fully than I do. I felt less anxious about the look on Ms. Washburn's face.

But I still had trouble falling asleep that night.

FOURTEEN

"Brett Fontaine was a good businessman. He was a loving husband. He was a good friend. And he was a man of integrity and humility. His loss will be felt by all of us for the rest of our lives."

I had merely been planning to ask for directions to the restroom in order to wash my hands, but the man in the suit was mumbling his words seemingly into his necktie. His head was bent and he was speaking quietly and quickly. He looked up at me after he was finished. "Did you hear that?" he asked.

"Yes," I said.

"What did you think?"

That was an interesting question. "About what?" I said. I honestly wasn't sure whether the man was asking about what he'd been saying or about his necktie, which was dark blue and matched the somber tone set by his black suit.

"About my eulogy. How did it sound?" The man was wearing a black *yarmulke* which was affixed to his hair with a bobby pin.

"It sounded very quiet and rushed," I told the man. When Ms. Washburn and I had decided to attend Brett Fontaine's funeral, I had not expected to be pressed into service as a critic of oratory.

"I don't mean the delivery," the man said. "I have to get up and say that in front of the crowd so I was rehearsing it to myself. I'm asking what you thought of the speech itself."

"I was just looking for the restroom," I said again.

"Perfect! I was going there myself. Follow me!" And the man headed through the outer door of the memorial home. I felt I had no choice but to go along since that had been my intent to begin with.

Ms. Washburn was parking her Kia Spectra and had suggested I go ahead. I had accidentally touched a chewing gum wrapper in Ms. Washburn's car and was anxious to wash my hands. Otherwise I would not have considered entering a public restroom I had never seen before. But now there was no choice so I followed the man in the black suit and the *yarmulke* and he did in fact lead me to a door designated GENTLEMEN. I did not dispute the idea but was certain some males who were not at all refined must have passed through this portal at some time or another.

It was not that the facility, the Crescent Hill Memorial Home in Somerset, was at all disreputable or had an unsanitary appearance. It was simply the mathematical idea that all people who opened this door were genteel that was unlikely. It was entirely possible, although not certain, that one person who walked over the threshold today could be a murderer.

The man in the black suit turned to me as he walked. "The eulogy," he said. "Tell me how you thought it sounded." I had already responded to that specific question but was now aware the man was asking something other than what his words might have indicated.

"I thought it sounded like something a person would say if he did not know Brett Fontaine very well," I told him.

The man's mouth flattened out and his eyes took on a sad expression. "I was afraid of that."

I walked to the row of sinks and chose one that looked less recently used than the others. They were all in a good state of repair and looked freshly cleaned, which was reassuring. I turned on the hot water and waited for it to warm.

The man, who had gone off to a corner where I thankfully could not see him, walked back toward me and took up a spot at the sink to my left. "What do you think I could do to fix the speech?" he asked.

He seemed preoccupied with his eulogy for Brett Fontaine, about whom he seemed to know only the most basic of facts. I had been researching Mr. Fontaine for only three days and already had a better sense of him than the man in the black suit was exhibiting.

"If you are insecure about the eulogy, why must you give one at all?" I asked. "I assume the speeches are voluntary." The water had reached the desired temperature so I began to wash my hands, which made my skin feel much better.

"Not for me," the man in the black suit said. "I'm the rabbi."

That had not occurred to me. Indeed, it had not struck me that Brett Fontaine might be Jewish, although that did not make a difference to my research. What bothered me was that I hadn't known it until now.

I finished my task and reached for one of the towels—unfortunately cloth and not paper, which bothered me because I didn't know who had used it previously—left on the countertop. Reluctantly and gingerly I dried my hands and then turned toward the rabbi.

"Bolster your assertions with facts," I said. Then I turned and walked out of the restroom before he could ask me another question.

I met Ms. Washburn at the main entrance. "What should we be looking for today?" she asked me as we walked into the memorial chapel and took seats in the second-to-last pew. I wanted a vantage point for the whole room.

"Mostly we want to see who Mr. Fontaine's 'inner circle' might be," I said. "Look for those who spend the most time talking to his widow, those who offer eulogies, and those who make the most public displays of being upset about Mr. Fontaine's death. They will be the most likely suspects in our research."

"Are you thinking that someone who shows emotion in public is automatically a possible killer?" Ms. Washburn asked.

"Not necessarily, but it is the display that makes the difference," I said. I wondered if her tone was challenging. That is not always easy to identify. "If he or she is particularly interested in having us see the emotion, it might not be genuine."

"Interesting," Ms. Washburn said. I did not know exactly what message she was attempting to deliver. I doubted she found my thought any more interesting than others I have conveyed, yet she didn't usually feel compelled to comment on most of them.

But she didn't say anything else and I could not properly respond, given that I did not understand the situation clearly. In one minute and sixteen seconds the memorial service began.

Virginia Fontaine had already entered the chapel before Ms. Washburn and I had arrived. She was seated in the front pew. There was no casket on display; apparently Brett Fontaine's body had been released by the medical examiner's office in time to undergo cremation because there was an urn made of copper on a stand near the podium.

I noticed Leon Rabinski in the pew directly behind Virginia. He was not conversing with her and sat very still in his dark suit. I could not see his face so I can't report on his expression.

Detective Monroe was not present. I had wondered if the investigator might attend the memorial, but he did not either because he felt it would not enhance his understanding of the case or because he had already decided Virginia Fontaine was the killer and therefore any further observation was superfluous.

The room's capacity was roughly two hundred people but it was far from filled. A white-haired woman in a blue suit with a hat that no doubt held a veil was sitting next to Virginia. I assumed she was Brett Fontaine's mother. The three rows behind them, aside from Leon Rabinski, appeared to be accommodating family members. It was impossible to tell which ones were from Brett Fontaine's family and which, if any, were representing Virginia's.

On the opposite, or left side from my vantage point, there were fewer guests. Ms. Washburn and I sat near the rear doors and we represented precisely 10 percent of the people occupying seats in this half of the chapel. Those who were seated here were scattered, mostly in couples. There were no children present, something I thought was significant and fortunate. Under such circumstances young people are easily bored and tend to act out, or "create a scene," as Mother used to say about me.

In the eighth row back—which placed him six pews ahead of Ms. Washburn and me—sat a man, alone, in a dark sports jacket and denim jeans. I considered pointing him out to Ms. Washburn, who had insisted I wear a business suit and a tie. The suit was not a serious inconvenience for me, but I have a special dislike of neckties, which I feel are unnecessary articles of clothing that serve no practical purpose and make one's throat feel constrained. I pulled at mine thinking about it. But I felt that the comparison would not make Ms. Washburn, who was being unusually silent, any more amiable.

I did notice the man in jeans when he'd walked by us, however. He was in his thirties by my estimate and had long, unruly hair that flopped over the collar of his jacket. He appeared to squint at the podium as if struggling to see it clearly but did not avail himself of a closer pew, despite there being many seats empty ahead of him. He sat fully back in the pew and crossed his right leg over his left knee. He spoke to no one else in the chapel.

Being sure not to speak too loudly I touched Ms. Washburn lightly on the arm and pointed the man out to her. "He is not the same as everyone else in the room," I told her.

Ms. Washburn took a long look at the man. "He's a lot more informal," she noted.

"Anything that stands out could be significant," I said. "We should make an effort to find out who that man is."

Ms. Washburn turned and looked at me with an air of importance. "He's not displaying any outward emotion," she said. I was beginning to understand that my observation about displays of grief might have in some way been responsible for Ms. Washburn's sudden distant mood.

"That is not the only thing we should note," I explained. "It would only be one example, and even then, not a sure sign of guilt, just interest." I felt that better explained my original statement.

But Ms. Washburn did not seem better convinced. "Uh-huh," she said, then sat back and crossed her arms. Her mood was endangering my ability to adequately observe the event because I was thinking about two things at once, something that does not come to me easily.

"Ms. Washburn," I began. But she put her finger to her lips in a gesture meant to stop me from speaking further. She pointed discreetly toward the podium.

The man I'd met earlier who had identified himself as the rabbi was making his way down the center aisle and toward the podium, which he reached quickly. He appeared to be in a rush, like a man trying to get an unpleasant task completed as quickly as possible in an attempt to forget it had ever happened. I wondered if this was his first memorial service over which to preside.

He cleared his throat as soon as he reached the dais. I believe this sound was intended to quiet the gathered assemblage but it went unnoticed by most of the people in the room including Virginia Fontaine, who was engrossed in a conversation with the white-haired woman and therefore not looking toward the podium.

Finally the rabbi noticed a microphone attached to the podium and pulled it toward his mouth. "If we may begin," he said, and his voice was amplified far too loudly. Many spectators winced at the sound and there was some feedback from the sound system. This might explain why the rabbi never finished his sentence to explain what would happen if "we" were allowed to begin. He held up his hands. "Brett Fontaine was a remarkable man and we are here today to celebrate his life."

It occurred to me that this hardly looked like a celebration: The gathered group was subdued at best. The white-haired woman appeared to be sobbing. The man in jeans was looking away entirely and seemed to be thinking about something other than Brett Fontaine and whether or not he was remarkable. I wasn't puzzled but I felt the rabbi's choice of words was questionable.

"Born into difficult circumstances, he managed to grow into an ambitious and successful man with real estate holdings in three cities," the rabbi continued. "His properties brought shelter to those staying away from home for the first time."

That was probably inaccurate, in that most first-year college students are required to live in dormitories and on-campus housing. It was fairly clear the rabbi was trying his best to expand upon what was undoubtedly thin information and "spin" it into a complimentary speech about Mr. Fontaine. But from a professional point of view it was obvious he had not done enough research on his subject and was probably working from the newspaper obituary that had been published the morning of the funeral.

He went on for approximately nine more minutes and I did notice he had changed the closing of his eulogy, perhaps at my suggestion. "It is a deep sense of loss we're all feeling at this moment," he said. "Brett was a son, a husband, and a friend or colleague to everyone here. Our lives are diminished by his absence. But his buildings will continue to house students for years to come, and perhaps in that unbroken line we will find some solace. Brett is gone, but the good he did goes on."

The rabbi stopped then and waited thirteen seconds as if expecting applause but got none. Finally he seemed to compose himself again. "Is there anyone else who would like to speak?" he asked.

Having never met Brett Fontaine and only knowing of his existence for three days, it seemed inappropriate for me to volunteer. I looked at Ms. Washburn and she shook her head, understanding the question I was asking with my expression. I was relieved at her reaction because it showed she was still communicating with me despite having some issue that was making her act a bit distant.

There was a slight buzz through the gathered assemblage after the rabbi asked for volunteers to speak. But before anyone else could acknowledge a desire to do so, the man in jeans stood up and strode to the podium with what could only be described as a sense of purpose. The white-haired woman saw him, perhaps for the first time at the service, and gasped.

The rabbi moved to the side and walked down from the dais to the front pew, where he sat on the opposite side of Virginia Fontaine and the white-haired woman. The man in jeans pushed his hair away from his face and did not clear his throat as the rabbi had done. He had no need to do so. The room was silent again.

"My brother Brett was no saint," the man said. "He was a cheater and a liar and he cared about no one nearly as much as he cared about himself." If this was his idea of a suitable opening for a eulogy, I wondered if Brett Fontaine's brother would be considered a person with an autism spectrum disorder. He did not appear to understand what was rude, and if I could make that observation it was probably much more obvious to the others in the room.

"Brett thought he was smarter than most and maybe he was," the man in jeans continued. "He thought he was better-looking than a lot of men and women seemed to agree with him. It bothered him that he wasn't richer than he turned out to be but he always figured the next deal he made would take care of that because Brett believed he was entitled to anything he wanted."

Perhaps I had been too lenient in my initial assessment of the eulogy being delivered. It was probably one of the least complimentary orations I had ever heard.

"But there was something about him that made you forgive the guy over and over," Brett's brother said. "He asked for loans and didn't pay you back. He stole your girlfriend and never even apologized. He borrowed your car without permission, dinged it up, and told you it was already that way when he took it. But no matter what, when he came back the next time, his head hanging down because he knew he'd been a jerk, you always let Brett back in. Because that was his saving grace—he was a jerk, but he was our jerk. And he knew it."

The man in jeans turned and addressed the metal urn directly. "I'm gonna miss you, bro, even though I don't know why. You treated me about as badly as anyone ever has and all these years I loved you for it. I'll miss the phone calls in the middle of the night asking whether you'd made a mistake marrying Ginny."

There was an audible intake of breath throughout the room. Virginia Fontaine put her hand to her mouth and bit on a handkerchief she was holding. The white-haired woman looked down as if unable to bear the sight of the man in jeans. There was an audible guffaw from a woman sitting in the pews to our right, in the last row.

I noticed one man two rows in front of me smiling what I would have to describe as guiltily. He put his hand over his mouth immediately to cover his amusement. There was clearly something funny about the idea that Brett Fontaine had questioned his choice of wife, but I could not identify it.

"I'll miss the drunken nights you cried over your old girlfriend, the one who died in the car crash," the man in jeans went on. Leon Rabinski's eyes glared at him and a prominent vein showed in his neck. "I'll miss the times when your business was going down the tubes and you'd call me for advice."

Times? In the plural? It would have been significant if Brett Fontaine's business venture had failed once, but the man in jeans suggested there were more instances. My check on Mr. Fontaine's business, at least under his name, seemed to have been inadequate or mistaken. I took a deep breath.

Ms. Washburn appeared to notice the rise in my anxiety level. She put her hand on my arm and quietly asked, "You okay?" I nodded and repressed the feeling that I had failed. It was something I would have to address later when I had time.

"Maybe that's the genius you had, Brett," the man said. He appeared to be struggling to keep his composure but was not crying. If this was an act, it was a very convincing one. "You could do all these things that I'd hate anyone else for doing, and you made me love you for it. So damn you, my brother. And bless you too. I'm sorry to see you gone. And I'm sort of relieved at the same time. That's you, Brett. That's you."

The man in jeans immediately left the podium and walked back to his pew, where no one waited for him. He did not interact with Virginia, the white-haired woman, Leon Rabinski, the rabbi, or anyone else in the room. He sat down and resumed the exact position he had affected before, one leg swung over the other, staring away from the podium and the assembled mourners.

The rabbi, eyes wide, took a long moment—seven seconds—to compose himself and walked back to the podium. He looked out over the group.

"Does anyone *else* want to express a few thoughts?" he asked.

There was absolutely no response at all.

"Then thank you all for coming," the rabbi continued. He said there would obviously be no internment and mentioned that Virginia and Brett's mother, Iris, would be sitting *shiva* at Virginia's home that night and the next day. He nodded to the group and left the podium. The rabbi walked to Virginia Fontaine and offered his hand. She took it and they spoke too quietly to be heard from this distance.

Ms. Washburn looked at me after surveying the stunned assemblage. Almost no one had moved. Some were staring at the man in jeans. Others were devoting a great deal of energy to *not* looking at the man in jeans. Some put their heads down. Those who were speaking were doing so in hushed tones. There was a slight buzz of sound in the chapel.

"So," she said, "was that the kind of emotional outburst you meant?"

FIFTEEN

"It seems odd that we didn't know about Brett Fontaine's brother," I said to Ms. Washburn. "He is not mentioned in any of the obituaries and no one we have interviewed so much as suggested there was a sibling."

We had returned to the Questions Answered office after the memorial service had ended. My first impulse had been to interview a number of the spectators at the event, but Ms. Washburn had said that was not an appropriate place to gather information through questioning. The thought did not make sense to me but I often defer to Ms. Washburn regarding such matters.

I had insisted, however, on talking to the man in jeans. He was the closest to where Ms. Washburn and I had been sitting and seemed the least likely to be offended by my research into his brother's murder. Ms. Washburn was not interested in accompanying me, saying it would be good practice for our separate efforts on the question. She decided to stand outside the inner door and observe people as they exited.

I walked up to the man as he sat, seemingly relaxed, gazing out through the chapel's window toward the parking lot, where a number of guests were already finding their vehicles and leaving.

He noticed me because I was blocking his view, although why he thought it interesting was not clear to me. "You are Brett Fontaine's brother?" I said. A quick Google search on my iPhone had not unearthed any information on such a man.

"Yeah." The man in jeans did not stand and, much to my relief did not extend a hand to be shaken. But he also did not say anything more than that.

I searched my social skills training for an appropriate way to elicit a more helpful response. "I am sorry for your loss," I told the man.

That seemed to focus his attention. He looked at me. "Are you a cop?" he asked.

I didn't understand the question immediately but then realized my phrase had been something police officers and detectives often say to those they encounter during an investigation. "No," I answered. "Allow me to introduce myself. I am Samuel Hoenig, proprietor of Questions Answered."

The man in jeans looked up at me but did not directly react to the information I had given him. "You a friend of Brett's?"

"No. We never met."

That appeared to confuse him; his expression was one I'd seen fairly frequently in my life, with one eye looking at me and the other narrowed in thought, almost winking. "So why are you here?" he asked.

"I have been asked by your brother's widow to answer a question and this seemed like a good opportunity to gather information," I told him. That was probably something Ms. Washburn would have said was not tactful. I saw no other truthful answer to offer.

"I'll bet it is," the man said. "What have you found out so far?"

There was no advantage in sharing information with the man in jeans, particularly since I did not know if anything he had said was true, including his claim to be Brett Fontaine's brother. But I felt it would be inadvisable strategically to refuse sharing information. Studies have shown that most people tend to respond more favorably to those who appear to be cooperating with them or sharing their interests.

"So far the only person who has spoken to me is the rabbi," I told him truthfully. "He does not have much information to share."

The man in jeans grinned. "He's someone who got a phone call yesterday to come and preside over the funeral of a man he never met. Brett wasn't even a little religious and never attended temple after his bar mitzvah, as far as I know." He leaned back, giving the impression he was enjoying the moment. I would bet his favorite Beatles song was "Revolution." The single version, not the one on the White Album.

"I've been trying to determine who some of the people who came here today might be," I said. "Do you know most of them well?" It seemed likely he would; surely many of the attendees were relatives of Brett Fontaine, and therefore him as well.

The man stood up and turned toward the emptying chapel to survey the few people left other than ourselves. He sighed a bit theatrically. "I don't know most of them," he said. "But Pete Belson? Do you know him?"

"I have heard of him. Your brother met him in college." That was an attempt to show that I had actually gained some information about Peter Belson. It is important to establish one's abilities as a professional.

"Pete's a piece of work," the man in jeans said. The expression can indicate that the person being discussed is an impish prankster or someone who is difficult to deal with. "You should definitely talk to

Pete. He's the one that started the whole thing with Melanie Mason being a ghost."

I'm not sure I adequately disguised my surprise at his remark. My expression must have betrayed me because the man in jeans laughed lightly.

"Mr. Belson made up the story about your brother's college girl-friend?" I managed.

Again a chuckle, but the man in jeans did not look at me; he was taking stock of what now was otherwise an empty chapel. "Do you believe in ghosts?" he asked.

I was not sure if he expected a response, but it seemed disre-spectful to ignore the question. "I do not," I said.

"Good. Neither do I. So that leaves one conclusion to reach, don't you think?"

I could think of seven conclusions to draw from that information but I chose the most likely one. "Brett Fontaine was mentally ill?" I asked.

This time the laugh was rueful and the man in jeans shook his head. "I don't think Brett was crazy." Without explaining himself he turned back and looked at me closely. "Did I get your name?"

My sensibility was being tested. I had been clear about telling the man in jeans my name before but felt my best course of action was to do so again. "Allow me to introduce myself. I am Samuel Hoenig, proprietor of Questions Answered."

He took my hand and then let it go. "And what is the question you are trying to answer?"

I suppose I could have told him such information was confidential but I did not. "I have been asked who killed Brett Fontaine," I said.

The man in jeans nodded. "I figured as much. How's that going so far?"

This time I felt it was best not to disclose any information because certainly Brett Fontaine's brother, after the eulogy he had delivered, could not be ruled out as a suspect in the killing. "I don't believe you have introduced yourself," I said, changing the subject. "What is your name?"

The man in jeans smiled. "Patrick Henry," he said.

———

"Well, clearly his name isn't Patrick Henry," Ms. Washburn said later in the Questions Answered office. "Could it be Patrick Henry Fontaine?"

I stared at my computer display, which was filled with seven separate web page images pertinent to the question we were trying to answer. "I have already looked into that possibility," I told Ms. Washburn. "There were two men of some significance to American history with that name, both of whom had died by the early twentieth century. I can find no evidence anyone named Patrick Henry Fontaine is currently alive in the United States, and probably not anywhere else on Earth."

Ms. Washburn chewed the end of her ballpoint pen, a habit I find disturbing so I averted my gaze from her direction and looked back at my screen. Brett Fontaine's birth name was Neil Silverman but his father Myron had changed the family name two years after Brett was born and assigned new names to everyone in his family except his wife Sarah. The reason for the change was not clear.

"What do you think he meant when he said there was one conclusion that could be drawn from you not believing in ghosts?" Ms. Washburn asked.

"I'm not certain he was doing anything other than trying to understand me," I told her. "I think he said that to see what I thought the one conclusion might be."

Ms. Washburn made a very small grunting noise in her throat. "It's not always about you, Samuel," she said. I was about to suggest that I was aware of that fact but she did not pause. "He had something in mind that he wanted you to guess or something. Why do you think he gave you a fake name?"

I ignored the idea that the man in jeans had somehow changed my name because I understood what Ms. Washburn was asking, but it was a distraction. I was looking at a web page devoted to legends of ghosts and spirits in northern New Jersey but did not find what I was seeking immediately. "It should be easy enough to ask Virginia or one of his relatives what his name is, so it seems there is no advantage in not divulging his name," I admitted. "It's possible he simply enjoys manipulating people and doesn't like to answer questions."

"Well, I found out a few things while you were talking to him," Ms. Washburn said. "Peter Belson was at the service. I didn't get to see him because he must have left before I went outside, but Virginia Fontaine stopped to talk to me for a minute."

That seemed oddly uncharacteristic of Ms. Fontaine. "At her husband's memorial service she decided to answer questions about his murder," I said.

It had not been intended as a question but Ms. Washburn apparently thought it had. "I guess she saw me and thought I was there for a reason, because I was," she said. "Anyway, she said Peter had been at the service sitting with some of Brett's family. He got to know some of Brett's younger cousins when they were in college."

"Did Ms. Fontaine give you any contact information for Peter Belson?" I asked.

"She did." Ms. Washburn stood and walked to my desk. She sat in Mother's armchair because she knows I don't mind when Mother is not present. "This is easier than turning my neck every time we want to talk."

I thought it was just as easy to converse without looking at each other but that is one of the "quirks" the neurotypicals feel make me a person with a syndrome. In Ms. Washburn's case, I think she simply wanted to ease the tension in her neck.

"Virginia gave me a phone number and address for Peter as well as for a high school friend who wasn't there, Debbie Sampras, who Virginia said Brett kept in touch with. She said she doesn't think Debbie had anything to do with Brett's death, but she might know more about his possible affair with Melanie Mason."

Ms. Washburn's mention of the deceased woman as a possible lover for Brett Fontaine tried my patience. I wanted to say that was a ridiculous waste of time, but I knew Ms. Washburn believed in such things and had been taught to be tolerant of viewpoints other than my own no matter how absurd or based in fantasy they might be.

Besides, I enjoyed kissing Ms. Washburn and wanted to be able to continue.

"Perhaps this is where we should divide our efforts," I suggested. "If you will contact Debbie Sampras, I will get in touch with Peter Belson. Did Ms. Fontaine provide an email address for him?"

Ms. Washburn smiled but not in a delighted way. "You don't get out of it that easy, Samuel. No, Virginia didn't give me an email; you'll have to call Peter Belson on the phone." She seemed pleased at my discomfort at the idea. I'd seen that look before; it comes when Ms. Washburn believes she is helping me to "broaden my horizons."

"I will do so." If I did not show my dread of the phone call, it might convince Ms. Washburn that I had indeed made a leap and therefore was not in need of more "help." "But I take it Ms. Fontaine did not give you any information on the man who called himself Patrick Henry?"

Ms. Washburn shook her head. "I didn't ask about him because you were talking to him at that moment. It never occurred to me that he wouldn't want to tell you who he was. He said he was Brett Fontaine's brother, but Virginia never mentioned a brother, not even on her client intake form."

"Perhaps we should ask her now."

Ms. Washburn frowned. "I don't want to tell her we don't know who he is," she said. "It'll make us seem less competent than we really are, and I'll bet there are other ways to find out."

That seemed a reasonable concern given our lack of progress on the question to this point. It was best, then, to move to the next point.

"Did Ms. Fontaine have anything to say about the eulogy the man in jeans delivered?" I asked.

"She was pretty shaken. I didn't ask her about it." Sometimes I think Ms. Washburn's concern for the feelings of those we encounter in answering questions slows the process down but she always manages to get the information eventually. And I do have to admit that she knows when I am alienating a subject because I am not terribly concerned about his or her emotions. "But I have a hunch."

Before I could ask to what she was referring, Ms. Washburn stood and walked to her desk. She sat down and began punching keys and moving the mouse attached to her computer. I went back to the search on cemeteries because it seemed the best way to solve one of my own problems at the moment. Ms. Washburn's hunches usually proved to be useful. I would wait until she had confirmed or denied the one she was clearly trying to verify now.

Her search took less than three minutes, which I assumed meant it had been successful. If the evidence was proving her wrong, Ms.

Washburn would probably have continued looking in order to confirm that she had guessed incorrectly.

"Here," she said, pointing to her screen, which I could not see from where I sat. "I was right."

The idea here, from Ms. Washburn's point of view, was to demonstrate to me how intelligent she was (which I already knew) and to convey information at the same time. I walked to her desk and took up a position behind her chair so I could see what she was doing on the screen.

"I looked up the college yearbook for Fairleigh Dickinson the year Brett Fontaine graduated," she said. Indeed, the screen showed young men and women, dressed identically in the cap and gown associated with a commencement ceremony. "See anybody you recognize on this page?"

I scanned the faces. I am not especially skilled at analyzing facial features because I try to avoid looking at faces when possible. There are also some studies that suggest those of us with a difference in our neurological systems tend to look at faces in ways that most people do not. So trying to find a photograph depicting a face that might be similar to another I had seen was a very difficult task for me. I studied the page for fourteen seconds.

Ms. Washburn understood. "I'm sorry, Samuel," she said. "I forgot because I was trying to show off. Look at this picture." She indicated one of the photographs and enlarged it on the screen.

The photograph was approximately twenty years old but after some observation the face was recognizable. "That is the man in jeans," I said.

"I think it is." Ms. Washburn, proud of her achievement, was smiling widely.

"But the name beneath the photograph is Anthony Deane," I noted. "Is he a half brother of Brett Fontaine, or a brother who was adopted by another family?"

"No. Let me show you something." She called up a second screen with an image of another graduate from what I assumed was the same yearbook. His was a face I had seen only in photographs at that day's memorial service.

"That is Brett Fontaine," I said.

Ms. Washburn nodded. "Now look at the list of affiliations under each of their names." She positioned the two photographs side-by-side on her display.

"They both belonged to something called Sigma Pi."

"That's exactly right, Samuel. I'm guessing they were not related by blood. They were fraternity brothers."

SIXTEEN

"We were all brothers at Sigma Pi." Peter Belson sat behind his desk at Rt. 4 Chevrolet in Paramus and smiled into his web camera. "Brett, Mike, and me. There were maybe sixteen or seventeen others, but we mostly hung out by ourselves."

I had arranged this FaceTime chat, as such a conversation is called, with Belson once Ms. Washburn had left to interview Debbie Sampras, Brett Fontaine's high school friend. Debbie lived in Spotswood, which was considerably closer to the Questions Answered office than Paramus, and Ms. Washburn owned and operated a car. I did neither and Mike the taxicab driver had told me when he drove me to the office this morning that he could not be called upon to take me to Bergen County today, "not if I want to keep making a living." He might be back in time to drive me home, he said.

Belson had seemed content to communicate this way, telling me on the phone that he would have to "duck out" if a potential customer wanted to be shown a vehicle or if one of his sales staff needed advice or permission to make a deal. He preferred the flexibility and I was unable to travel the distance, so this was the best way to conduct our business. Although his title was director of advertising, he had told me he was also a "floor representative," or a member of the sales force.

"Why was that?" I asked. "Were you not friendly with the other members of the fraternity?" The question was probably not relevant to the question I had to answer, but it might shed some light on the type of relationship the three men had.

"Oh, we were friendly enough," Belson answered. He was a man in his late thirties with short hair that was graying but not receding. He wore a business suit and tie which he repeatedly pulled at and a wedding ring on his left hand that he occasionally turned on his finger as if to remind himself it was still there. "We just got along really well and the other guys were basically okay. I haven't kept in touch with any of them except on Facebook."

"But you did keep in touch with Brett Fontaine and Anthony Deane," I said. I thought I was presenting the information as a statement, but Belson seemed to think it was a question.

Before I could finish by asking when he's last seen either of his fraternity brothers—a title I felt was deceptive if not blatantly incorrect—Belson said, "Well, I kept in touch with Brett. I haven't seen Tony probably in two years. We just didn't have that much to talk about once we weren't in college anymore. You know, again on Facebook we'd run into each other and ask how things were going but that was about it."

"How often did you see Brett Fontaine, then?"

"Actually see each other, be in the same room? Maybe once or twice a year, not that much. With social media and cell phones we kept in touch, but I live up here and Brett was down there…" He did not complete his thought.

"Anthony Deane suggested that you started a rumor about Mr. Fontaine's college girlfriend being a ghost," I said. The statement was intended to take Belson by surprise.

His lack of an emotional reaction indicated it did not. "I never said that," he said. It seemed he'd been expecting me to bring it up. "I said that Mel was haunting Brett, but I didn't mean it literally. He just never stopped asking about her. She died in a car crash and he wouldn't shut up about her, him with a wife and everything. It seemed a little weird, to tell you the truth."

Had he not been telling the truth until that last point? That was a common expression but I never knew if it was being used literally or figuratively. I assumed in this case Belson was trying to establish a rapport with me and used the phrase in that context.

"You knew Mr. Fontaine and Melanie Mason when you were all in college," I said, not letting Belson speak before I added the question, "Why did their relationship end?"

He sat back in his chair and seemed to look out over the dealership, which I could not see. "Oh, why does any college love affair end?" he asked. I was hoping he did not expect an answer, since I had none and did not wish to research the subject. "Brett and Mel were the tightest couple around for a while but then he decided that was it and he called it off."

"And he did not explain how he made that decision?" Romantic relationships have always been a source of endless confusion for me. I have never understood how they begin, what forces in a person make them continue, and why they end. Until Ms. Washburn kissed me the first time I had considered the prospect somewhat intimidating. Letting a person into the most private aspects of one's life seemed incredibly inconvenient and potentially embarrassing. How Brett Fontaine, or any other person, could engage in a relationship to that point and then decide it should end appeared to hold no rational basis.

"He said he got tired of her, that she was always asking him questions," Belson answered. "If I remember—and it's been a long time—Brett said Mel had started to criticize everything he did and it was making him crazy."

I assumed he did not mean the relationship was literally driving Mr. Fontaine into a state of mental illness, but that he was using the expression to convey a certain frustration or anger that arose within it. But the idea of being asked questions as a basis to end what had been, according to Belson, a satisfying relationship to that point was intriguing.

Still, the romance between Brett Fontaine and Melanie Mason did not seem to hold significance to my question until much more recently. "You said that lately Mr. Fontaine had acted obsessed—that was your word, I believe—with Melanie Mason." It was not meant as a direct question; I simply wanted Belson to elaborate on that point.

He complied immediately. "Like I said, Brett started talking about Mel all the time. He'd text me and email me because like I said, we didn't really see each other that much, and who has the time to talk on the phone, right?" I did not answer that question. "Strange questions about was Mel faithful to him when they were together, did she ever say what she really thought about him, had I heard anything from her before she died."

"Had you been in touch with Melanie in the years after you received your degree?" I asked.

"No, not really. Once Brett broke up with her I really didn't have that much contact. You know, at the time I thought maybe I'd ask her out myself but I thought Brett would get mad so I forgot about it. Then I heard she got married because Brett told me. I think he went to her wedding."

I made a note on the pad at my right hand to ask Virginia Fontaine if she and her husband had attended the wedding of Melanie Mason and Leon Rabinski. "Yes," I said. "She was the wife of a close business associate of Mr. Fontaine. Do you know Leon Rabinski?"

Peter Belson very visibly twitched his mouth and looked up and to the left, indicating he was trying to remember something. Some people believe it is possible to determine if a person is lying or telling the truth based on the direction of such a glance, but others indicate that excessive hand movement is more indicative of a person trying to distort the truth. "Rabinski? I don't think so. He and Brett were working together? And he was married to Mel? That must have been weird."

Another aspect of romance that eludes me is the concept of jealousy. While a relationship is ongoing there is a logic to feeling angry at someone who seems to be trying to damage it. I still don't entirely understand it, but I can at least imagine the concern about a threat to something the person in question uses to ground him or herself emotionally.

But once the relationship has ended, there is no longer a connection (at least romantically) between the two people. Why one should feel threatened by a new suitor to one's ex-lover is difficult to grasp.

"But Mr. Fontaine had married as well, before Melanie and Leon Rabinski," I pointed out. I'm not sure if I was asking to further my research into the question or to better understand the dynamic between two former romantic partners. "Shouldn't each of them have simply accepted that the other had moved on to a more successful relationship?"

Belson wrinkled his brow. "I'm not a marriage counselor and I'm not going to pass judgment on Brett and Ginny's marriage. Wouldn't you be weirded out if your ex married someone you were working with?"

I didn't see how some hypothetical situation with which I was unfamiliar should have a bearing on this interview. "I don't know," I said honestly. It was best to move on quickly. "Did Mr. Fontaine's questions about Melanie begin before or after she died?"

The tone of Belson's voice and his facial expression seemed to indicate I had said or done something mildly inappropriate or at least surprising. "After," he said. "As far as I can tell, immediately after. And it went on right up until he ended up dead too." His voice choked unconvincingly on the last phrase.

"Do you know of anyone who was angry at Mr. Fontaine?" I asked.

"Someone who'd want him dead? Absolutely not. Brett was a great guy." Belson's eyes shifted to the left. He seemed to be paying attention elsewhere.

That was not the picture that had been painted at the memorial service I'd attended. "Anthony Deane did not seem to express that sentiment yesterday," I said. "Why did you choose not to attend the memorial service?"

Belson continued to look to a spot off-screen. "I had to work. I'm sorry, Mr. Hoenig, but there's a salesman waiting for me. I have to go."

"One last question," I said.

"No. I don't have time." And with that Belson disconnected the FaceTime session. I looked at my screen for three seconds.

When Ms. Washburn is not in the office I have a tendency to speak my thoughts aloud. Some find it a distraction so I do it only when alone.

"That was an odd conversation," I said. "I wish I could have seen his hands."

SEVENTEEN

"Debbie Sampras had been a friend of Brett Fontaine's since high school," Ms. Washburn said. "She said he never got over Melanie Mason and was obsessed with her since they broke up at Fairleigh."

Since she had returned to the Questions Answered office, Ms. Washburn had been typing her notes on the Debbie Sampras interview into her computer file for the Fontaine question. But she was telling me what she had learned even as she preserved the information digitally. I had given her the data I had gathered through my FaceTime conversation with Peter Belson.

"The two stories don't appear to intersect at any point," I said, mostly so I could hear the thought out loud. "Belson said that Brett Fontaine was the one who ended the relationship with Melanie Mason, and that he'd known her even when she was married to Leon Rabinski, but did not become, as both Ms. Sampras and Belson put it, *obsessed* with her until after she had been killed in the vehicular incident on Route 22."

"Maybe he was obsessed with her the whole time but it came out after she was dead because he'd married Ginny and wanted to think he'd moved on," Ms. Washburn suggested. She continued to stare down at her notepad—Ms. Washburn does not record interviews but takes extensive notes in a version of shorthand she created for herself—while she typed and spoke. I marveled again at her ability to multitask, something I would have found overwhelming or impossible.

"If that is the case, why did he end the relationship at all?" I asked.

"Debbie said he didn't," Ms. Washburn answered. "She said it was Melanie who broke up with Brett. He told Debbie about it because they were that close, but he told the rest of his friends and anyone else who would listen that he couldn't stand how Melanie clung to him, but it wasn't true."

I mused on that while examining a photograph of a gravestone whose inscription was worn but still readable. "Why would he do that? Why not simply tell the truth and say that Melanie had ended their romance?"

To my right I heard Ms. Washburn chuckle. "Some men just can't admit to their truest emotions, Samuel. They cover up the pain and pretend it's someone else's fault or someone else's problem."

"Odd." The stone did not reveal anything especially useful so I moved on to the third newspaper account of Melanie Mason's death that I had discovered. The first two had simply been reported from reading a police blotter on the accident and it showed. They were written by two separate people but were almost identical. I wondered if this one would be different.

"It's a lot more common than you think," Ms. Washburn said. I don't know how but she managed to convey wordlessly the message that she was now looking in my direction. She had stopped typing. Curious, I looked at her. "But Debbie said more than that. She told me that she thought Anthony Deane had killed both Brett Fontaine *and* William Klein."

Clearly Ms. Washburn's interview with Debbie Sampras had been more productive than mine with Peter Belson. That was both encouraging and disturbing. "Why would he do that?" I asked. "How could Deane have even known William Klein? He was dead for years before Brett Fontaine met his wife Virginia."

"Anthony Deane is the link," Ms. Washburn said, a slight grin of triumph (or what I saw as triumph) on her face. "He knew Virginia when she was married to William Klein and it was at his stand in the Metuchen farmers' market that Brett asked Ginny to marry him."

"He might have known Virginia Fontaine when her name was still…" I tried to remember the name she had included on her client intake form.

"Virginia LoBianco," Ms. Washburn said.

"Yes, thank you." I answered. "Because Anthony Deane knew Virginia LoBianco or Virginia Klein does not mean he was at all familiar with her first husband. Why does Debbie Sampras believe that he had something to do with William Klein's death?"

"Because Debbie says he was always in love with Virginia, was angry that she married men who weren't him, and he visited William the day he fell off the fire escape."

I stood up. "I believe we should take a trip," I said to Ms. Washburn, "assuming you are not tired of driving today."

She reached for her purse. "Where are we going?"

"To the New Brunswick police station to see Detective Monroe."

———

Detective Jack Monroe did not want to have a meeting with Ms. Washburn and me, and he made that very clear when he walked into the waiting area where the police dispatcher was in touch with officers in cruisers and on the street. She had told us to wait for him and it had taken him eight minutes to walk through the locked door and say he didn't want to see us.

"I have a homicide to work," he said. "I don't need amateurs coming through here trying to solve it themselves. I already had enough information. Only one of you was on the scene when it happened and we've already talked to you." He looked at Ms. Washburn. "If I have any further questions, I'll get in touch. Now, go home." He turned to walk back through the door to the bullpen where his cubicle was located.

"We have a link between William Klein's death and Brett Fontaine's," I said as quickly as I could. It is possible I said it more loudly than I had anticipated, since voice modulation is not something I do especially well.

Monroe stopped in his tracks and turned to regard me. "What's that?" he said.

Ms. Washburn stood, perhaps to look more defiant. It certainly seemed that way to me. "We'll tell you when we're inside," she said.

Monroe took a deep breath and seemed to think. He shook his head, perhaps involuntarily. "All right," he said. He made a sweeping gesture toward the door, which he opened when the dispatcher unlocked it from within her bulletproof compartment. "Let's hear what you've got to say. But it better be worthwhile."

We wasted no time following him back to the area designated as his workspace. Once there he gestured, somewhat limply, toward the two chairs in front of his desk and Ms. Washburn and I sat. Monroe maneuvered himself through the cramped space and sat behind his desk looking stern. "What's the link?" he asked.

"A man named Anthony Deane. He was a member of the same fraternity at Fairleigh Dickinson University as Brett Fontaine and he introduced Mr. Fontaine to his wife, Virginia. We have a source who says Mr. Deane visited William Klein the day he died, so he knew both of Virginia's husbands. He bridges the gap."

Detective Monroe sat back in his chair and looked at the rather badly stained ceiling. There had clearly been some kind of incident involving water in this building sometime in the past, probably three to five years. He made a discontented noise softly as if feeling a mild ache and then turned his gaze toward Ms. Washburn and me.

"Why do you people come here and ruin my perfectly good case with outside facts?" he asked.

I could not answer because I had no idea what an outside fact might be. Ms. Washburn, who I'd noticed had been watching the detective with a look in her eye that indicated she might not hold him in the highest regard, crossed her arms. That was never a sign that Ms. Washburn was pleased.

"Why do you just want to confirm your suspicions and not find the truth?" she asked.

"Hey." Detective Monroe tilted his chair forward and rested his elbows on the desk in front of him. "I follow the case where it goes." There was no evidence he had been doing so, but we had not been able to watch him constantly since Ms. Washburn found Brett Fontaine's body on High Street. The detective picked up a ballpoint pen from his desk and fished a notebook from his top drawer. I noticed the open file regarding Brett Fontaine's murder on his desk and examined what I could from this distance and vantage point. It was difficult to see clearly. "What's the name of your source on this?" he asked.

"We keep our sources confidential," Ms. Washburn told him. I was aware of no such policy and almost pointed that out to her, but she spoke again quickly, perhaps anticipating my impulse. "But we don't want to impede an ongoing police investigation. I'll tell you what: We'll be glad to trade the information for some of yours."

The detective, beginning to understand the person he was dealing with, looked cross. "You realize I can go to a county prosecutor and get a subpoena compelling you to tell us," he said.

"Do you really want to go through all that paperwork?" Ms. Washburn asked. Her tone was concerned, empathetic. It was interesting to watch her bargain with the detective.

Detective Monroe clearly was no fan of doing paperwork, which Ms. Washburn must surely have concluded by looking at his paper-covered desk and the piles of forms on either side of him. His mouth twisted a little. "What is it you want to know? And you realize my asking that does not mean I'm saying I'll trade."

Ms. Washburn and I had discussed this possibility during traffic light stops on the way to the police station. "We would guess you had officers canvass the whole street where Brett Fontaine's body was found," she said. "I was the one who discovered his body, but it isn't possible absolutely no one else saw anything. We want any relevant information your officers collected from the street canvass. We don't need all the names and addresses, just the ones that saw something. For that we'll give you the person who knew Anthony Deane and Brett Fontaine well enough to connect the two and place Deane on High Street the day William Klein died. If your records show someone meeting his description on the street when I was following Brett Fontaine, you might very well have your killer all wrapped up in a neat package."

"I still think the wife did it," Monroe said.

"It is not wise to reach a conclusion when there are not sufficient facts," I told him. "What you have regarding Ms. Fontaine is circumstantial evidence, which I will admit is compelling but has considerable weakness if you were to arrest and charge her. I'm sure the prosecutor would tell you that if he or she has not already."

Monroe took a thumb drive out of his desk drawer an inserted it into a USB port on his desktop computer. "She had motive and she could have had opportunity," he said in something very close to a mumble.

"But there are no witnesses I know of who are saying she was at the scene when Brett Fontaine's body was left there," I pointed out. "And there is the issue of height. Ms. Fontaine is not a small woman but she stands only about five-foot-five. If Mr. Fontaine was tall, and my records indicate he was six feet, she would have had a very difficult time inflicting the kind of wounds that killed him."

"She could have stood on a box." Monroe, having moved his mouse and saved a file to the drive, removed it from his computer. He held it up in front of Ms. Washburn. "Now, who's this mysterious source of yours?"

"We want to see the file you put on there first," Ms. Washburn responded. "For all we know you just gave us snapshots of your trip to the Grand Canyon." That seemed unlikely but I did think confirmation was a vital component of the bargain she had made.

"I gave you what you asked for." Monroe sounded offended. "Check it for yourself." He handed Ms. Washburn the thumb drive. She removed her laptop computer from her tote bag and handed it to me. I inserted the drive as soon as the computer was functioning. After a very cursory look, I nodded to Ms. Washburn; the file was what Monroe had promised.

"Our source is a woman named Debbie Sampras," Ms. Washburn said. She had called Debbie before we left the Questions Answered office and obtained permission to give her name to Monroe. Debbie, she said, had been eager to tell her story but had not been contacted by any member of the New Brunswick Police Department. "She was a high school friend of Brett Fontaine's and she stayed in touch with him until he died. She was at his memorial service. She knew him and she knew Virginia. She believes Anthony Deane was in love with Virginia Fontaine but she wasn't interested in him. Debbie thinks he killed both of Virginia's husbands."

Monroe listened to Ms. Washburn first with an air of interest and then, as she continued, a look of skepticism. Or at least that was what Ms. Washburn told me his expression had meant when I asked her about it hours later.

"She thinks?" he said. "How does she know any of this?" It was not unreasonable for a detective to ask for evidence that would be useful in court. But Monroe's tone was belligerent, almost mocking. I have become better at recognizing the modulations people use in speech than the meaning of their facial expressions. I am not always capable of expressing those modulations myself, Mother has told me.

"Debbie was around the whole time," Ms. Washburn explained. "I only spoke with her once, today, but she was very close to Brett and he told her things that apparently even his other friends didn't know. She's convinced Anthony Deane is the killer. I don't know about that, but I think it's at least worth talking to her."

Monroe stood up. I did not understand the maneuver until Ms. Washburn stood as well. Apparently it was the detective's way of signaling that the meeting was concluded and we should leave. I got to my feet but did not walk toward the bullpen.

"I'll talk to her," Monroe said as Ms. Washburn took three steps and then turned to look at me questioningly. "But I'm telling you, the wife did it."

"I have one last question," I said as Monroe noticed Ms. Washburn's look and followed it to me. I did not give the detective an opportunity to say he was too busy or that we'd already gotten as much information from him as he was willing to give. "Did the medical examiner find any traces of olive oil at the scene where Mr. Fontaine's body was discovered?"

Detective Monroe's eyes almost closed and his eyebrows moved toward each other. "How did you find that out?" he asked. "The ME's report hasn't been made public yet."

"Thank you," I said. "That was all I needed to know."

EIGHTEEN

"Olive oil?" Ms. Washburn asked.

She had just driven her Kia Spectra into the driveway of the house I now shared with both of my parents. Ms. Washburn had declined to join us for dinner, largely I believed because it had been a long day and she knew I would probably be talking about Ms. Fontaine's question until I could put the pieces of the puzzle together in my head. That was a metaphor. There were no pieces of a puzzle in my head. I assume you knew that.

"I believe olive oil might be the key to discovering where Brett Fontaine was actually killed," I explained. "There were photographs of the scene on Detective Monroe's desk which he did not attempt to conceal from us."

"I saw them," Ms. Washburn said. The car was still running but she had safely placed it in the Park gear and engaged the parking brake. We were not in danger of moving. "They were pretty gruesome, but I didn't get any connection to olive oil out of them."

"There was more blood on the pavement than there should have been," I pointed out. "The medical examiner concluded Mr. Fontaine had been beaten to death somewhere other than the sidewalk on High Street. That meant he was probably not bleeding at all when his body was arranged there. The consistency of the blood on the pavement was wrong."

"Wrong?" Ms. Washburn bit her lower lip, thinking. "You believe it wasn't blood at all? They used something that looked like blood? Wouldn't the ME have figured that out immediately."

I nodded. "That is why I believe that there was blood on the sidewalk. But not as much as there would have been if Brett Fontaine had been killed there. I think the killer or killers collected some of his blood—so it could properly be identified as his when his body was found—and mixed it with something to make it appear to have more volume than it actually contained."

It took Ms. Washburn a few moments—six seconds—to absorb the information I'd given her. "And you think what they mixed it with was olive oil? Why?"

"I don't think it was pure olive oil; that would have been too easy to spot and would not have looked authentic," I said. "But there was a spot very near Mr. Fontaine's right hand where the pool of liquid took on an appearance very much like that of consumer olive oil. I think it had started to separate from the solution, or had not been mixed into it adequately."

"So if we find olive oil, we'll find the place where Brett Fontaine was killed?" Ms. Washburn looked perplexed. "You think somebody beat him to death with a tire iron in the cooking oil aisle of a supermarket?"

"I most certainly do not. I believe there was a somewhat secluded alternative location nearby. Tomorrow, I propose we retrace your route from that day and see if there are any likely venues."

Ms. Washburn pondered that. "Okay. But I also want to go talk to Virginia Fontaine and maybe Brett's mother tomorrow."

"Then we should get started early. Can you pick me up at eight?" I reached for the car door release.

"You leave the house every day at eight, Samuel. That's not early."

I stopped in my motion. "But most days we do not drive directly to the route we wish to follow," I pointed out.

"Of course." Ms. Washburn's voice had an air of something like sadness in its tone.

I stopped and looked at her. "Ms. Washburn, is something wrong? Is there something that is troubling you?"

There was a two-second hesitation. Most people would not have noticed. "No, Samuel. I'm just tired and tomorrow is going to be a long day. I want to get home and relax."

I was somewhat suspicious of her response but realized I had no fact-based reason to doubt her word. I opened the door and got out of the car. "Rest well, Ms. Washburn," I said.

"You too, Samuel."

I closed the car door and Ms. Washburn had the vehicle in motion before I had reached the flagstone path to the front door.

Once inside I found my mother preparing dinner as usual and Reuben sitting at the kitchen table watching her do so without offering to do so much as set the table. I did that without being asked but set it for two people.

My mother glanced over and frowned. "You haven't left a place for yourself, Samuel."

"I am not hungry, Mother. Thank you for cooking dinner for me, but I believe I won't be eating right now."

She stopped what she was doing at the stove and walked to me. "Are you feeling all right?" she asked.

"I am perfectly healthy," I told her. "I simply need to think about some things and they are occupying my full attention at the moment. Food is not something very high on my list of priorities this evening."

Mother searched my face but did not seem to find what she was looking for. She glanced at Reuben. "Is there a reason you don't feel like eating with us?" she asked.

"None other than the one I've already stated. I believe I will go upstairs to my apartment and work. If I feel the need to eat later, I will come downstairs and heat up the chicken you have prepared, Mother. Thank you again."

I turned to walk to the stairs but Reuben stood up and touched me on the arm, something I would have preferred he not do. I stopped and turned to face him mostly because I wanted him to remove his hand, and he did.

"Is it me?" he asked.

The question was nonsensical. Was *what* him? I had no context to formulate an answer. "I do not understand," I said.

That should have been clear enough, but apparently it was not. "I meant, is it me?" he responded, doing nothing but repeating himself. After four seconds during which I did not respond, he added, "Am I the reason you don't want to eat dinner?"

Everyone I knew—with the exception of Mike the taxicab driver—was behaving in some fashion I did not recognize or comprehend. My mother was being unusually harsh in her assessments, Ms. Washburn was acting distant and somehow disturbed by elements I did not notice, and now Reuben was asking me ridiculous questions.

"Of course you are not the reason I am not eating dinner now," I told him, although it should have been obvious enough that the question would never have been asked. "I need to work and have no appetite at the moment. I can't begin to imagine why that might be somehow your doing." Having answered his question, I walked to the stairs and up to my attic apartment.

Work had until now been my driving force, the thing that occupied my mind almost constantly. Now it was becoming my refuge, where I could forget the strange emotional actions of the neurotypicals and immerse myself in the logic and physical reality of answering a question that dealt strictly with facts.

I began by delving deeper into the reports of Melanie Mason's death, the only one of three I was currently researching which had no suggestion of foul play. It was the second of the three deaths, but the one that seemed to have set much of the subsequent activity in motion.

According to the one newspaper account that had been written by a reporter doing something more than regurgitating the police report, Melanie Mason had been traveling east on Route 22 in Union when another vehicle, much larger than the one she was driving, miscalculated the flow of traffic on an onramp from the westbound side of the road. Unique to highways in New Jersey, Route 22 incorporates onramps into the left lane of traffic which lead to a higher rate of collisions than on virtually any other such road in the state.

When the larger vehicle—a 2009 GMC Sierra truck—hit Melanie's 2013 Subaru BRZ, it was traveling at approximately 17 miles per hour. Melanie's car, however, was going considerably faster, at 62 miles per hour. Her car spun away from the truck and into the center lane, where it was hit again on the passenger's side by a 2011 BMW 335i, traveling at a rate of approximately 54 miles per hour. That car pushed Melanie's Subaru for 22 yards before it came to a stop.

Unlike vehicles in accidents on television or in motion pictures, real cars do not explode in flames whenever they are struck. In fact, anytime a vehicle does catch fire it is because the fuel line is ruptured and something ignites the gasoline underneath the damaged car. Unfortunately for Melanie Mason, that was the case in this accident.

Her body had been so badly burned, according to the written account in the *Courier-News*, that identification could not be made even with dental records. Instead shreds of clothing and a partially melted wedding band were used.

There had been a funeral, as Virginia Fontaine had told Ms. Washburn and me, but all that had been buried was a small urn with some of Melanie's ashes and her engagement ring, which she had not been wearing at the time of the accident. The melted wedding band was kept by Leon Rabinski.

I decided to seek out a photograph of Melanie Mason. Because the picture Virginia Fontaine had shown us was of her husband getting into an automobile with an open passenger door and no visible person on that side of the car. I had never seen her face. A quick Google search—the simplest kind of internet research—would provide that view, although I knew facial features were not something especially enlightening to me.

Unfortunately, it quickly became obvious that Melanie Mason was not an uncommon name. Even when I added the middle name I'd found in the obituaries (Samantha), the field of photographs was not narrowed by much. I would have to ask Peter Belson or Anthony Deane if either of them had a photograph, vintage or otherwise.

In the meantime I decided to sift through the few hard copy documents I had on my desk. I had brought any paper articles I had in the Questions Answered office home because I knew I would be working on this question tonight, and I had printed out a few at home in previous evening sessions.

There was precious little of note in the small stack to my right hand side. A copy of the incorporation form for Fontaine and Fontaine showed nothing I did not already know. The medical examiner's report on William Klein's death reported a finding of considerable blunt trauma consistent with a fall from the height of the fire escape and did not suggest foul play. Anthony Deane's birth certificate proved only that he had been born twenty-nine years earlier and that his parents were Estella Llewellyn Deane and Peter Deane of Denville, New Jersey. That information seemed to have no relevance to the question at hand.

When I lifted that sheet, however, I found something I had not expected. A single sheet of paper, smaller than the standard copy size I use in my printer, folded in half vertically and a light green shade, had been inserted into the pile. I did not recognize it and had no idea how it had been included in my work stack. Before touching it I put on a pair of latex gloves from a box I keep in my closet to avoid contaminating the paper if it turned out to be evidence in a criminal matter like the death of William Klein or Brett Fontaine.

Using a pair of tweezers from my desk drawer I carefully examined the paper. Because it was folded with nothing written on what was now its "front," there was little information. There was no watermark or random ink blots on the outside of the sheet. The only data, if there were any at all, would be found by unfolding the prepared message. I hoped there would be some writing inside.

The tweezers might make an indentation if I closed them firmly enough to open the sheet so I relied on my fingers in the gloves to do so. And I was rewarded with a handwritten note on the inside of the green paper.

It read: *Meet me at the Hillsdale Cemetery in Scotch Plains at nine thirty tonight. MM.*

MM? Out loud I whispered, "Melanie Mason?"

NINETEEN

"WHERE IN THE CEMETERY?" Mike the taxicab driver asked. "The place is over a hundred acres. That's a lot of ground to cover."

"One hundred and twenty-five acres," I said, having done some research on the facility before calling Mike to ask if he could drive me to the spot. "And I believe I know where to look. Melanie Mason's grave is on the eastern side of the cemetery."

There was no explanation of the initials MM on the green note I had discovered in my stack. Of course I did not believe Melanie Mason herself had left the note, but clearly someone wanted me to believe she had done so, possibly to deflect suspicion. It would be interesting to find out who, if anyone, would meet me at the designated spot.

Mike had initially been reluctant to make the thirty-minute drive to Scotch Plains after a full day of driving the taxicab and I was about to call Ms. Washburn to ask her to fill in. But when he heard I was intending to have a rendezvous with a mysterious figure claiming to be a dead woman, he said I should ask no one but him for transportation. The bulge in his jacket indicated he had thought to bring his handgun with him. I knew there was a shotgun well concealed in the cargo area of the Prius he had converted into a taxicab.

I was especially glad he had decided to accompany me because the cemetery officially closed to public visitation at four thirty p.m. This led me to wonder why the person who had left the mysterious note in my packet would have chosen a much later hour for our meeting. Mike, luckily, knew of a back entrance he said was used for delivery of equipment and supplies that would be open at night. Funerals tend to take place in the morning, so many such deliveries are made during off-hours to prepare for the next day's events. Mike had turned off the headlights on his taxicab and we had driven through the open gate without incident. Then he had maneuvered us, according to an interior map I had downloaded, toward the area of Melanie Mason's grave.

"I'll head in that direction, but do you have a more specific area in mind?" Mike asked.

"Yes. I have the plot number. I can guide you once we are in the area."

It had taken us approximately six minutes to find the correct area. Once there we looked at the plot but the car path was too far from the graves to make out any names carved into the headstones. Mike turned off the engine but switched on the headlights to illuminate the immediate area. There were no lights on in the cemetery itself.

I wondered why Ms. Washburn and her friends had thought such a place was an appropriate spot to enjoy themselves as teenagers but no obvious advantages came to mind.

"What do you think?" he asked me.

"I don't see anyone standing at any of the graves," I answered. "I suppose we should get closer."

Mike followed me as I approached the designated area where Melanie Mason's grave was located. He turned off the headlights on his taxicab before we made our approach saying he wanted to preserve the energy in the battery. We had brought flashlights with us that were more powerful and reliable than those contained in our smartphones.

"What's the map say?" Mike asked. I had learned to accept the use of the word *say* when discussing printed material despite its inaccuracy. It was probably less practical to expect the common usage to change due to logic than to turn one's attention to more consequential issues.

"I am following it to the site," I told him. "If you follow me it should take only another minute or two."

Indeed, within forty-eight seconds we were standing in front of a nondescript tombstone marked MELANIE SAMANTHA MASON. It offered the years of her birth and death and included a quote suggesting that those who die reach a more satisfactory level of existence afterward. It was not terribly enlightening.

"This must be the spot the person referred to in the green note," I said. I did not want to reach for my iPhone, although I did pat my front pocket to reassure myself of its presence. I worry about losing important objects I have obtained and resisted purchasing a cellular telephone for years until Ms. Washburn had convinced me I could be counted on to retain it. So far she had been correct. "What time does your phone indicate?" I asked Mike.

He knew I expected accuracy and not an estimate. "Nine twenty-eight," he said.

"Well, whatever is supposed to happen will happen in two minutes."

Mike, behind me, sounded more tense than usual. "How do you think they snuck the note into your take-home pile?" he asked.

"The sheaf of papers is kept on my desk during office hours and then comes home with me in a folder every night," I said. I had given the matter some thought but had not reached a definitive conclusion. "It had to have been someone who was in the Questions Answered office today or in Ms. Washburn's car on the way home tonight."

"Well, you'd have seen anyone in the car," Mike said. "Who besides you and Janet was in the office today?"

That was the puzzling part. "No one."

Mike remained silent. I saw the beam from his flashlight sweep the area.

"Perhaps there are further instructions on the gravestone itself," I said, musing aloud but also to explain to Mike, who thinks of himself as my protector in dangerous situations, why I was approaching the grave to examine it more closely.

I was only a few feet from the stone when a voice, from an indeterminate direction, became audible in the area. It was a woman's voice and not one I had heard before.

"Samuel Hoenig." The tone, if I was interpreting it correctly, was conversational. Whoever this woman might be, she was attempting to attract my attention and not to threaten me. Nonetheless I heard Mike's feet rustling as he turned in a full circle with his flashlight trying to locate the speaker.

"I am Samuel Hoenig," I said, feeling it was not necessary to introduce myself and choosing instead merely to identify myself so she would not mistake Mike for the person she was addressing. "Who is speaking?"

"I am Melanie Mason," the voice said.

I saw no reason to pretend I believed that. "You are not," I answered. "Melanie Mason is dead."

"Yes. I am."

The woman was not speaking in long enough sentences for me to accurately locate the source of the sound. Had remote speakers been set up in this area? Was some technological device projecting the voice from a higher elevation nearby? I scanned the area above our heads for 360 degrees with my flashlight and saw no such point that made sense as an origination spot.

"You are asking us to believe that you are speaking from literally beyond your grave?" I asked.

"I don't care what you believe," the voice said. "I am who I am."

Mike moved closer to me. "Do you see anything?" he asked.

Clearly, he was asking whether I had managed to find anything relevant to our situation. He knew I was capable of sight. "Nothing that helps," I answered.

"Who's your friend?" the woman's voice said.

I ignored the question because I felt it was best not to give the person or people behind this dramatic event any more information than was necessary. "I assume you are the person who placed the note in my folder today," I said. "What was your purpose in doing so?"

"He's cute," she continued. Was the voice prerecorded and therefore incapable of dealing with unexpected responses?

"Why did you set up this meeting?" I insisted.

"You're investigating Brett's murder," the voice said. I could not determine if that was an answer to my question or another predetermined recording. The pattern of speech was not personal. Still, the question about Mike made me think it was more probable the voice was operating from a remote location with a view, however dim, of the gravesite.

"That is the reason?" I asked. I noted that Mike had not spoken except in a hushed tone since the person claiming to be Melanie Mason had made herself known. He is a keen observer but does not care to participate until needed. "Why is my research into Mr. Fontaine's death important to you?"

"Because I killed him."

That seemed unlikely. "You purport to be a woman who died in a vehicular incident three years ago, and you then say you murdered Brett Fontaine this week," I said. "How is that physically possible?"

"I'm a ghost," the voice said.

"There is no such thing as a ghost," I said. "That is not a physical possibility. Tell me where you murdered Brett Fontaine, if you are going to insist that is something you did."

There was a pause of eight seconds. "I don't need to tell you anything," was the eventual reply.

"You don't know where he died because you didn't kill him," I suggested. "Why don't you reveal yourself so we can discuss this face-to-face?" Actually, the last thing I would have wanted was to look Melanie Mason—or whoever was playing her in this fiction—in the face. But the expression was valid and appropriate for use under these circumstances. If the person did arrive, I would have had to quell my unease and look at her directly simply to store the image in my mind.

But that was not about to happen. "I can make myself visible when I desire it," the voice said. "But I do not desire it now. I killed Brett so he could be with me forever."

This conversation was becoming increasingly absurd. "You can make yourself visible merely by leaving your current hiding space and walking to this spot," I told the voice. "I have no desire to play a role in your Gothic melodrama. Come and speak to me and we will settle whatever differences you believe we have."

"We have differences." That was certainly vague.

I saw Mike the taxicab driver, eyes still wary of the surroundings, drop to his knees to examine an area of grass approximately six inches to the right of Melanie Mason's headstone.

"Then come out and discuss them," I said. It seemed the best strategy, or at least the one that would result in irritating the woman

149

pretending to be Melanie Mason to the point that she might make a rash decision and reveal herself.

"I will not play your game," the voice said. "You are warned. Stop investigating Brett's murder."

"Why should I?" I said in an attempt to prod her further.

"Because if you don't, I will kill someone close to you."

Mike looked up quickly and got to his feet, an expression that implies one has left his feet behind, which was certainly not the case. He stood. His flashlight beam resumed its slow 360-degree sweep of the area. With his free hand he gestured that I should continue to engage the woman we heard in conversation.

"I don't understand why the research into Mr. Fontaine's murder would upset you," I said as Mike walked to a position six feet from Melanie Mason's grave and continued his flashlight sweep. "If you are the ghost of Melanie Mason and you did indeed kill him, there is no authority that can possibly threaten you. Why does it worry you that we will find the truth?"

I believe it is important to reiterate that I did not believe this woman to be a ghost because there is no evidence that such beings exist. I was using her own statement against her in this argument.

"It doesn't worry me," the voice said. "It makes me angry. You don't want to see me when I'm angry."

"I can't see you now," I pointed out. "If you are a ghost and you wanted to threaten me, why was it necessary for me to come here? Why didn't you come to my home?"

Mike looked at me and shook his head violently. I realized then I might have planted an idea in the woman's mind that I would prefer not be there.

"I don't need to come to you. I can kill your girlfriend without coming to you."

That suggestion did not immediately frighten me. It was possible the woman playing the role of Melanie Mason was, as the expression goes, bluffing.

"I have no girlfriend," I said.

"Oh yes, you do," she answered. "She shows up everywhere you go. I was expecting her tonight instead of the cute guy. What's his name, again?"

"What is your favorite Beatles song?" Changing the subject seemed a worthwhile pursuit at this moment.

The response came without any hesitation. The woman might have anticipated the question and prepared an answer in advance.

"'Maxwell's Silver Hammer,'" she said.

It was possible I was talking to a homicidal maniac.

TWENTY

"Melanie Mason's ghost talked to you about me?" Ms. Washburn sat on a very functional sofa I recognized from having once thumbed through an Ikea catalog. "She said she was going to kill me?"

I had insisted Mike the taxicab driver take me to Ms. Washburn's apartment after the purported voice of Melanie Mason had stopped speaking. It seemed the revelation of her favorite Beatles song had been her last communication, as we had heard nothing from her after that. Mike had said it was important to let Ms. Washburn know we were on the way because it was late in the evening and she might, as he put it, "be sleeping or something she doesn't want us to see."

It was the first time I had visited Ms. Washburn's residence. The apartment was in a complex of similar units and was a clean, simple and adequate shelter. She had moved here after divorcing her ex-husband, Simon Taylor.

Ms. Washburn had actually asked two questions, but I chose to respond to the second exclusively, assuming my previous statement had answered the first. I shook my head. "She did not say she was going to kill you."

"That's true," Mike agreed. "She said she *could* kill you without coming to Samuel's house, but she never said she was going to."

"That's very comforting." I am reasonably certain Ms. Washburn meant that comment sarcastically. I was standing next to the sofa on which she was sitting and Mike had leaned against the jamb of the nearest door, one that led to another room I could only assume was Ms. Washburn's bedroom. That was his typical stance; he liked to stay on his feet and keep a vantage point taking in the whole room. "Why does she want to kill anyone?"

Ms. Washburn has a penchant for asking questions about an interaction that I cannot definitely answer. It is one of the reasons I prefer to have her along on interviews. She will ask about the aspects of an issue that would not occur to me.

"I did not ask that question, but she was quite clear in communicating that we should cease our research into Virginia Fontaine's question," I said. "That appeared to be the message."

"Oh, yeah," Mike said. "That was the message."

Ms. Washburn looked at my hand, which was resting on the arm of the sofa near her own. Her gaze seemed to follow up my arm to my face and when she looked at me her expression had a tinge of disappointment in it. It was not the usual smile she presents when she looks at me. I was confused.

"Then maybe we should stop," Ms. Washburn said.

That suggestion added to my astonishment. Ms. Washburn had never for a moment considered backing away from a question before, even when her own safety had been threatened. Now she was saying the research into Brett Fontaine's murder should not be continued.

"It is never a good idea to stop because someone wants us to stop," I said. "Surely this means we are getting close to a truth that the murderer or murderers would prefer not be disclosed."

Ms. Washburn withdrew her hand from the arm of the sofa. "That's the point," she said. "A ghost is telling us to quit the investigation. She says she's the killer. It's not somebody who can be caught or charged. It's someone who has the ability to come and kill us with impunity. This isn't like anything we've ever faced before, Samuel."

I was so stunned that I do not even know the number of seconds before I could find a way to respond. "A ghost?" I said. "You believe this was really the spirit of Melanie Mason contacting me in the cemetery? I am surprised, Ms. Washburn."

She turned her head so as to be facing away from me. "I know what you think, Samuel, but from the beginning of this question we've disagreed. I am certain there are ghosts and you're certain there aren't. I wish this experience had changed your mind, but apparently you won't even believe your own eyes."

"We did not see anything at all," I said. "There was nothing to believe."

"Your own ears, then. You heard her voice."

The conversation in which I was engaged was disturbing on a number of levels. First, it is always difficult when Ms. Washburn and I disagree seriously because I trust her judgment and believe she has my best interests at heart. With the new aspect of our relationship, it was additionally worrisome because now I was arguing with a woman for whom I had complex and unfamiliar feelings. But the idea that Ms. Washburn was so willing to perpetuate an unproven, unscientific, non-empirical theory like the existence of ghosts at the expense of a question we were researching was especially shocking to my system. I felt my left hand, the one not resting on the sofa, begin to move involuntarily. I tried to control the motion before Ms. Washburn, who luckily was looking in the opposite direction, could notice it.

My next words would be pivotal in the direction of this discussion so I took great pains to choose them carefully. "I believe that what we heard in the cemetery is easily explained without the assumption that an undead spirit was talking," I said. Before Ms. Washburn could respond I looked at Mike the taxicab driver. "Mike, you told me on the drive here that you saw something on the ground near Melanie Mason's grave. What was it?"

In the interest of full candor, Mike had already explained his thoughts on this subject. But I wanted Ms. Washburn to hear what he had to say from him and not me. She clearly believed that my judgment was prejudiced in the area of ghosts, and it would have been possible if there were even the slightest possibility that such beings exist.

"It was very well hidden, I'll give them that," Mike answered. "But what I found was a little round disc, covered in wire mesh, that I think covered a small audio speaker. There were probably a lot of them in that area and I think they connected to a wireless transmitter of some kind that sent the sound from a remote location not too far away. There might have been cameras near the grave so they could see us, or they were close enough and had the right night vision equipment to see us in the dark."

Ms. Washburn looked at Mike and I believed—although she has since denied it—that I saw tears in her eyes. "You too?" she said.

"I'm just telling you what I saw."

"No, you're also making guesses about transmitters and night vision equipment and hidden cameras," Ms. Washburn said. She stood up but did not move toward either Mike or me. "That's a level of paranoia I wouldn't have expected from you."

I hardly believed Mike's analysis was evidence of mental illness. "I'm sorry you feel that way," he said, and continued to lean against the doorjamb.

Ms. Washburn shook her head. "I'm not trying to insult you, Mike," she said. She walked to the door and addressed him directly. "But don't you see you're doing the same thing to me? When you and Samuel dismiss my ideas out of hand, you're saying I don't know what I'm talking about. You're not respecting my intelligence and you're pretty much ridiculing me for thinking a different way. And that hurts."

Mike took a moment but did not change his expression. "Janet, in the part of Afghanistan where I was stationed most of the people believe in the jinn, kind of a genie, something you can sort of wish to and sometimes your wish will be granted. We joked about it when we were back at the base but over my three tours, I have to tell you, I saw some stuff happen that I can't explain to this day." He paused and took a breath. Ms. Washburn looked up at him. "So when I tell you that I saw something that could have been part of a speaker system in the ground around that grave, I'm here to tell you that's what I saw. It's not because I believe or don't believe in anything. It's because I found it in the ground."

Very quietly, Ms. Washburn asked, "What did you see in Afghanistan?"

Mike's smile was not a typical one. "That's a story for another day."

Ms. Washburn nodded and walked back toward me. "I'm sorry," she said. "I was so upset thinking a ghost was after me personally that I took it out on you and I shouldn't have. Please forgive me, Mike."

He barely twitched an eyebrow. "There's nothing to forgive."

Ms. Washburn smiled at Mike, turned toward me, and held out her hand, which I realized she wanted me to take. I held hers in mine gently. This was not like a business handshake. I was getting used to the gesture but did not always understand its emotional significance. This time, however, I did. Ms. Washburn was reaffirming my special status in her life. I wondered how I should feel about that and decided to think about it later when I got home. It would be quieter there.

"Samuel," Ms. Washburn said. "I need to apologize to you too. I've been cranky and I had no legitimate reason to be. Sometimes I expect more of you than I should, or expect it sooner than I should, because you're always progressing. I can't dictate when you'll grow, or how. I shouldn't have done that."

I honestly did not understand the supposed offense to which Ms. Washburn was alluding, nor did I understand her assertion that I was growing, as I was a mature adult. But I felt it was best to say the same thing as Mike because it had gotten a positive reaction for him. "There's nothing to forgive," I said.

Ms. Washburn blew a little air out, not quite a sigh but almost a laugh. If she had done so more loudly it would have been accurate to say she had snorted. "Thank you, Samuel," she said. "The question now is, how seriously do we take this ghost's threat?"

I pondered whether repeating that ghosts do not exist would be a worthwhile tactic and rejected it. Perhaps Ms. Washburn was speaking figuratively. "I think we should take any threat seriously," I said. "Will you feel unsafe staying in your apartment tonight?"

Mike's eyebrows rose briefly.

"Maybe," Ms. Washburn said. "But I don't have family in the area and I'm not going to let this nut job drive me into a hotel. You don't pay me enough."

"Perhaps you could stay in my attic apartment for the duration of this question," I suggested. It seemed the most logical choice available to us. "We might do best if we were in constant contact until we know what this encounter at the cemetery means."

This time Mike's eyebrows rose and stayed risen. But he remained silent.

Ms. Washburn's eyes looked at my face carefully. "Do you know what you're suggesting, Samuel?" she asked. "I've seen your apartment, and there is only one bed."

"There is a very comfortable sofa in the den," I told her. "I will be glad to use that until such time as we can resume our normal arrangements."

"I have a cot in my place, Janet," Mike the taxicab driver suggested.

"I think I'll take Samuel up on his offer, thanks," she answered. "But I do appreciate your saying that."

"No big," Mike said.

"I'll need to put a few things in a bag," Ms. Washburn said. She began to walk toward Mike, who moved out of the doorway leading to her bedroom, then stopped and looked at me. "What's our plan in the morning?" she asked.

"I think we need to visit two police departments and one cemetery superintendent," I said.

TWENTY-ONE

"I DOUBT ANYONE HAS been installing sophisticated electronics on our grounds without my knowledge." Stephen Manfred, superintendent of the Hillsdale Cemetery, was a thin man in a business suit. He appeared to be roughly sixty years old but had a full head of brown hair I suspected was not currently displaying its natural color. "That kind of underground construction would require permits and those permits would have to come through me." I assumed he meant that he had the authority to grant or seek out those government documents and not that he would pass them through his body.

Ms. Washburn, Manfred, and I were walking from the path where Mike had parked his taxicab the night before toward the headstone marking Melanie Mason's grave. Mike had given me instructions regarding the locations where I should seek out the wire mesh indicators that audio speakers were being used in the area. It would still be difficult to find such small mechanisms under full-grown and groomed grass.

"I expect that the people who did this did not ask you for permission." We reached the gravesite. I knelt in the spot I thought I'd seen Mike do the same the previous night. Very carefully I ran my right hand over the grass, bending back the blades so the soil beneath could be seen. Initially I did not see the type of mechanism Mike had described. "I believe the necessary electronics are small and wireless, making them fairly easy to install surreptitiously."

Ms. Washburn did not kneel beside me to look, which was certainly acceptable. This was a very delicate search. Having two people do it might actually make the task more difficult. She stood with Manfred to my left and behind me.

"To get any decent level of sound quality, wouldn't that kind of thing be awfully expensive?" she asked.

"It doesn't matter because the things aren't there," Manfred insisted. "There's no paperwork on it at all."

"It would be a relatively high-end system, yes," I told Ms. Washburn as I meticulously moved my hand slowly over the grass and watched its progress. "I imagine the people who did this had a decent amount of money to spend and are hoping to do better."

"You think this is all about money?" Ms. Washburn said.

"Most killings, even robberies gone wrong in the street, are about money or domestic issues," I said without citing the statistics from the Federal Bureau of Investigation that had helped me form that understanding. "William Klein's death might have been an accident or it might have been about his wife, but Brett Fontaine's was almost certainly about money. Ah!"

My fingers felt the small disc before I saw it. It was as Mike had said: round, flat, and covered in the kind of wire mesh one sees on a microphone head. It couldn't have been more than four centimeters in diameter and it was planted flush with the ground. No one who wasn't searching for the mechanism would have made note of it. I mentally noted Mike's ability to observe and notice things. I had asked him to join the staff at Questions Answered (although it would have been difficult to find the funds to pay him a salary in addition to Ms. Washburn's and my own) but Mike preferred driving his taxicab, saying he enjoyed the rides and never knew what the next day would bring.

I pulled lightly on the disc but it was difficult for my fingers to close on its sides because it had embedded itself very snugly in the plot of earth. I did manage to pull on it successfully after seven attempts and it was not hard to extract the disc—and what was under it—from the ground.

"What's *that*?" Manfred asked. He sounded shocked.

I stood and extended my hand for him and Ms. Washburn to see the mechanism. Underneath the disc I had pulled from the ground was a short wire which no doubt acted as the sensor for the audio signal being sent from a remote location nearby. "It is a receiver and an amplifier," I said. "Someone broadcast a voice to this gravesite from an area near here."

Ms. Washburn turned to look behind her, which appears to be the natural impulse for someone who feels she is being watched. "Where?" she asked.

"It is difficult to say at this moment," I told her. "I will have to do some research to determine the range of a device like this one." I looked toward Manfred. "Is there Wi-Fi access in the cemetery?"

"Of course not," he answered. "This is not a coffee shop."

"But your office is less than three hundred yards away," I noted. "Do you have Wi-Fi there?"

"Sure."

"They could be transmitting through that signal," I mused aloud.

"It can't be," Manfred insisted. "There's no authorization."

"I believe whoever planted this device installed others as well," I said. I knelt again and began a search approximately one foot to the left of the area where I had discovered the disc. "In my opinion they are in violation of your regulations, Mr. Manfred."

"I can't believe it," he said. His head was shaking at the very thought. The fact that a man had been murdered did not seem as astonishing to him as an infraction of his cemetery's stated rules.

Within twenty-three minutes I had located four more devices identical to the one I had first unearthed. I left them in their positions so as not to alarm the people who had made such an elaborate effort to convince us—and no doubt others—that Melanie Mason was speaking from another realm of existence. One of the devices was embedded in a tree behind the gravestone. I assumed there were a number of others in the immediate vicinity that I did not uncover, as the sound the night before was not localized. It had not seemed to emanate strictly from beneath my feet.

Ms. Washburn and I returned to the cemetery office with Manfred, thanked him for his time, and got back into Ms. Washburn's Kia Spectra to begin the next leg of our day's travels. I sat beside her as she drove and this time in the car her silence seemed more distant than usual; it was not simply about paying attention to the road. In fact, once I had to point out to Ms. Washburn that a traffic light had changed its signal from red to green.

When we were stopped in a similar situation I asked, "Is something bothering you, Ms. Washburn?" It is not usually my habit to start a conversation in the car but her expression was somewhat troublesome to me. It seemed like she was preoccupied with a topic other than safety behind the wheel.

"I'm okay, Samuel." The light illuminated green and she began to drive again.

I said nothing more until Ms. Washburn had parked the Kia Spectra in the parking lot of the Union Police Department. Detective Monroe, when we'd telephoned, had flatly refused to see us so we bypassed that part of our planned agenda and went directly to the authorities who would have records of the automobile accident that claimed Melanie Mason's life.

But before we opened the car doors, I said, "I have noticed that you are somewhat less animated than usual. Are you concerned about your safety?"

Ms. Washburn, who had been reaching for the door handle on her side, stopped and turned toward me. "Sure I'm concerned," she said, "but I don't think it's changing the way I'm acting. I'm just tired, Samuel."

"Was the bed not comfortable?" Ms. Washburn had indeed spent the night in my attic apartment, protesting all along that she, as the guest, should be on the sofa in the den. But Mother and I had prevailed in that argument. I had slept on the sofa with only a slight difficulty relaxing. It had never occurred to me that Ms. Washburn might not have slept well.

"No, it was fine," she answered. "There's a lot going on right now and I have trouble turning my mind off at night. Do you understand what that means?"

I smiled. "Better than most, I imagine."

Ms. Washburn smiled in return. "Then I don't have to explain further."

"I suppose not. Why don't we go inside and see what we can find out. Perhaps we can answer this question today and you can return to your apartment."

We entered the building, a roomy, modern facility that offered a noticeable contrast to the building in which Detective Monroe worked on a daily basis. When Ms. Washburn explained our request to the officer behind the desk in the reception area, we were directed to the Motor Vehicle division. That unit would have kept records of traffic incidents rather than crimes.

There, Officer Joanna Johnson said most records for Rt. 22, being a state highway, would be kept by the New Jersey State Police, but copies of those reports pertaining to the municipality in question would be retained. I told her the date and location of the incident that claimed Melanie Mason's life and she did a search on her desktop computer.

"That accident was investigated because of the loss of life," she reported. "But it was pretty straightforward. No indication of foul play. The driver of the other vehicle walked away with minor injuries. It was the fire, not the impact, that killed that woman."

"May we get a copy of the incident report and any subsequent filings on the collision?" I asked.

"It's public record. Printing out now." She pointed to a printer in the enclosed space behind her where other uniformed officers were milling about with their work of the day. One was pouring a cup of coffee for himself. Officer Johnson stood and pressed the security code into a keypad to open the door, then walked in and picked up the pages from the printer tray. She brought them back out to the area where Ms. Washburn and I stood.

I briefly scanned the top page she handed to us for the name of the police officer who had first arrived on the scene of the incident. "Is Officer Palumbo still stationed here?" I asked.

"Yeah. That's him right there." Officer Palumbo was the coffee drinker among the group.

"Can we speak to him?" Ms. Washburn said.

Officer Johnson considered the question. "In what capacity are you guys here, again?" she asked. "Are you private investigators or something?"

Before I could explain Ms. Washburn said, "We've been asked by a member of the family to look into it. Nobody thinks anything was wrong with the report. We're just looking for a little extra detail than we're going to find in the document." Given that the report we'd been handed was only two pages long, I believed Ms. Washburn's assessment was valid, even if we had not been employed by any member of Melanie Mason's family.

The officer took a moment to think and said, "I'll ask him." She did not wait for a response and returned to the glass-paneled area, where she walked to Officer Palumbo and spoke briefly to him, once pointing in our direction. Palumbo took on a neutral expression, shrugged, and followed her out into the waiting area.

"I'm Nick Palumbo," he said, not extending a hand to be shaken. "That accident was a few years ago, wasn't it?"

"Three years," Ms. Washburn answered.

Officer Palumbo appeared to be focusing more favorably on Ms. Washburn than on me. I had seen this happen before when she and I had encountered male interview subjects. He smiled. "I don't know how much I can help you. It was pretty routine and I'm not sure how much I remember that isn't in the report."

"Is there somewhere we can sit for a moment?" Ms. Washburn asked. She smiled back at Palumbo in a way I had also witnessed before. Quite often we were able to get more complete information from the person we interviewed after she had done so. It was not a smile she had ever shown me personally.

Palumbo led us to a separate waiting area where there were seven seats, none of which was occupied at the moment. He sat next to Ms. Washburn and I sat on her opposite side. "We haven't had a chance to read the whole report yet," Ms. Washburn said.

"I have," I interjected. "And there are a few questions I would like to ask."

Officer Palumbo scowled a bit, taking his attention away from Ms. Washburn. "Like what?" he asked.

"With only a wedding band, how was it possible to positively identify the body?" There was little point in leading up to the most important question I would ask. It was better to divert Officer Palumbo from his scrutiny of Ms. Washburn.

"There were a few other items. You'll see them listed in the report." I had in fact noticed that section and had been unimpressed. Among the evidence Palumbo was citing were the ashes of a paperback book and the melted remains of a cellular phone so badly burned even the manufacturer could not be identified.

"Yes, I saw those," I said with what I hoped was a pleasant tone in my voice. "They wouldn't conclusively identify Melanie Mason."

"That's true," he said. "But there was a fingernail that apparently held a shade of polish Mason actually made herself. She didn't sell it and she didn't give it away; she kept it all for herself."

"That is persuasive but hardly definitive," I suggested. "There are scenarios under which the fingernail could have broken off days before. How could you be certain the woman in the car you finally recovered was Melanie Mason if such utter destruction was visited upon the body?"

"Let me ask you a question, Mr. Hoenig." Palumbo had ceased examining Ms. Washburn's face and focused his gaze upon me with a much different expression upon his face. "If that woman *wasn't* Melanie Mason, who was she? No other woman of that general age or size was reported missing in this county for weeks before or after the accident. If Melanie Mason was somewhere else, why didn't she come forward and let us know she wasn't dead? She would have had no money, no car, her bank accounts and credit cards would have been canceled, her marriage would have been basically over. How come we haven't heard about the missing woman or Melanie since then?"

Ms. Washburn, who had initiated this conversation but had looked slightly perturbed when Palumbo was staring at her, cleared her throat. "Those are very good questions, Officer," she said. "But I think what my colleague here is saying would be that you have circumstantial evidence to show that Melanie Mason died in that car crash. Was that enough, in terms of procedure, to close the case and decide against investigating any further?"

Officer Palumbo put his hands down flat on his thighs and produced a slapping sound that I'm not sure was his original intention. He looked at me still, not Ms. Washburn. "Are you saying that I didn't do my job?" he demanded.

"I am suggesting no such thing," I answered. "Obviously you have done and continue to work as a police officer in the borough of Union. And as you pointed out, the investigation of the incident was left to the State Police and not this department. I am attempting to answer a question and Melanie Mason's death is somehow central to the research Ms. Washburn and I are doing in the pursuit of that answer. What I am trying to understand is how certain those who investigated the collision—from the time you first arrived on the scene to the time the State Police decided to discontinue questioning the incident—were in determining that Melanie Mason is indeed dead."

Palumbo squinted at me like Clint Eastwood in many motion pictures. "Do you have any evidence that she isn't?" he asked.

"Last night I had a conversation with a woman who said that she is the ghost of Melanie Mason," I told him.

The officer blinked twice and blanched a little. "It happened to you too?"

TWENTY-TWO

"He had a conversation with the ghost too?" My mother settled into what she calls her easy chair in our living room after we finished lunch. I saw no feature or quality that made this particular piece of furniture any less difficult than another but I have learned not to question Mother on such terms, largely because the answers to such queries are usually not as interesting as the words she uses themselves.

Ms. Washburn and I had come back to the house to eat and would have left immediately afterward, as I usually do, if not for Mother's intense interest in the question Virginia Fontaine had asked. She had insisted on hearing all the details and then ushered us into the living room to sit down "and rest my knees," which were not supposed to hurt anymore.

"Officer Palumbo said he had been at the gravesite himself only once before and had heard the voice of Melanie Mason speaking to him," Ms. Washburn explained. She and I were seated on the sofa and Reuben Hoenig, wearing socks but no shoes, was scratching the sole of his left foot and listening from the overstuffed chair to Mother's left. "He said she had told him she was at peace and that he shouldn't worry about her. The officer said he never mentioned the conversation to anybody before today because he was afraid the other police officers would think he was crazy."

"Why was he there in the first place?" Reuben asked. "What was he doing at this woman's grave?"

It was a question I had asked Palumbo myself earlier in the day. "He said the case had bothered him because it was such an unlikely accident, one that should not have resulted in a flaming car and a dead woman. Palumbo told us he had gone to Melanie Mason's funeral and had then come back to the gravesite three weeks later seeking closure. In the words he supposedly heard the 'ghost' speak, he said he thought he had found it."

"So he didn't get a note like you did," Reuben said, still concentrating on his foot.

"No." I saw no need to elaborate, but it did raise an interesting question: How did the person pretending to be Melanie Mason's ghost know Officer Palumbo would be visiting at that time? Ms. Washburn and I would have to discuss that later. I found myself feeling uncomfortable discussing my work with Reuben.

Mother sat back and put her hand to her mouth in a gesture of pity or empathy. "The poor man," she said. "I'm glad that made him feel better."

Her sentiment made no sense. "The words he heard were lies," I reminded her. "There is no ghost of Melanie Mason. We found the technology that had been used to carry the sound from another location to the area of the headstone. Officer Palumbo no more heard the spirit of a dead woman than I did last night."

Mother looked especially concerned. "You didn't tell him that, did you, Samuel?"

Ms. Washburn looked away. I did not understand why she did that.

"Of course I did," I said to Mother. "He is an officer of the law and an investigator of crimes. Letting him think he had heard a supernatural spirit when he clearly had not would have been a disservice to him and the badge he wears."

"Janet," Mother said wearily.

"I couldn't stop him, Vivian."

"What did the officer say?" Reuben asked.

"He suggested I was lying," I told him. "I don't understand how he might have come to that conclusion. I never lie and I certainly couldn't have been dishonest about the existence of a mythical supernatural creature. His suggestion was completely insensible."

"How did that go?" my mother asked Ms. Washburn.

"About how you'd expect."

Mother closed her eyes for a moment. "Samuel," she said slowly, "you simply can't go around telling people that what they believe in their hearts is foolish."

"I don't believe I used the word *foolish*," I said. "The suggestion was something more like *unrealistic*."

"Did you tell him about the speakers and the antenna?" Reuben asked me. He stopped scratching the sole of his left foot and began on the sole of his right foot. I considered suggesting a strong foot powder but did not know if such a comment might be considered inappropriate. Certainly scratching one's foot in the company of others couldn't be thought of as polite, but the situation had never arisen in my presence before.

"I did. Eventually I believe Officer Palumbo realized I was speaking from a position of factual evidence. He said there was nothing he could do about the false voice of Melanie Mason because the cemetery is not within his jurisdiction and neither is the accident. It still falls under the purview of the State Police after three years."

"What *could* he do?" Mother said. "Because I know for a fact you didn't walk away from that conversation without him promising to help you somehow."

Reuben put both his feet back on the floor, which helped me focus on the conversation. "He agreed to look into sales of such sophisticated wireless transmission and reception equipment between the time Melanie Mason died and the time he believed he heard her voice at the gravesite," I said.

Mother smiled. "I'm never not proud of you, Samuel," she said.

It made me feel better that Mother did not seem to consider me an embarrassment, as I had thought she did a moment before. But my reading of Ms. Washburn's mood was less positive and less definitive. I had been having great difficult predicting her reactions for two days.

"So what's our plan now?" she asked me.

I thought it would be wise to defer to her judgment. "This has been chiefly your question to answer from the beginning," I said. "What do you think we should do?"

Ms. Washburn did not smile broadly but it was unquestionably a more satisfied expression on her face. "I think you had a good idea when you suggested we retrace my steps the day I was tailing Brett Fontaine," she said. "Let's drive the route now and see if we can find a likely place he was killed before they dumped his body on High Street. Maybe we can figure out how he did it."

"I believe that is a very good plan," I responded.

Ms. Washburn's face did not lose any of its pleasure when she said, "Of course you do. It was yours."

———

"Olive oil," Ms. Washburn said. "You think there was olive oil being used at the place Brett Fontaine died."

"The evidence would certainly suggest that is the fact," I agreed. "Detective Monroe bore out that theory."

We were in Ms. Washburn's Kia Spectra at Brett Fontaine's former home, now the sole property of his wife, Virginia, in Highland Park. Ms. Washburn had said it was not worth our time to question Virginia again in the matter until we had more evidence that would pertain directly to her. She was, after all, still Monroe's prime suspect in her husband's murder. I usually believe it is always better to talk to each participant in the question as often as possible, but given the strange mélange of facts we had gathered so far, I agreed that Virginia did not seem to be at the center of the question (speaking metaphorically) but somewhere to one side of that point. If such an image is appropriate.

"Let's look for places that deal in olive oil, then," Ms Washburn said.

"Where did Mr. Fontaine go first that day?" I asked.

"He went to his office," she said, starting the Kia Spectra's engine. "Should I drive extra slow?"

"I don't believe that should be necessary," I said. "You were driving alone that day and could not possibly have noticed every building you passed. With me in the car it should be possible to analyze our surroundings in real time. Drive as you would to avoid being spotted as you followed his car."

There was no need for a Global Positioning System device today. Ms. Washburn had driven this route before and we were traveling over territory that was not at all foreign to her. She proceeded from memory toward the building which housed the office of Fontaine and Fontaine in New Brunswick, a short drive from where we had begun.

The buildings we passed in Highland Park were first residential structures but became more commercial when we reached Raritan Avenue, the commercial center of the borough. I scanned the storefronts and occasional office buildings as we went, but the only one that might have regularly dealt in olive oil was a pizzeria just before Ms. Washburn took the car onto the Albany Street bridge, the most direct route into New Brunswick, the Middlesex County seat.

"Should we even be paying attention to buildings we just pass?" Ms. Washburn asked. "He couldn't have been killed with several blows to the head while he was in motion in his car. It had to be when he stopped."

"Astute reasoning," I said. "How many times did Mr. Fontaine stop in his travels that morning before the car he had been driving headed to High Street and you discovered his body?"

Ms. Washburn, breaking with our established behavior of speaking only when the vehicle was not in motion, said, "Three times. Once at his office, then at a bodega to get a cup of coffee, and then at his first rental property on Wyckoff Street."

I chose not to continue with her pattern and waited until we had stopped. "It is possible any of those could be the spot where he was killed, although the office seems the least likely, especially given the presence of olive oil. That would not be a typical element found in a real estate company's headquarters. Still, we need to consider each one as we reach it, and to evaluate the areas surrounding each."

In another three minutes Ms. Washburn pulled the car up to the curb directly across from the office of Fontaine and Fontaine Real Estate. She did violate the law by parking the Kia Spectra in front of a fire hydrant, but there were no available legal parking spaces on the street and she said she would move if fire department representatives needed to use the hydrant. "Besides," Ms. Washburn said, "I don't think we'll be here very long."

"Indeed. I believe we can continue on our route now," I said.

"Already?"

I made a point of looking at each building on the street including the one directly to our left. "There are no likely spots for Brett Fontaine to have been assaulted here," I said. "The buildings are very close to-gether. Notice that there are people prominently walking on both sides of the street. This is approximately the time of day when Mr. Fontaine was killed. It is unlikely the event could have happened without anyone at least hearing something unusual. The police would probably have been notified, but Detective Monroe had no record of any such call having been made."

Ms. Washburn put the Kia Spectra's transmission back into the Drive gear. "So we're looking for a spot where there would be more space between the buildings or with less foot traffic, is that it?" she asked.

"Yes, and the availability of at least some olive oil," I answered when it was appropriate.

"The bodega would probably have olive oil," Ms. Washburn noted.

"Agreed."

Luckily, after a six-minute drive we found a parking spot two buildings south of the bodega where Brett Fontaine had stopped on the morning he was killed. The business, which according to the sign over its doorway was named B-B-Big Food, was a small space, contradictory to the name, horizontally three doors north of the nearest corner. It was, as are most such enterprises, crammed with products on shelves from ceiling to floor with very little space for customers to maneuver through its aisles.

Ms. Washburn turned the engine off and we walked to the door-way of B-B-Big Food. "Should I look for the olive oil right away?" she asked me. "Is that the idea here, or is there something else we are looking for?"

"The entire floorplan of the store is significant, but it will proba-bly be best for us to divide our focus," I answered. "You search for the spot where olive oil might be found and I will walk through the store to see what I might observe that would be significant to the question we are considering."

"Should we go in separately? Should I wait a minute after you go in?"

"Why?"

Ms. Washburn thought for exactly one second. "Good point," she said.

I held the door open for Ms. Washburn, as I have been taught it is what one does when a woman is entering one. This is a social construct that appears to have survived the thought—in my view, quite correct—that women are equal members of society and do not require special treatment. Customs are fluid things, rarely based on empirical data.

Once inside the store Ms. Washburn moved to the left and began scanning shelves of various products to determine where bottles or cans of olive oil might be displayed. I took the cramped route to the right of the store from the perspective of a customer entering the business and simply observed the conditions of B-B-Big Foods on what I could only assume was a typical day.

It was an unremarkable store, a neighborhood bodega meant to serve basic needs. The only fresh produce was represented by a bowl of red apples on the front counter and another of slightly overripe bananas to its right. Otherwise virtually every product in the store was in a sealed container of some sort.

There was a rather elderly man of Asian descent behind the counter, watching a small television playing a program that to my ear sounded like it was being broadcast in Mandarin. I approached him while observing the rest of the surroundings: One door behind the counter, no doubt leading to a storage area, clean if not necessarily neat shelving and floors, very little free space. The aisles were narrow and made me somewhat uncomfortable. I felt my left hand begin to move involuntarily and since the movement was slight and made me feel better, I did not check it.

"Excuse me," I said when I reached the counter. The man did not turn down the volume on the television but he did look in my direction. He said nothing. "May I ask about your cleaning procedures?"

The elderly man looked at me with an expression I took for concern but turned out to be suspicion. "Are you from the Health Department?" he asked.

"No. Allow me to introduce myself. I am—"

"You want to buy something?" The man was glancing at the television screen but still directing most of his attention at me.

"I do not," I said. "I am Samuel Hoenig, proprietor of—"

"If you don't want to buy anything, why should I listen to you?"

It was a fair, if not a polite, question. "A man who purchased coffee here recently was murdered," I said. "I am—"

"You think a guy was killed because I sold him coffee?" The man looked angry.

"I do not think that at all. I am wondering if you remember anything about the man."

The elderly man looked again at his television and then regarded me with something resembling derision. "A guy comes in and buys a cup of coffee and I'm supposed to remember him? You know how many people come in here every day and buy coffee?"

I looked to my left but did not yet see Ms. Washburn approaching. "I have no idea," I told the man. "But perhaps you might recognize him from this photograph." I had saved to my iPhone a photograph of Brett Fontaine provided by Virginia. I showed it to the man, who regarded it briefly and shook his head.

"Not a regular," he said.

"Did he buy any olive oil?" I asked.

"I just told you I didn't recognize the guy and now you want to know about him buying olive oil?" The man shook his head. "If you

176

don't want to buy anything, just go, okay? I'm working." He sat back down and paid more obvious attention to the television, whose screen was not visible to me. I did not know enough Mandarin to decipher the dialogue being spoken by the actors.

With no other interrogative techniques at my disposal, I walked back in the direction I had seen Ms. Washburn taking after we entered the store. I found her sitting on the floor of the most distant aisle to the left. She was perusing various bottles of olive oil. I did not understand the perplexed expression on her face.

"There appear to be only two brands available in this store," I pointed out. "Is there a reason you seem to be thinking so deeply about them?"

"I'm trying to figure out what could have happened that makes sense," Ms. Washburn responded. "Brett Fontaine walks into this store and toward this aisle. Someone comes up behind him and beats him to death with a tire iron. When he falls he knocks over a bottle of olive oil, which is in plastic, from the bottom shelf. It falls maybe three inches to the floor and breaks, getting enough olive oil on Brett that the autopsy report will show it mixing with his blood. Then the killer dresses up in Brett's clothing and somehow carries him out of the store, blood and olive oil dripping all over the place, gets him into his car and drives him to Wyckoff Street, presumably in the trunk of the car, gets out dressed as Brett, goes to the property he owns there, does *something*, gets back in the car so I can see him being Brett, drives to High Street in the hope that I'll get caught in a two-minute traffic jam, which will give him enough time to lay Brett out on the sidewalk in front of the building where Virginia Fontaine's husband first died so I can find him. Is that about it?"

"Perhaps this is not the stop where Mr. Fontaine was murdered," I said. "Let's go to Wyckoff Street."

"Help me up."

TWENTY-THREE

THE PROPERTY ON WYCKOFF Street—whose full address I have been asked not to divulge—was a typical one in this area of New Brunswick, where students of Rutgers University often spend their post-freshman years. It was not very new, not especially well maintained despite Virginia Fontaine's suggestion, and had two front doors, one for each of the apartments contained within the structure. It sat on a residential street that also included a small warehouse which appeared, from our vantage point four doors away in the Kia Spectra, to have been closed by its owner at least a few years previously. It was, in other words, not a very notable property or area.

"Is this where you parked the day you were following Brett Fontaine?" I asked Ms. Washburn.

"No, I wasn't able to get this close that day," she said. "I was there, by the oak tree." She pointed toward a mature oak on the opposite side of the street.

"What did Brett Fontaine do when he got here?" I was unable to see much of the rental property from this position so I opened the door of the Kia Spectra and stood next to the vehicle. My height added a little to my viewing ability, but not much. The leaves from the completely sprouted trees were making everything on the other side difficult to see.

"I couldn't see him perfectly because I didn't want to be obvious about watching him," Ms. Washburn answered. "So the trees didn't exactly block me out, but they weren't making it any easier. I saw him get out of his car. He was parked there." She indicated a spot on the other side of the street where no legal parking appeared to be available.

"How did he do that?" I asked. "He would not have been allowed to park his vehicle there."

Ms. Washburn smiled and shook her head. "He did it by not caring about stuff like that, Samuel." She also exited the Kia Spectra and walked around the car to join me. "But he walked over there and went into the building he owns. Owned. You know."

"You saw him go inside?" I was paying more attention to the closed warehouse than the residential property, but I was interested in her answer.

"More or less. He walked in that direction and then I saw his feet turn toward the house."

"Did you have your photography equipment with you?" I asked. Ms. Washburn is a former photographer for the *Home News-Tribune*, a local daily newspaper.

"Of course, but I didn't think a picture of his shoes would have been all that interesting." Ms. Washburn looked at the house and then at me. "Why? What are you thinking?"

"You are probably correct. Photographing Mr. Fontaine's feet would not have provided much in the way of useful information."

Ms. Washburn clapped her hands loudly, causing me to glance away from the warehouse and back at her. "Samuel! What are you looking at?"

I looked to the left and then to the right, and then to the left again. I would have walked to a crosswalk but none was marked on the roadbed. "Come with me," I said to Ms. Washburn, and then proceeded across the street.

She did not question me, probably assuming I wanted to have an unobstructed view of the property owned by Fontaine and Fontaine. Instead I stopped once we had reached the opposite sidewalk to consider the unused warehouse.

"Why are we here?" Ms. Washburn asked. "Brett went into the other house."

"We can't be certain of that," I told her. I pointed at the warehouse. "Notice the sign."

Ms. Washburn looked up. Over the front entrance of the warehouse was an admittedly dirty and long-neglected sign reading, in what had once been white letters over a black background Triple A Cannery Storage.

"I give up," Ms. Washburn said. "So they stored cans here a long time ago. What does that have to do with…olive oil?"

"Exactly," I answered. Ms. Washburn has always been quick to connect pieces of a question's facets. "If there was, for example, tuna being stored for distribution here, it might very well have been packed in olive oil. Surely the facility would occasionally suffer some damage or a shipment would have been compromised. Olive oil could certainly be so well saturated into the floor that it would show up on the body of a man who had been beaten severely inside."

"But how can we be sure Brett went inside?" Ms. Washburn asked. "I didn't see him head this way."

"Could you have seen if he changed his direction after walking a few steps toward the house?" I asked.

Ms. Washburn considered the question. "Not from the angle I had. You saw what it looked like. With cars parked on that side of the street and the leaves on the trees hanging low, I had a very small window to look through."

I looked at the warehouse again. It was obviously in a state of near collapse. The metal on the hinges and fixtures on the front door had rusted. Again I questioned the wisdom of traveling anywhere without at least two pairs of latex gloves. I felt my head begin to shake as it does when I am frustrated or angry with myself. The inside of my lower lip scraped against my teeth.

"Samuel," Ms. Washburn said gently.

Her voice made me refocus my attention and emotions. My involuntary responses eased but did not immediately cease entirely. I remembered to breathe. I closed my eyes for a moment and counted to three slowly. Then I looked at Ms. Washburn again.

"Thank you," I said.

"What was bothering you?"

"I am angry at myself for not bringing latex gloves," I explained.

"Why do we need latex gloves?"

"Because we need to go inside the warehouse and observe the scene."

Ms. Washburn reached for the canvas tote bag she had brought with her. "I have some latex gloves, Samuel," she said.

I should never have doubted it.

With our hands protected—I had two gloves on each hand—we approached the warehouse door, which a quick attempt indicated was locked, chained, and padlocked. That was not unexpected.

"Is there another way in?" Ms. Washburn asked, I believe rhetorically. She walked toward the left side of the building and looked down into the alley beyond. Then she turned back toward me and shook her head negatively. I did the same, more carefully, on the right side of the warehouse. There was no obvious entrance there, but there were windows lining the wall, approximately six feet from the pavement of the alley.

"There are windows," I said when Ms. Washburn was again by my side.

"On the other side too. Should we try to climb up and break in?"

"That would not be my first choice," I admitted. "There must be a loading dock in the back. Did you see an entrance for trucks on your side?"

"Yeah. There's a very wide skirt in the curb by the parking lot. Must be to allow bigger vehicles in for deliveries. Maybe there's a way in back there."

I was not enthusiastic about the experience but saw no alternative. We walked into the alley and then all the way along the side of the warehouse. I concentrated very diligently on not looking down for fear of any urban creatures that might have inhabited this space. Ms. Washburn made no noise to indicate she had been startled so I simply chose to believe there was nothing there. It seemed a very long time, but in truth we reached the rear of the warehouse in seventeen seconds.

There was a small parking lot, presumably for employees. The white paint delineating individual spaces had almost completely faded and could be seen only when one was making a specific effort to do so. But the roadway was clearly intended to allow for deliveries, as were the two large loading docks that took up almost the entirety of the back wall.

"This was where they had stuff delivered for sure," Ms. Washburn said, and although she was stating the obvious her comment did start my mind imagining what the operation must have been like.

There would have been at least ten employees working in the facility at any given time to accommodate a warehouse of this size. I could envision men and women opening and closing the bay doors in incidents of extreme temperatures during both winter and summer. Inside there would be forklift operators bringing the deliveries to the designated spaces.

A door to the left side of the bays would have been where the supervisors and company executives would have entered. Because there was a roof over that entrance, the door was not as badly damaged or rusted as the ones in front. I walked toward it.

"There is no chain or padlock," I said aloud, although I'm not certain Ms. Washburn could hear me. She stood approximately thirty feet to my right and behind me. It sometimes helps my process to hear the words out loud. "There are no visible hinges; they must be on the inside." With my peripheral vision I saw Ms. Washburn examine something on the rocky ground in front of her and bend down on her left knee. "There do appear to have been security cameras here but I would be very surprised if they were still operational."

Ms. Washburn reached for something and stood up but I was concentrating on the door. "If this is indeed the place where Brett Fontaine died, someone had access to the building. There is no sign of forced entry," I said.

At that moment I saw violent movement to my right and instinctively stepped back. That was the right move to make because suddenly a large rock was being pushed hard into the lever being used as a doorknob. The impact, coming with an impressive strike downward, instantly caused enough damage to the mechanism that the lever was obliterated and the door showed an open hole where it used to be.

Ms. Washburn, holding the stone in her right hand, pushed out two large breaths. "That oughta do it," she said.

Indeed, now I could work the lock from the inside, being careful to wear the latex gloves, and within a minute we were inside the warehouse. "I marvel at your ability to take a situation in hand, Ms.

Washburn," I told her as we stepped from the parking lot into the building.

She shrugged. "Sometimes it's just the simplest thing that works."

As we had expected, the warehouse was almost entirely empty. It was a large open space with very little interior construction cutting into its utility. There was what appeared to be an office to our right and almost nothing else in the building other than wooden pallets that had no doubt kept the stock off the floor in the case of flooding from heavy rain. Those ringed the perimeter of the warehouse. Other than that and two obviously unused forklifts, there was nothing here.

There was also, even after the long time this warehouse had been out of use, a rather overwhelming smell of fish. I found myself breathing through my mouth.

"What are we looking for?" Ms. Washburn asked.

"Any trace of violence," I suggested. "A dark stain on the floor or walls. Something that could have been used as a bludgeon."

We walked farther into the center of the open space. "You don't think the tire iron was the murder weapon?" Ms. Washburn said.

"I do not have enough information to form an opinion yet, but it seems unlikely to me."

"That sounds like an opinion."

I did not respond because I thought it might have been an attempt at banter, something which does not come naturally to me. I try to avoid it. Instead I diverted my attention to carefully scanning the floor for signs of Brett Fontaine's murder. The odor in the air was not helping. I began to worry that I might vomit.

For the first six minutes there was nothing unusual Ms. Washburn or I noticed in the warehouse. A quick look behind the door of the office, which was unlocked, showed an absolutely empty room, not even a desk or chair. I made a mental note to check on the ownership of this building and how long it had lain dormant.

When we had split up to better cover the main floor Ms. Washburn called to me from the eastern side. "Samuel. I think I've got something."

I walked to her side. It was a fairly sizable distance but I did not run as it was clear whatever Ms. Washburn had discovered would not be in danger of leaving anytime soon. When I got to her approximately thirteen seconds later I saw the evidence she had mentioned.

There was a distinct area indicating there had been a liquid on the floor and the stain was not very old. But more importantly there was also a metal grappling hook, the kind used to help workers move large crates more efficiently. It lay on the floor near the dark stain, which was approximately seventeen inches in diameter.

"Did you touch anything?" I asked Ms. Washburn.

She looked at me with a curled lip. "Of course not. This is not my first dead body, Samuel. With you it's become a habit."

I must have looked horrified because Ms. Washburn immediately touched my arm and said, "Oh Samuel, I didn't mean anything by that. It was just a joke."

It was best to shake my head to indicate her comment had not hurt me emotionally. "I think now we have a clear course of action," I said. "Take two steps back and call the police."

We took two steps back.

TWENTY-FOUR

"How did you get in here?" Detective Jack Monroe did not sound pleased and he did not look pleased.

"The lock on the back door was broken," Ms. Washburn interjected quickly. Of course what she said was true, but she left out the fact that she was the one who had broken it. "We came in to look around and found what you're looking at now."

Monroe looked down at what we believed to be a bloodstain and the grappling hook. "How do I know you didn't bring it with you?" he asked.

I was momentarily stunned by the question but Ms. Washburn had no such hesitation. "Are you serious? You think we came here to plant evidence just so we could make your day more complicated?"

Monroe held up his hands defensively. "Easy, lady. I have to ask."

It occurred to me that he did not in fact need to ask that question but there was no point in stating the obvious. "We have touched nothing," I said.

"I would hope so," Monroe answered. He bent at the knees and squatted next to the wet area, which had already been isolated with yellow police barrier tape. Two uniformed officers stood by. Monroe looked toward the door where Ms. Washburn had obliterated the handle to allow our entry. "Crime scene should be here any minute."

"I thought Brett's murder was a state case now," Ms. Washburn said. She definitely knew that was not true. I wondered if she was trying to elicit information from Monroe that he would not otherwise divulge.

Monroe looked up at her with an odd expression I could not classify. "It would be the county's Major Crimes unit and we haven't been told that yet. So you don't know what you're talking about."

"Wouldn't be the first time," Ms. Washburn said. "So if the county's going to get involved, why are you here?" She was unquestionably baiting Monroe.

He did look annoyed. "We don't know what we have here yet," he said. He pointed toward the outline on the floor. "This could be chocolate syrup for all we know."

"It is not," I said. "It is Brett Fontaine's blood. He was killed here."

Monroe, apparently satisfied that he had posed as a brilliant detective long enough, rose to his full height again and looked at me. "I'm a member of the New Brunswick Police Department and a detective," he said. "I need concrete evidence before I can make a claim like that. I can't just decide based on a hunch."

There was much of his statement I could have questioned. For one thing, why evidence should be made exclusively of concrete was baffling. But I decided to concentrate on the thrust of Monroe's argument, which I found particularly troublesome and possibly insulting.

"I am not operating on a hunch," I told Monroe. "The presence of olive oil mixed with Mr. Fontaine's blood, even in trace amounts, would lead us to this building, which was used as a warehouse for products packed in that substance. No doubt you have noticed the odor of fish in this facility."

"So there's olive oil in the ME's report," the detective said. "So what? He could have been killed at a pizzeria or there could have been olive oil spilled on the street where he was found. It didn't even have to be that recent, if you're making the argument that it was here. This place hasn't been active in two years."

Ms. Washburn stepped forward to confront Monroe. "That's true, but there was so much olive oil spilled here over the years that it's probably on every surface of this building. Right, Samuel?"

"Yes. No doubt each of us will have a very thin coating on the soles of our shoes when we leave here today. Perhaps an examination of Mr. Fontaine's shoes on the day he died will indicate he was here as well."

"Finding that grappling hook doesn't prove anything," Monroe said. Perhaps he was changing the subject to learn something or to avoid discussing olive oil any further. "Fontaine was killed with something much more blunt than that thing."

"You'll notice the stain on the hook shows on its handle," I pointed out. "I believe the killer used it backward, holding the sharp point in his or her hand and the larger end as a bludgeon. I think a forensic examination of the wounds will bear out my contention that Mr. Fontaine was not killed with a tire iron."

Monroe's lips became thin; he was pressing them together. "I think I've learned all I can from you two," he said after a sizable pause. "You can go."

As we walked out Ms. Washburn said quietly to me, "I guess you got him madder than I did."

We were back outside and in Ms. Washburn's Kia Spectra shortly thereafter. "Detective Monroe has an odd tendency to reward any assistance we give him with scorn," I said as Ms. Washburn started the engine.

"Some people have difficulty getting in touch with complicated emotions," she answered, and then we did not speak because she was driving.

We returned briefly to the Questions Answered office because we had not been there at all today. Much of our business can be done with the use of smartphones and Ms. Washburn's laptop computer when there is a Wi-Fi signal nearby, but being in our headquarters makes things easier and more efficient. I do not like to stay away from the office for an extended period of time for fear I have missed something, or that a potential client might walk in off the street. Or more accurately, the parking lot.

I did a few quick calculations on the question of the world circumnavigation while Ms. Washburn spoke on the phone to Virginia Fontaine to keep her abreast of our progress. She made an appointment to see Ms. Fontaine the next morning and another to talk to Leon Rabinski again regarding his alleged affair with Virginia. I could hear her side of the conversation as I worked on my desktop computer.

When she had completed her calls I suggested we drive back to my home, as Ms. Washburn was still staying there for security purposes. Ms. Washburn had suggested returning to her apartment because there had been no further communication from the person pretending to be the spirit of Melanie Mason, but I was wary of making assumptions and said she should stay at least one more night.

"All right," Ms. Washburn said, "but I'm not making you sleep on the sofa again." I assumed she would change her thinking on the subject and did not object, waiting for the subject to be broached again later in the evening.

"You made two appointments for interviews tomorrow morning," I said as we left the office. "Are you assuming we will conduct those sessions separately?"

"That was the plan, wasn't it?"

"I will have to ask Mike the taxicab driver if he is available at that time," I mused aloud. Ms. Washburn simply nodded; yes, that was what I would need to do.

When we arrived at my home, Mother had not yet finished preparing our dinner. Ms. Washburn said in a voice my parents could not hear that it would be rude to excuse ourselves and go to my attic apartment. That was typically my custom when there was an interval like this, but I acceded to her view and sat with Ms. Washburn and Reuben Hoenig in the living room where Mother, with the kitchen door swung open, could hear the conversation.

Ms. Washburn recounted the afternoon's activities. There was no comment from Reuben, although he looked interested, but Mother sounded aghast. "You broke into a warehouse?"

"It was an abandoned warehouse, and we needed to observe a crime scene the police had not yet discovered," I explained. Ms. Washburn signaled to me with her hands palms up and raised them, indicating I had not spoke loudly enough for Mother to hear, so I repeated what I'd said at a higher volume.

"You didn't have to yell," Mother said from the kitchen. I resolved to practice modulating my voice more stringently.

"So you broke the case for the cops," Reuben said. He rarely looked at me but often at Ms. Washburn, whom he appeared to find fascinating.

"We do not break cases; we answer questions," I told him. I had made similar statements to him on eight previous occasions. "And in this instance, we merely located the scene of the crime. We still do not have enough information to form a theory on its perpetrator or perpetrators."

"Well, what about that?" Reuben asked.

"We still have to gather a good deal of data," I explained. "Officer Palumbo should soon have some information on the electronic equipment Mike and I found at the gravesite. And we will continue to talk to those who knew Brett Fontaine, although I'd like to concentrate on those who also knew Virginia's first husband, William Klein."

"That means we have to find Anthony Deane," Ms. Washburn said. "And he seems to be very serious about not being found. I've looked up everyone with that name I can find and there are none listed in New Jersey. We know he had a stand in a farmers' market in Metuchen years ago, but we don't know if he still lives here and neither does his fraternity brother Peter Belson."

Reuben seemed to ruminate on the problem. "From what you told me the person who thinks this Deane guy killed both husbands is the high school friend…Donna?"

"Debbie Sampras," Ms. Washburn corrected him.

Reuben pointed at her like a teacher whose student has found the correct answer. He snapped his fingers. "Debbie Sampras," he said. "What do you know about her?"

"Ms. Washburn interviewed her in person," I said. "I'm sure it was a very thorough conversation based on her recounting."

"I'm not questioning your work, Janet," Reuben said. "I'm saying someone who's that anxious to pin two murders on another person just because she thinks he had a crush on the woman in the middle probably has her own agenda."

"We have not ruled anyone out as a suspect," I reminded Reuben.

"No, of course not." He moved his head back and forth, nodding almost to the side as if considering and agreeing at the same time. "Do we know anyone else who knew them both in high school?"

"We?" I said.

Ms. Washburn quickly responded, perhaps in an attempt (which, if so, was successful) to distract from my question. "I've looked through the class roster but I haven't found anyone else who seems to have kept in touch with Brett Fontaine," she said. "There certainly weren't any other high school friends at his memorial service."

"Maybe what you need is somebody who kept in touch with this Debbie Sampras," Reuben suggested. "They might know more about her thinking and how she really felt about the guy who died."

"Are you suggesting that Debbie Sampras killed Brett Fontaine out of jealousy?" I asked. "Is it your assertion that just because they were of opposite sexes they couldn't simply have been platonic friends?"

Reuben sat back in his chair. "Samuel, I'm surprised at you. It's obvious we don't have enough facts yet to form a coherent theory; you said so yourself. I'm trying to suggest an area you don't seem to have pursued yet because you have been looking elsewhere."

Ms. Washburn looked thoughtful. "I can see who Debbie's friends are on Facebook. Maybe some of them are mutual friends of Brett Fontaine's. His page hasn't been deleted yet." She reached for her laptop computer.

"That can wait until after dinner." Mother appeared in the kitchen doorway. "I made brisket." I must have looked slightly panicked. "Don't worry, Samuel. There's something for you too."

As we stood to walk to the dining room, where I had helped Mother set the table, Reuben stroked his chin and asked, "You're splitting up for these meetings with people tomorrow?" Only his tone indicated to me he was asking a question.

"Yes. Ms. Washburn and I have concluded that we can be more efficient if we sometimes divide the interviews."

Reuben looked at me with an expression I could not decipher. "How are you going to get to yours?" he asked.

"I will contact my friend Mike the taxicab driver," I said. "He might be available."

Reuben waved a hand to declare the matter settled. "I'll drive you," he said.

"I think that's a very good idea," Ms. Washburn said, smiling.

I did not know what food Mother had prepared for me, but my appetite was fading.

TWENTY-FIVE

"Why did you marry my mother?" I asked Reuben Hoenig.

We were sitting in the front seat of my mother's car in the parking lot of a Dunkin' Donuts across the street from the Union Township police headquarters. Officer Palumbo had left strict instructions to wait here until he could make his way to us because he did not want his extracurricular investigation known by his colleagues in the police department. So far we had been waiting seven minutes in silence, which I was now breaking.

Reuben looked at me with a questioning expression. "I loved her," he said. I waited for a more detailed explanation but apparently he felt that statement was sufficient.

"And yet you left her for twenty-seven years," I pointed out.

"I still loved her. It was a different set of circumstances that made me go. It had nothing to do with the feelings we had for each other." Reuben sat back in the driver's seat and stretched his neck a bit, first to the right to face me and then to the left to look out the window. "I understand why you're angry with me, Samuel, and I don't blame

194

you. If my father had done to me what I did to you, I'd have been just as mad."

He was missing the point, as he had in virtually every conversation we'd had since his return. "This is not about me and it's certainly not about me being angry with you," I told Reuben. "I am trying to understand how you decided to marry a woman because you loved her enough to commit to a lifetime together, but found that emotion did not stay strong enough to keep you with her for a very long period of time."

"It was because I loved her that I left."

That made no sense at all but I had no time to respond because I noticed Officer Palumbo walking toward the parking lot. He had told me to meet him inside the Dunkin' Donuts but I do not drink coffee and had no desire for a doughnut this early in the day. I'd chosen to wait outside until he was visible. Now I stepped out of the car and walked to the entrance of the store.

I arrived at the door almost exactly as Palumbo did the same. "Go inside," he hissed at me. "I told you to wait inside."

"I didn't want a coffee."

"Just go in."

I did as he instructed, grateful that Reuben had not—as he'd suggested on the ride here, despite my obvious discomfort about conversing while the vehicle was in motion—accompanied me inside. Palumbo took up a position in the line, which was currently three customers long including him, and indicated I should stay behind him, which I did.

As he waited his turn (something I had seen other uniformed officers eschew in other such establishments before), Palumbo spoke to me quietly without looking back. "I looked into the electronics you gave me," he said. "You're lucky. It's a very specific and limited brand.

There isn't much of that stuff sold in this country, let alone in the state."

Assuming I should not respond verbally I nodded and waited for Palumbo to say more. He was not looking in my direction, however, so he did not see the signal. "Do you hear me?" he asked.

"Yes."

"Okay. I traced the receiver you pulled out of the ground and found the compatible sending unit from the same company. As far as I can tell, since the time of the accident I worked on Route 22, there have been only three sets like that sold to customers in this state, all online."

I did not want to draw attention to myself but felt I should communicate to Palumbo that I had heard and comprehended what he'd told me. "Yes," I mumbled.

"I don't know all the people you've been looking at for this murder you told me about, but I wrote down the names of the three people who bought the stuff. The paper is in my left hand. I'm going to leave it on the counter when I order. Don't say anything and don't look at me or signal me. Just order whatever you want and pick up the paper. Let me know later on if it helps."

The customer in front of Palumbo walked away and he advanced to the counter. He put both hands out palms down and leaned on the counter as he ordered a large black coffee and a bran muffin. When the employee working there walked off to collect his order Palumbo did not turn to face me but he moved his left hand. A small folded piece of white paper was left on the flat surface.

Palumbo paid for his order, leaving me as the next customer in line, and walked out of the store. This was perplexing for me because I did not want to purchase anything available at the Dunkin' Donuts outlet. The employee, wearing a headset to hear orders from the drive-through window, looked at me. "Yes?"

I closed my hand around the folded paper Palumbo had left on the counter. "I…I…" I could not think of a socially appropriate way to end the encounter.

From my right I heard Reuben Hoenig's voice. "He'll have an iced decaf, light with one pink sweetener, and a glazed." I turned to see Reuben standing directly to my side as the employee nodded and walked off to fulfill his order.

"What are you doing here?" I asked. "We had agreed you'd wait in the car."

Reuben made a face to indicate he did not think much of that agreement. "I wanted an iced decaf and a glazed."

The Dunkin' Donuts employee brought back Reuben's order, took his money, and thanked him when Reuben left a dollar in the tip jar. I tried to determine the best way to clean my hand after having rested it on the counter.

I insisted he sit at a table to eat and drink before getting back into Mother's car. I would have been petrified with fear if he'd attempted to do either of those things while driving. "So whose name did he write down?" Reuben asked once we were seated. I put two paper napkins down under each elbow on which I was leaning.

"You knew what Officer Palumbo said?" I asked.

"Sure. I was standing right behind you. You just didn't notice me."

I was beginning to feel like a man whose powers of observation were inferior to most. Given that Ms. Washburn had recently implied I was something of a liability during certain interviews, my self-esteem was not very high at this moment. I felt a slight tremor of frustration in my neck and concentrated on halting it.

"So what does the paper say?" Reuben was nothing if not direct.

I opened the tight fist on my left hand and extracted Officer Palumbo's note, folded into the size of a credit card. First I looked in every direction around the Dunkin' Donuts to be sure no one who might have an interest in Brett Fontaine's death or Officer Palumbo's work might be watching. Most people in the establishment were buying coffee and leaving immediately thereafter.

I placed the paper on the table which was doubly useful in that it acted as a barrier. I unfolded it carefully and smoothed it out on the surface. There were, as Officer Palumbo had indicated, three names on the list, each with an address and phone number supplied.

The first and third were names of people unfamiliar to me, although I made a note to research each one when I returned to the Questions Answered office. But I did believe immediately I would find nothing of significance to the murder of Brett Fontaine attached to either of those people.

The second name on Officer Palumbo's list was that of Leon Rabinski.

"Isn't that the guy we're going to see next?" Reuben asked me. I nodded. "Well. That conversation just got more interesting." He sat back and took a bite of his doughnut, looking unusually pleased with himself.

TWENTY-SIX

"I don't know anything about audio equipment," Leon Rabinski said.

Although he'd been reluctant to have a second conversation with me—and had in fact asked if "the pretty blonde" would be a more suitable representative of my business—Rabinski had agreed when I had promised not to ask him personal questions about his marriage to Melanie Mason. He had not delineated what might constitute a personal question, however, and that was making me slightly anxious because my own definition might not match Rabinski's.

Reuben Hoenig had offered to accompany me as a "liaison," but I had declined his suggestion. One does not usually bring a parent to a business meeting. Mother told me that.

"And yet there are records of you purchasing this very specialized type of electronic component designed to send and receive audio at a remote location," I reminded him. "If you did not buy it, how do you account for the online records?" I felt it was not personal to ask Rabinski about the sound equipment as long as I did not mention it was used at his late wife's gravesite.

"I don't know." Rabinski crossed his legs, which can sometimes be seen as a defensive gesture. "Maybe someone hacked my credit card."

We were sitting in the den of Rabinski's home on a tree-lined street in East Brunswick. The large windows of the room, which might at one time have been a screened back porch, overlooked a small area of woods and, in the distance, a pond. Occasionally the quack of a rather insistent duck could be heard. It was very distracting.

"Were there any other suspect charges made on a credit card of yours during that period?" I asked. "According to the documents I have, it would have been during the month of September three years ago." A quick check of the information Officer Palumbo had supplied on my iPhone during the ride to Rabinski's house had supplied most of the records available on the purchase in question.

"I don't remember." Rabinski was looking through the window, probably trying to locate the verbose duck. "It was a few years ago."

"Do you remember having to report any fraudulent charges to your credit card company any time in the past?" I asked. Rabinski's denials and the sound of the duck were raising my level of irritation, which is always a concern for someone like me.

"Look, Mr. Hoenig. I don't know what you're talking about and I don't really want to go on talking about Melanie and her death if I don't have to. And I *don't* have to. So why don't you just go home and I'll get back to what I was doing?" Rabinski nodded toward a desk in the opposite corner where his computer was open and running, although at the moment the screensaver function had been activated. It was randomly displaying photographs, clearly from Rabinski's own collection, as many of the images included his face.

"Mr. Rabinski, I agreed not to ask you about your marriage because I have no desire to make you uncomfortable." That was true in principle; in fact I did not especially care if Rabinski felt awkward or not. It was simply going to be less productive a conversation if he decided to stop speaking at all. "So please, if I have crossed a boundary, let me know and I will not do so again."

I was well aware my line of inquiry had done no such thing. This was a tactic, sometimes successful, meant to make the person being questioned feel more at ease to facilitate more revealing responses. I did not know if it would work in Rabinski's case, but since he was attempting to ask me to leave it seemed unlikely to do any harm.

"It's not that I'm annoyed. I just don't have anything that can help you and this feels a lot like a waste or your time and mine."

There are certain indicators when a person is lying. I am not especially expert in this study but I have done some research on the subject and Dr. Mancuso has pointed out a few during our weekly sessions. Still, there are some that are particularly obvious.

Rabinski was scratching his nose.

While it is possible to do so for reasons other than to cover up an untruth, with no noticeable insect bite or other skin abrasion on the bridge of the nose, scratching that area repeatedly is one of the more recognizable signs of lying.

This led to unspoken questions: If Rabinski was not being truthful about the audio equipment at Melanie Mason's grave, why was he doing so and what was he concealing? The other thing to consider was how to best coerce him into giving up this strategy and telling the truth. I will confess to wishing for a moment that Ms. Washburn was there to consult.

There didn't seem to be many options and people become uncomfortable with long gaps in a conversation. Rabinski looked at me and asked, "So are we done here?"

"I don't believe so," I answered. "I think you are lying. Leaving before I get a satisfactory answer would be unproductive and frustrating. So please. If you would simply explain the purchase of the electronics I've mentioned, I believe I can leave you to return to your daily activities."

As I spoke the word *lying* I saw Rabinski's eyes widen. He sputtered, something that is not usually heard in conversation. It took him six seconds to compose himself after I had finished speaking.

"I think we've finished our talk," he said. He stood up.

I sat where I was.

"Mr. Hoenig, I hate to be rude but I will have to insist that you leave," Rabinski said. He folded his arms and looked toward the door. But I did not move. "Please. Now."

"I think it would be a key strategic mistake for me to leave without an explanation. May I see records of your credit cards for the past two years? That would show any activity that might have some relevance to this question." I had realized that sitting as still as possible and letting Rabinski be the more agitated party in the situation was having an effect. Whether it would prove fruitful was not yet clear.

It became more understandable a moment later when Rabinski exhaled with some drama and dropped his arms to his side. "Okay, I bought the speakers and the transmitter," he said. "But I was just buying it for a friend and didn't use it myself. I don't even know how to use it, to tell you the truth."

At that moment I believed he was indeed being honest. But he was not being totally forthcoming. "Who is the friend?" I asked.

"I beg your pardon?"

"You said you bought the equipment on behalf of a friend. Who is the friend who asked you to do so?"

Rabinski pursed his lips. "Mr. Hoenig, in the interest of absolute honesty, this is what I will tell you: There is no chance at all you'll be getting that information from me. If a crime was committed by purchasing that stuff, I'm guilty. Call the cops. If not, it's time for you to go. Believe me, I'm not going to tell you more than that."

"Did you receive a substantial insurance payment after your wife's death?" I asked.

Rabinski spoke very slowly and through clenched teeth. "I said I'm not going to tell you anything more."

"Your percentage in the ownership of Fontaine and Fontaine clearly increased after Brett Fontaine's death, and there are reports that the company is about to be purchased for a very large sum of money," I pointed out. "You seem to have benefitted financially from Brett Fontaine's death."

"That's a fortunate result of an unfortunate event," Rabinski said. "Are you accusing me of something?"

"I am not. Were you having an affair with Virginia Fontaine?"

"I'm not going to speak to you anymore."

I believed him so I left.

When I settled into the passenger seat of my mother's car, Reuben looked at me with an expectant expression. "So?"

That was an unspecific question. "I don't understand," I said.

"What did he tell you?" Reuben asked.

"Mr. Rabinski admitted to purchasing the audio equipment but he would not reveal the person who asked him to do so." I could not pinpoint the catalyst for the emotion but I found myself feeling somehow embarrassed over my failure to name Rabinski's friend. Saying that to Reuben had been difficult and I was not able to understand why.

"Who do you think it was?" Reuben asked.

"My best speculation would be that it is a woman and someone with whom Mr. Rabinski might be having a romantic relationship, but that is only speculation," I told him. "I do not have enough facts yet."

"That seems to be the problem, for sure." Reuben sat back and looked through the windshield in thought. "Do you want me to go in there and squeeze him?"

How Reuben giving Rabinski a hug would produce any information was a mystery to my sensibility. "No," I answered. "Please just drive me to the Questions Answered office."

"Sure? I can be really good at persuading people." Reuben had worked for some unsavory people during the years he'd been away. I chose not to consider what he might have meant by his remark.

"Please. Just drive."

TWENTY-SEVEN

REUBEN HAD SUGGESTED STOPPING for lunch but I was anxious to get back to my office, to confer with Ms. Washburn and especially to avoid having lunch alone with Reuben again. Once in the office (to which Ms. Washburn had not yet returned), I dedicated myself to a search for Anthony Deane. I'd found a slight glimmer of hope by the time the bells over the entrance to the office rang and Ms. Washburn walked in.

"Virginia Fontaine is a tough cookie," she said immediately. I understood her statement was a metaphor but I was not clear on its current relevance.

"She is our client," I reminded Ms. Washburn. "If she is withholding information from us, we can exercise the clause in our contract that allows us to sever the relationship."

"It's not that bad," she said as she hung her jacket on the back of her chair and sat at her desk. "But I don't understand why she doesn't want to tell me about her ownership of the business. Why would it go to Leon Rabinski and not Virginia?"

"Usually when someone tries very hard not to answer a question it is because that person believes the answer will be somehow damaging," I said. I was calling a web page up on my screen and found what I had hoped would be there.

"Yeah, but if she's hiding something, why did she come to us in the first place?" Ms. Washburn asked. "She could easily keep things quiet by not asking for help at all."

I took a screenshot of the page. "You assume she's hiding something that might implicate her in Brett Fontaine's murder," I said. "She might have things to hide in other areas that are equally dangerous or embarrassing."

Ms. Washburn shook her head. "It doesn't make sense."

"Look here." I pointed at the screen. "I might have found a way to locate Anthony Deane."

Ms. Washburn stood and walked to my right side to see my computer display, which I angled to better accommodate her viewpoint. This was one of the random moments that occurred more frequently now when I felt the urge to kiss Ms. Washburn. But we had agreed that would no longer happen in the Questions Answered office so I redirected my thoughts toward the screen.

"What is this?" she asked. "It looks like they're trying to sell me tires."

"You are not wrong," I assured her. "This is the website for a company devoted to that pursuit. It is based, as you can see, in Darby Township, Pennsylvania. That is roughly a ninety-minute drive from here."

"Close enough to come for Brett Fontaine's memorial service," Ms. Washburn said. She was following the same line of thought as I had to reach this web page.

"If one clicks on the *About Us* link for Darby Tire, a list of the company's top personnel is presented. See here." I moved the cursor on my screen to a particular spot.

"Tony Deane," Ms. Washburn read.

"Precisely. By focusing on businesses within easy driving distance and using various nicknames for *Anthony*, I was able to find two Tony Deanes. The other was a woman living in Morris County and a photograph of her confirmed she is not the person for whom we are searching."

Ms. Washburn read the description aloud. "*Tony Deane started as a mechanic at Darby Tire ten years ago and is now the marketing manager for the company. Tony has helped us grow the business from one location to four in a very short time.*" She looked at me. "There's a phone number for his direct line."

"I think this might be better handled face-to-face," I said. The Skype interview with Peter Belson had left me feeling that I had missed something and I did not want to repeat that error. "Is it possible for you to drive to Darby tomorrow?"

Ms. Washburn said she could do so and we agreed to start out as early as possible. With Ms. Washburn staying in my home it was possible to save up to seventeen minutes in the morning that would normally be consumed in our separate commutes to the Questions Answered office. I avoided pointing that out because Ms. Washburn had seemed less than enthusiastic about spending another night in the house. For reasons I couldn't pinpoint, I was much more secure having her under the same roof.

"Have you had any luck finding other high school classmates of Debbie Sampras and Brett Fontaine?" I asked.

Ms. Washburn, who had bent over slightly to observe my monitor, stood up. "Yes," she said. "There were two intersections in the friends area of Debbie and Brett's Facebook pages. One is a woman who lives in Seattle, Marlyn Beebe. But the other is a guy not far from here, in Westfield. His name is Neil Betts."

"What do we know about Neil Betts, as Reuben Hoenig would ask?" That was my attempt at humor. Ms. Washburn seemed to understand because she chuckled lightly.

"From what I've been able to dig up, Neil is an agent of the IRS working out of their Newark office," Ms. Washburn said. I found it was easier for me to concentrate on what she was saying when she was at her own desk more than eight feet away. My personal urges involving her were less pronounced. I always wanted to hear what she was saying but from here it was less difficult to make that the priority. "He's married with two children. Apparently he runs a Facebook group for people who graduated high school with him and the others."

"Is there contact information for Mr. Betts?" I asked.

"I friended him on Facebook and sent him a private message explaining what we've been doing and asking if there is anything he might be able to add to what we know so far. I'm waiting to hear back from him."

"Please let me know when there is a reply," I said.

"Of course, Samuel."

I told her of my visit to Leon Rabinski's home and my mixed results. "He obviously knows more than he is saying. He outwardly admits to knowing more than he is saying. I can't help wondering if he might have said more if you had been there, Ms. Washburn."

Ms. Washburn, who had been looking at her screen, turned toward me with her brow wrinkled and a concerned look in her eyes. "I doubt that, Samuel. Why would he tell me more than he told you if he doesn't want to divulge the name of the person he bought the audio equipment for?"

"Because you are more likable than I am and that makes a difference in getting subjects to offer more information," I said.

Ms. Washburn turned her chair so she could face me. "I don't think I'm more likable than you are, Samuel. You can be very engaging when you want to be. You just don't always want to be."

I stood up. It was time to begin a round of exercise walking. I begin relatively slowly and increase the pace after two circumnavigations of the office's perimeter. "I think there are times when my personality is something of a mystery to most people," I said.

"If I'm so accessible, how come Virginia Fontaine won't talk to me?" Ms. Washburn asked.

"It is a good question. Perhaps we chose our subjects badly." I began my second trip around the office and Ms. Washburn returned her gaze to her screen. It must be difficult to keep track of me as I move in and out of her line of sight.

"You mean you should have talked to Virginia and I should have gone to Leon Rabinski's house?" she asked.

My breath was starting to feel a little more strained; that is normal. "Precisely. Mr. Rabinski, you'll recall, reacted badly to me the first time we met, while Ms. Fontaine, aside from my reliance on facts in questioning the existence of ghosts, was not at all averse to my working on her question."

Ms. Washburn considered that point for twenty-seven steps. "You might be right, Samuel. But there's nothing we can do about it now. We just have to be sure to think before we decide who's going to talk to whom in the future."

My fourth trip around the office is when speaking starts to become slightly more difficult. "Or…we could go to the interviews… together…as we used to."

I happened to be directly in front of Ms. Washburn's desk; she looked up. "But I thought we agreed that splitting up was a more efficient use of our time."

Now I was in the area of the office nearer the drink machine and the pizza ovens. "It is not…more…efficient…if we are not able to…get better results," I said. "Perhaps…we make a more successful team."

I could not see Ms. Washburn's face but there was an unmistakable sound of pleasure in her voice. "Maybe so, Samuel. Maybe so."

She worked rather diligently while I completed my rounds and accepted my offer of a diet soda when I purchased a bottle of spring water from our drink machine. From the sound of the bottle dropping we were running low on spring water; it was fortunate that Les the drink machine man would be delivering more the next day.

I fell rather heavily into my chair after giving Ms. Washburn her bottle of diet soda. Exercise is important, but it often feels like it does more harm than good. My physician Dr. Levine would disagree. Science is constantly evolving but facts must be respected.

"Samuel," Ms. Washburn said, "what does it mean when a person goes missing and nobody reports until a year later?"

That seemed a random hypothetical. "To what are you referring, Ms. Washburn?"

"I was looking into what Officer Palumbo told us about no other women being reported as missing or dead around the time Melanie Mason died in the car crash," she said. "And just like he said, I didn't find anyone. But a year later a homeless man told a cop in North Plainfield that a woman he knew had vanished from their spot under an overpass. The guy said he hadn't told anyone because nobody had ever asked him, but he thought maybe the cop would know because he was a cop."

It took me a moment to piece together the information she had given me. "Ms. Washburn, I believe you might have just answered a very important part of this question."

"I did?"

"Yes, and that means we should call Mike the taxicab driver."

Ms. Washburn's eyebrows dropped slightly. "I'm driving us both to your house, Samuel."

"We need Mike for backup," I said. "We are going to have another conversation with Melanie Mason."

TWENTY-EIGHT

My mother and Reuben Hoenig had wondered why Ms. Washburn and I were rushing through dinner, even after I'd explained that we'd be leaving shortly. Ms. Washburn had suggested we not divulge our plans for fear of worrying Mother. I had agreed because I was concerned Reuben might try to tag along with us.

Mike the taxicab driver was his usual reliable self, arriving in the driveway of my mother's home at precisely the time I had requested. Tonight he knew precisely how to reach the gravesite in question, and the back gate of the cemetery had once again been left open. I wondered if Stephen Manfred would have approved of that practice, but it allowed us the opportunity to reach Melanie Mason's grave after sunset.

"The last time she invited you," Mike pointed out. "How can you be sure she'll be watching for us now?"

"I don't know for certain," I admitted. "We did not uncover any motion sensor or underground equipment that might alert someone at a remote location, but we know that Officer Palumbo had not arranged a conversation ahead of time when he supposedly heard Ms.

Mason's ghost speak. Whoever is speaking had been in place when he arrived."

Ms. Washburn was staring at the headstone and looked like she was unusually nervous. "Are we sure it's not Melanie?" she asked.

I walked to her and, as I had seen in motion pictures and television, put my arm around her shoulders. I spoke quietly to avoid Mike overhearing me. "This is just like going with your high school friends," I said. "Pretend we are here to have a good time."

"When I did that I saw a ghost," Ms. Washburn insisted.

"I think not, but either way, you will not see one tonight. This area is wired for sound. If there were such a thing as a ghost, she would not need to rely on electronic equipment."

Ms. Washburn looked up at me. "That's true, isn't it?" Her face gained confidence. "Thank you, Samuel."

"You have your flashlight?" Mike called over. "Maybe we can attract someone's attention, and hopefully it won't be the cops."

We both reached for the flashlights I'd purchased earlier, ones with especially bright beams visible from a remote location. I took two from my pockets and handed the extra to Ms. Washburn, who seemed still transfixed by Melanie Mason's headstone.

"Ready?" Mike asked.

I nodded and he turned on the powerful flashlight at the same time I lit my own. We pointed the beams into the sky and began to move them in a circular fashion, slowly, around a fairly wide area above our heads. We continued this movement for twenty-six seconds.

Looking at Ms. Washburn I could see she was not participating. The third beam might not have been necessary but I did not know how far away our targets might be situated, or even if they were watching at all. Every bit of light we could generate would help.

I walked to the spot where Ms. Washburn was standing and nudged her lightly on the right should. She looked at me. "The flashlight," I said.

"Are we sure we want to tell her we're here?" she asked.

"Certainly. If what you found this afternoon is an indicator, this could be essential to answering Ms. Fontaine's question." I kept moving the flashlight in a generally circular pattern.

Ms. Washburn nodded. She turned on her flashlight and added her beam to the ones being generated by the devices in my hand and Mike's.

While we created the pattern and waited for a response, I made it a point to stay close to Ms. Washburn. I had noticed a slight tremor in her flashlight's beam and a tight-lipped expression on her face. These are indicators that a person might be experiencing anxiety. Having studied romantic relationships through motion pictures and television, I assumed it was expected of me to be close to Ms. Washburn if she was feeling especially tense about the situation even if I did not expect it to be at all dangerous to any of us.

Perhaps distracting her would also help ease her worried demeanor. "Have we found any evidence that Virginia Fontaine and Leon Rabinski are lovers, as Detective Monroe suggested?" I asked.

"Nothing, but that's not the kind of thing somebody advertises," Ms. Washburn answered. Concentrating on my question seemed to help her relax even as we created our aural light show. "Debbie Sampras didn't know anything about it, but she wouldn't because she was friends with Brett and he'd be the last person to know if his wife was having an affair."

"Unless he did find out and that's what got him killed." Mike the taxicab driver had been listening from his station some nine feet northwest of me. "People get awfully testy about stuff like that."

"Wouldn't a husband be more likely to commit violence on the woman who betrayed him rather than she or her lover killing him?" I asked. It was an honest question because there is only so much one can infer from depictions of relationships in motion pictures or television programs, which are largely fictional.

"You think Brett would be justified in killing his wife if he found out she had an affair?" Ms. Washburn asked, an edge in her voice I did not recognize.

"Not at all. I don't think anyone is ever justified in taking another person's life. But I believe he would have a reason to be angry with his wife. Of course, Ms. Fontaine did not seem homicidal when she was telling us her husband was dallying with a dead woman. It is possible I'm not reading the situation accurately."

From every direction there was suddenly a voice, the same one Mike and I had heard in this spot before. "You are trying to summon me, Samuel Hoenig?"

Ms. Washburn froze in her tracks. Mike the taxicab driver immediately extinguished the beam from his flashlight and stood still, his hand resting on the pistol he had secured in a holster strapped to his left shoulder.

I did the same as Mike but was carrying no weapon, although he had offered me one. I am not licensed to carry a gun. "Turn off your flashlight," I whispered to Ms. Washburn. She did not move. "Ms. Washburn," I said. That seemed to focus her attention and she turned off the beam. I felt her hand encircle my left bicep. If we had to flee quickly, that would make running more difficult, but I did not remove Ms. Washburn's hand.

"I did wish to have a conversation," I said in what I hoped was an appropriate tone. "You left many questions unanswered the last time we spoke."

"I don't have to answer your questions. My message was clear. I wanted you to stop investigating Brett Fontaine's death and you didn't listen."

I did not care for the words this woman was choosing. "I did not understand your objection. We are simply trying to discover the truth. How does that threaten you?"

"I'm not threatened. I'm annoyed."

Ms. Washburn's hand tightened on my upper arm.

I decided to try to redirect the conversation. "Who are you?" I asked.

"You know who I am."

The audio equipment Leon Rabinski had purchased was obviously of very high quality. Even with the one speaker I had removed no longer functioning there was no way to attribute a direction to the voice and no electronic interference or static. I marveled at the efficiency of the technology.

"I know who you said you are, but I am certain that is not the truth. You are not the ghost of Melanie Mason." The graveyard setting and the disembodied voice were effective, but the fact remained that I was talking to a completely ordinary living woman.

"I am the spirit of Melanie Mason," the voice said.

Leaning closely toward Ms. Washburn's ear I was very careful to whisper, "Is that Debbie Sampras's voice?"

Ms. Washburn shook her head fervently; no, we were not being watched by Debbie Sampras.

"Perhaps you are exactly that after all," I said more loudly, but without shouting. "Are you familiar with Anthony Deane?"

The woman, wherever she was, did not answer my question. "I have warned you. Now go to your home. If you value the people who live there, you will go immediately."

I felt unable to move. Ms. Washburn, fire in her eyes visible even in this darkness, said loudly, "What do you mean by that?"

There was no response.

My head was beginning to shake. My hands were undoubtedly flapping at my sides. I must have fallen to my knees because I felt strong hands pulling me up and looked to see Mike the taxicab driver on my right side and Ms. Washburn on my left.

"Let's go," Mike said. "Now."

I felt them pull me to my feet and I felt my legs begin to walk. I do not remember willing them to do so.

The drive to my home was not a long one. I tried calling Mother's cellular phone but the fact that the signal went immediately to her voice mail application indicated she had turned the phone off, probably to prepare for bed. I called the landline at the house but there was no answer. Sometimes my parents do not come back downstairs for a call, letting their answering device in the kitchen take the message.

When it came on with Mother's voice saying, "*I'm sorry I can't take your call. Please leave a message when you hear the beep*," I said, "This is your son, Samuel Hoenig. Please call my cellular phone immediately." Then I disconnected the call.

Ms. Washburn, sitting in the back of Mike's taxicab, could not quite reach to put her hand on my shoulder, but she did make an attempt. "It's okay, Samuel. I'm sure."

"Drive faster," I told Mike.

"Really?" He knew of my anxiety regarding exceeding the posted speed limit.

"Really."

With Mike's increased effort we arrived at my home in twenty-two minutes. I kept my eyes closed for most of the ride but it did not relieve my concern about my parents and the veiled threat issued by the woman at the cemetery. I found myself biting both my lips. Ms. Washburn made several attempts to reassure me that nothing sinister would be found when we arrived, but I could not help but mentally consider every possibility and there were many gruesome ones.

At first glance when we approached the house everything appeared normal. There was a light on in the living room, as Mother would do if I was out. There was another light upstairs in my parents' bedroom. No sign of anyone anywhere in or outside the house was visible.

"What do you think?" Mike asked as he put the taxicab's transmission into the Park gear and applied the parking brake. "I don't see anything suspicious."

"Our first priority has to be Vivian and Reuben," Ms. Washburn said. "I'll check on them." She opened the door on her side of the taxicab and started toward the house before I could object, over my own fears, that I should be the one to do that. Ms. Washburn knows when to take charge of a situation.

"Okay, then," Mike said as Ms. Washburn opened the front door with the key I'd given her when she'd agreed to stay for the duration of this research project. She went into the house and closed the door carefully behind her. "Let's you and I check out the grounds, shall we?"

I did not answer but opened the passenger door as Mike got out of the taxicab. Without discussing it we both reached for the flashlights we'd taken to the cemetery, although the porch light was also still lit.

Again, we did not discuss a course of action but both resorted to using gestures rather than speech to communicate in case there were prowlers in the area. Mike pointed to the east side of the house and gestured toward himself. Then he pointed his index finger down and made a sweeping motion in a semi-circular pattern toward the house. He would examine the east side and then go around to the back.

I nodded and made similar gestures regarding the opposite side of the house. We would meet in the back yard.

Mike started around, his flashlight scanning the property in front of him as he walked. I did the same until I reached the side of the house and Mike was no longer visible on his opposite path. After carefully examining every shrub my mother had planted in front of our house, I had seen nothing at all worrisome. That did not mean there would be no danger elsewhere.

I made my way toward the back very slowly. Since I was not certain what to anticipate, each square inch of the grounds had to be inspected, even if cursorily. The flashlight beam was indeed bright, making me worry that it might be a warning to anyone who had come to do us harm. I was very careful not to tread too heavily and tried to control my breathing, which I noticed was through my mouth at the moment.

Then my cellular phone buzzed.

The sound broke through the silence and momentarily panicked me until I realized what it was. When I retrieved the phone from my pocket I saw a text message from Ms. Washburn: BOTH VIVIAN AND REUBEN ARE FINE. HEARD NOTHING. WE'LL STAY INSIDE UNTIL WE HEAR FROM YOU.

Certainly that was a relief and I texted back to Ms. Washburn simply, THANK YOU.

When I reached the corner of the house after considerable effort to determine the property was secure I saw Mike the taxicab driver already in place behind the house. He seemed especially interested in something I could not see from my vantage point. His flashlight was pointed down at the foundation of the house approximately twenty feet from the back door.

Seeing no reason to scan the rest of the area with Mike already there I walked directly to his side. His facial expression was grim. He reached into his pocket and pulled out a pair of thin gloves, which he put on.

I approached him carefully, still running the beam of the flashlight along the foundation because that seemed to be the focus of Mike's concern. Before I reached him I saw what he was examining: four metal cans, red, displayed carefully end-to-end next to a white cloth of some kind. Mike glanced over at me as I walked to his side.

"Somebody doesn't like what you're doing," he said in a low volume. He pointed at the cans. "They're marked as pyrethroid, an industrial insecticide."

Something clenched in my stomach. "Flammable?" I asked.

Mike nodded. "Could be used as an accelerant."

The thought made my right hand flap a little at my side. "Do I need to evacuate the house?"

Mike bent down and, wearing the gloves, opened the spout on one of the red cans. I was a bit taken aback when he dipped his finger into the spout and then removed and sniffed it.

"Mike," I said.

He stood up. "It's water, Samuel," he said. "Whoever did this didn't want to set your house on fire. They just wanted to show you they could if they felt like it. They wanted to scare you."

"They succeeded," I said.

TWENTY-NINE

"They wanted us to know this was no empty threat," I said.

Ms. Washburn and I were in my attic apartment after having assured my mother and Reuben that there had been no real attack on our house and they should not blame themselves—as Mother had attempted—for not being vigilant enough while Ms. Washburn and I were out.

"Except the cans were full of water," she noted. Ms. Washburn was sitting on my bed, which was currently being used as her bed, while I was at my workstation just four feet away from her. "You couldn't come up with a worse way to burn a building down."

"The cans of insecticide were merely props," I reiterated. "The message was that we should take what we heard at Melanie Mason's gravesite seriously."

"I already was," Ms. Washburn said. "I'm glad you were there, Samuel. I was pretty freaked out."

I wanted to tell her that I would always be there when she was upset. I wanted to say that she should never be worried when I was there. But I thought saying such things might be too forward for the type of relationship we had defined and did not want to upset Ms. Washburn with ideas that I was envisioning something more serious than she.

Therefore I nodded and said, "The scene set there was designed to make the visitor feel uncomfortable. It was quite effective. If I had not known it was being manipulated from a remote location, I would have found it extremely disturbing myself."

"I knew, or at least I knew you'd said so." Ms. Washburn rested her chin on her right hand, fisted and supported by her knee. "I should have trusted your judgment, Samuel."

I saw no utility in that area of conversation. Ms. Washburn believed in me when others thought I was simply odd and awkward. She had touted my expertise to a client ten minutes after meeting me. I had no issue with Ms. Washburn's trust, but telling her that would be redundant.

"We need to focus on Anthony Deane, Debbie Sampras, and Virginia Fontaine," I said. "I know it was not Virginia's voice we heard at the gravesite and you are certain it was not that of Debbie Sampras. Another woman must be involved we have not heard about yet."

"Melanie Mason," Ms. Washburn said. I believe she was attempting to be amusing in a sarcastic fashion.

"Actually, I believe that is a possibility," I said.

Ms. Washburn looked at me without a clear expression on her face. "You think there is a ghost?"

"No. I believe it is possible, although so far unproven, that Melanie Mason did not die in that automobile accident, and that it was indeed her voice we heard amplified at the gravesite."

Ms. Washburn stood up and took a step toward me. "Samuel, you saw the pictures Officer Palumbo had of that car and the body inside. Frankly, they made me a little sick, but they left no doubt that the person in that car was dead."

It was now an uncomfortable social situation because Ms. Washburn was standing and I was seated. Should I rise just to meet her gaze? Would she think that somehow diminishing or insulting? I had another chair in the apartment, but Ms. Washburn had already been sitting on the bed. Should I point that out? Surely she'd seen it—she had in fact used it in the past. I found myself thinking of things other than the question at hand at this crucial moment.

"The person in the car was unquestionably dead," I answered, doing my best to focus. "Do you want to sit down?"

"I'm fine. Are you saying the person in the car wasn't Melanie Mason? Then who was it?"

I stood up to relieve the tension. "It is possible that it was the homeless woman whose story you discovered this afternoon," I said. "She would have been easy enough to convince and she was not missed for quite some time. It is even possible someone gave her Melanie Mason's signature nail polish to wear in the hope that would be an identifying factor."

Now Ms. Washburn, realizing the gravity of what I was suggesting, sat on the second desk chair. "You think the homeless woman was set up? They knew there was going to be an accident on Route 22? How could that be possible?"

I sat again in my desk chair, glad the sitting versus standing situation had been resolved. "Those are excellent questions," I said. "I wonder if Anthony Deane, Debbie Sampras, or Virginia Fontaine might be able to answer them."

Ms. Washburn nodded slowly. "It sounds like tomorrow is going to be a very busy day," she said.

"Indeed. If you are tired, I will go downstairs so you can prepare for bed."

Ms. Washburn reached for my hand. That is a gesture I normally try to avoid, but I held it steady and let her place her own on mine. "Samuel, I think maybe it's best if I go back home tonight," she said.

Immediately I had to deal with a flood of conflicting feelings. I did not want Ms. Washburn to leave. But I did miss sleeping in my bed. Sleeping on the sofa downstairs had been very different, and changes are not welcome to a person like me. I had very little time to settle on a proper response. "Why?" I asked. It was the best I could do. Her response would give me a conversational direction to follow.

"The reason I came to stay here to begin with was that we were worried about the ghost...whoever is speaking at that gravesite doing me some harm," she said. "I think what we've seen tonight proves that this house isn't safer than my apartment. So there's no reason for me to stay, is there?"

I could think of many reasons she should remain in my house but none of them had anything to do with security against the voice in the cemetery. I considered carefully and then said, "No, I suppose not. Your argument makes sense."

For some reason Ms. Washburn looked a bit disappointed, but it was possible I had misinterpreted her expression. She withdrew her hand from mine.

"Okay, then. I'll pack up my stuff and come pick you up for the drive to Darby in the morning." She stood and walked toward the bed, reaching underneath to pull her small travel bag from where she had stored it.

But as she spoke an idea occurred to me. "Perhaps you should stay just one more night," I said.

Ms. Washburn turned to face me. "Why?" she asked.

"Because we will be leaving at an early hour. It will be more convenient for you if we are together in the morning." That made practical sense to our research and would potentially keep Ms. Washburn here another night.

Again her expression changed to one of slight regret. "That is a point, but I do this all the time," she said.

"Just this once," I said. My tone might have sounded a little more like begging than I would have preferred, though it was not intentional.

Ms. Washburn sat on the edge of the bed and her lips pursed a bit. "I'll tell you what, Samuel. I think you have a point, but I don't like the idea that there could be danger wherever you and I go. If we stay here, it could put your parents at risk. So why don't you come and stay at my apartment tonight?"

That was definitely unexpected. I looked at my bed, which seemed awfully inviting. Then I looked at Ms. Washburn. Somehow this seemed to be a situation like those Dr. Mancuso would sometimes create when I was a teenager and young adult; it was a test to see if I would react like a neurotypical. I rarely did, but it helped me understand what was expected even if I could not provide it.

In this case, I felt Ms. Washburn was challenging me. Would I leave my comfort zone at her behest rather than ask her to do the same for me? I certainly did not wish to disappoint her but the prospect of staying in her apartment, her private space, was daunting. There were so many ways I might violate social norms.

In the end there was no choice. "That is a very sensible idea," I said. "I will put my necessary belongings in a bag."

Ms. Washburn looked surprised and I wondered if this was not the outcome she had hoped to see. But there was a slight smile on her face as well.

THIRTY

"Put your things anywhere."

Ms. Washburn made a vague gesture with her left arm as her right returned her keys to her pocket. We had just arrived at her apartment and were preparing to retire for the evening in anticipation of a long day of work starting early the next morning.

I looked around the main living area in the apartment and wondered where I might be sleeping tonight. The most likely spot was the Ikea sofa, which looked sturdy enough but might not accommodate a man of my height lying flat upon it. I put my travel bag down on the floor next to where I was standing and assessed the room. I saw no other natural areas to sleep other than the floor itself and I had not brought a sleeping bag. Perhaps Ms. Washburn owned one.

She draped her jacket casually over the back of a small club chair, the only other piece of furniture in the room other than a pole lamp and a small table in front of the sofa. There was no television. The kitchen was to my left, just large enough to allow for one person doing the cooking. Two barstools were set up next to a counter to allow for a quick meal. I saw no dining table.

The only other rooms were the bathroom and Ms. Washburn's bedroom.

It was difficult to know what I should ask and what I should simply take for granted. Ms. Washburn turned and looked at me. "Well, it's pretty late," she said. "I think maybe it's time to turn in, don't you?"

That was certainly an interesting question, although the answer was obvious. "Yes," I said. "That seems like a very good plan."

I was about to ask where I might be sleeping and if there was a blanket or large pillow I could lay on the floor when Ms. Washburn said, "Okay, then. Come on." She walked toward the door to the bedroom.

I stood absolutely still. "Where?"

"In the bedroom. It's late, Samuel. Let's go." She walked into her bedroom then turned and stood in the doorway looking at me. "Samuel?"

At last I understood. "Ms. Washburn, I would not have agreed to spend the night here if I'd understood I was putting you out of your own bed."

She chuckled. "You're not going to do that, Samuel."

That confused me. Did Ms. Washburn intend for me to sleep on the floor in her bedroom? "I don't understand," I said. She always responded well when I did so.

"You and I are going to sleep in here," she said, indicating her bedroom. "Don't worry."

That was even more baffling. Was Ms. Washburn suggesting we take our physical relationship to a much higher level? I was both intrigued and immediately frightened. "Don't worry," I repeated to myself.

"Come on in, Samuel," Ms. Washburn said. "It's okay."

Because I had been told to do so I walked into Ms. Washburn's bedroom, incapable of sorting the emotions rushing through my brain. I have read accounts in which people describe such moments in intricate detail but I couldn't possibly do so now. I was operating without my conscious mind and I believe my hands began to flutter at my sides.

Ms. Washburn, upon looking at me, broke into a laugh. "Oh, Samuel," she said. "I'm sorry. I didn't mean what I'm guessing you thought I meant. We're just going to sleep in the bed at the same time, that's all. There's plenty of room and no reason for one of us to be uncomfortable."

"So we're not—" I began. I could not think of a word that was not obscene or clinical.

A light chuckle. "No. Certainly not now, anyway. We have a long way to go, Samuel. This is just a question of practicality. We have two people and one bed. We might as well use it."

I exhaled. I'll admit to a moment of disappointment, but overall I was more relieved of tension than I was upset. "Should we create a barrier of some sort, a wall between us?" I asked.

Ms. Washburn managed not to laugh, which in retrospect I appreciate. "I don't think that'll be necessary," she said. "I think we can trust each other not to be overcome."

We did spend the night together in that bed. And while nothing of note occurred during that time (other than my discovery that Ms. Washburn snored), I did not sleep very much at all.

I was thinking about Melanie Mason. Mostly.

The next morning started at 6:20 a.m. and was devoted entirely to being dressed and ready to leave quickly. We were in Ms. Washburn's Kia Spectra and on the road to Darby, Pennsylvania at 7:02.

"How are we going to find Tony Deane once we get there?" Ms. Washburn asked. "We know where he works, or at least where he was working the last time anyone on the internet checked, but what if he's not there? We don't have a home address."

"His employer will have one. He or she might not want to give it to us, but we can see if there are ways to discover it without help."

"That sounds ominous." The light turned green and Ms. Washburn resumed driving.

We arrived at Darby Tire, the business that employed Tony Deane (whom we were assuming was the Anthony Deane I'd spoken to at Brett Fontaine's memorial service) at 8:47 a.m. It was larger than the usual car repair shop, which indicated to me there were offices for the whole company and not just this outlet in the building, but it was still configured like a tire store with bays to remove and install tires in the back and a small waiting area in the front where customers might purchase tires and amuse themselves while the new purchases were being installed. Ms. Washburn noted the sign in the window indicating the business did not open until nine. "I want a coffee anyway," she said, so we walked to a small coffee shop listed on Ms. Washburn's cellular phone.

I ordered nothing, but when we sat down at a table with Ms. Washburn's coffee and a croissant her phone buzzed. Ms. Washburn examined the screen and said, "Looks like Neil Betts has gotten back to me."

"Betts?" The high school chronicler of Brett Fontaine, Debbie Sampras, and others. "What did he say?"

"He's busy today at the IRS but will be happy to talk to me during his lunch break a little before noon." Ms. Washburn looked at her watch despite us both being keenly aware of the time. "We should be back by then, don't you think?"

"That depends on how complicated our search for Tony Deane becomes," I mused.

"I'll eat fast."

We were at the door of Darby Tire by 9:12. Once inside we approached the counter, where a man in a blue uniform shirt that bore his name, *Dave*, on an appliqué smiled at us as the potential customers he clearly thought we were.

"How can I help you?" he asked, unwittingly using the proper words. He did not yet know his assistance would not be required concerning the sale of tires.

Ms. Washburn, as has become our custom, approached Dave and spoke first. "Hi. We're here looking into a matter for a client of ours and one of the people we'd like to talk to is a man named Tony Deane. Does he work here?"

The man's face, smiling at the prospect of the day's first sale, darkened. "You're cops?" he asked. "Let me see a badge."

"We are not employed by any law enforcement agency," I assured him. "We are simply representing a private agency that has been engaged to answer a question. Mr. Deane might be able to help us with that question and we are anxious to discuss the matter with him. That's all." People we encounter often believe we are there to arrest someone when we have absolutely no authority to do so at all.

"If you aren't cops, why should I talk to you?" Dave asked. "Besides, Tony isn't here."

Ms. Washburn moved a little closer to the counter. "That's very disappointing," she said. "We drove almost two hours to get here first thing today. Can you tell us where he is? We won't take up much of his time."

"I don't care how much time you take," Dave said. "He's not here." He started to leaf through some forms on the counter, but it was clear he was doing that simply for our benefit. None of the forms were filled in.

"There's been a murder," I said. Ms. Washburn turned and stared at me with what looked like shock. Dave looked up from his forms and opened his mouth but said nothing. "Mr. Deane might be able to help us discover who committed the crime. Do you want to be the man who refused to let us speak to him?"

It was a bold stratagem but apparently an effective one. "He's in the offices, around the corner," Dave said quietly. He pointed in the direction to his own left, which I assumed indicated where one would find the company's offices. "Second floor."

"Thank you," I said. Ms. Washburn looked up at me and smiled as we left the building.

"I haven't been hiding," Anthony Deane told us.

Ms. Washburn and I were sitting in the cramped office that Deane called his own. The door was closed at the moment because Deane didn't want others to hear the conversation, which I understood. It was not related to the tire business. Ms. Washburn was obviously assessing Deane, as she had never talked with him before. I knew him from the memorial service, but this was a different version of the man.

At the memorial Anthony Deane had cast himself as the outsider, wearing jeans at the chapel and letting his long hair hang down. Here he was being careful to appear businesslike, his hair neatly pulled back in what is unfortunately being called a "man-bun," and wearing khakis and a denim button-down shirt with the company logo on the left chest.

"It took us some time to track you down, and the last time we met you told me your name was Patrick Henry," I pointed out. "You said you were Brett Fontaine's brother when you were simply a member of his fraternity. Those are not the actions of a man who wishes to be especially accessible."

Deane laughed. "I like you," he said. "You say what you mean."

"But you don't," Ms. Washburn told Deane. "You've been doing nothing but talking around the point since the first time you talked to Samuel. How about a straight answer for once?"

Deane smiled and laced his fingers behind his head. "I wouldn't count on that."

"You know something about Brett Fontaine's murder and you're withholding it," Ms. Washburn countered. "We can let the police know that."

Deane's face indicated he wasn't especially concerned about that possibility. "You can."

"You went so far as to say you were Brett Fontaine's brother," Ms. Washburn said. "Didn't you care at all about him?"

At that Deane looked angry. "Don't tell me what I cared about," he said. "Brett was my friend and yes, my brother. If I could I would personally beat the person who killed him to a pulp. So don't you dare tell me I didn't care."

"Then why don't you help us?" I asked, attempting to steer the conversation back into a useful direction. "Tell me why you said it was significant that I don't believe in ghosts, that it was all I needed to know. Is it because Melanie Mason is still alive?"

Deane was still glaring, but he turned his attention from Ms. Washburn to me. "You know about that?" he said.

"We do now," Ms. Washburn said, grinning a little too broadly in my opinion.

Deane dropped his hands to his sides and sagged a bit in his chair. "Look. I don't know who killed Brett, okay? But I do know that whole ghost thing was crap. Melanie didn't die in the car crash. She was just trying to get some money for that husband of hers. I don't think she liked him that much but he was ambitious and she didn't want to file for divorce because he was jealous or something. Said he'd kill her if she left him so she figured she'd just be dead. He'd get the insurance and she'd get a new identity. But I never saw or heard from her again after that. All because of her husband."

Ms. Washburn blinked twice. "Leon Rabinski?"

"That's what I was told."

I saw Ms. Washburn look at me. I think she wanted to exchange some sort of facial expression, but all I was feeling was a sense of confirmation. "Who told you that?" I asked Deane.

He did not resume his relaxed pose but he stopped glaring and looked through the window. There was nothing to see but the building next door but Deane appeared to find it fascinating. "I really can't say."

"I don't see why not," I said.

"Because I was asked not to and I'm not going to."

Ms. Washburn considered that for a moment and then looked at me, commanding my attention. "He's not going to tell us, but we can certainly guess," she said. "The only people in touch with Tony here were Debbie Sampras and Peter Belson. Debbie thinks Tony is the one who killed Brett *and* William Klein because he was in love with Virginia LoBianco Klein Fontaine."

Deane actually sputtered and sat forward in his chair, almost spilling a cup of water he had on his desk. "Debbie Sampras thinks *I* killed both of Virginia's husbands? She thinks I'm in love with Ginny?" He laughed. "That's so far off base."

"You're not in love with Ginny Fontaine?" Ms. Washburn asked. She smiled at me privately because her gambit had proven successful.

"Of course not." Deane spread his hands on his desk as if to push himself up to a standing position but left them there. "I'm gay. I came out fifteen years ago. If you like you can ask anybody who works here about my husband, Gary." He smiled at me with an air of triumph.

"Why would Debbie think that?" Ms. Washburn asked. "Is this something from before you came out?"

"You would have to ask Debbie."

"We will, believe me," I said. "So that means the person who gave you this information is Peter Belson."

Deane merely smiled and said nothing.

"Are you in touch with Melanie Mason?" I asked.

Deane, as neurotypical liars often do, looked away. "Of course not. She's supposed to be dead and I wasn't supposed to know anything more than that. I told you, I never heard from her again."

"You are not telling us the truth," I said.

His head pivoted quickly and he tried very hard to look at me angrily. "You calling me a liar?" Deane asked.

"On that point, yes I am."

Ms. Washburn looked at me as she often does, questioning my motivation or my choice of action. She believes in my abilities but is sometimes taken by surprise when I do not attempt to act like a neurotypical.

"Then I'm going to have to ask you to leave my office," Anthony Deane said.

Ms. Washburn and I stood. I opened the office door and we left without proper social cues indicating we were leaving. I thought that was an effective way to create a tense mood in Deane.

The building was not large and Deane's office was on the second floor, easily visible from the street. When Ms. Washburn and I reached the most logical vantage point I asked her, "What is he doing?"

"He's on his cell phone and he doesn't look happy," she answered.

That was exactly what I'd expected. "I imagine we'll be hearing from the ghost of Melanie Mason soon," I said.

THIRTY-ONE

Neil Betts called Ms. Washburn not long after we arrived back at the Questions Answered office. I had not been able to exercise yet this morning and was trying to make up for the lost time when I heard her say, "Hello, Mr. Betts."

Ms. Washburn conducted the conversation while I completed my thirteen trips around the office, and I was able only to hear the occasional question as I passed her. But she was certainly capable of handling the situation and I waited until I had purchased a bottle of spring water and was seated in my office chair before asking about her progress.

"Betts said he couldn't confirm much about Brett Fontaine, whom he doesn't remember all that well and wasn't on the class Facebook page," she answered, referring to notes she had typed into a file on her computer. "But he remembers Debbie Sampras and has kept in pretty close touch with her all these years."

"We are going to see Ms. Sampras later today."

"Three o'clock." Ms. Washburn confirmed the time I had already committed to memory.

"What does Mr. Betts have to say about her?" I took a small sip of the water. It is better after exercising not to take large amounts of liquid even if one's natural inclination is to do so.

"He says Debbie was the class gossip and she liked to stir the pot," Ms. Washburn said.

"I am not familiar with that expression." It is comforting that I don't have to hide my ignorance of some idioms from Ms. Washburn.

Ms. Washburn chewed on the end of a pen, so I averted my gaze. "It means she likes to be the center of attention by creating situations that might be dramatic."

"Like a playwright?"

"No. Like a meddler."

That I understood. "Very well, then. So was Mr. Betts suggesting that information we get from Debbie Sampras might not be reliable?"

"I think he was suggesting we might want to confirm anything she says with another credible source, as the journalists say." Ms. Washburn put down the pen, which I heard her rest on the surface of her desk. I looked in her direction. "I'm saying that just because Debbie tells us Tony Deane must be the killer is no reason to start fitting him for a prison jumpsuit."

Before I could mention that prison attire is not tailored for each inmate the bells over our entry door sounded and I looked up, as did Ms. Washburn. Virginia Fontaine was walking into the Questions Answered office.

She approached my desk, bypassing Ms. Washburn's, with a purposeful gait. As I stood to greet our client she held up a hand defensively, palm out. "Don't start, Mr. Hoenig," she said. "I'm here to withdraw my offer. I don't want you to look into Brett's murder anymore."

I began to wonder if my initial analysis of the situation had been in error; perhaps Anthony Deane was calling Virginia Fontaine after

Ms. Washburn and I had left his office. Was everything Deane had told us untrue? Could he possibly have been involved romantically with Virginia and not a man named Gary?

"What has led you to that decision?" I asked. "When a client decides to end our agreement it makes sense for us to understand if what we have been doing is somehow unsatisfactory. That way we can avoid making the same mistake again."

I gestured toward the client chair in front of my desk as Ms. Washburn walked over to join the consultation, but Virginia shook her head and remained standing. "I don't think I'm the main suspect anymore and I think we can leave it to the police," she said. "I just don't see the need for a separate agency to be looking into this matter."

Her choice of words was odd, which indicated she might have rehearsed the speech ahead of time. I have done the same thing when confronted with a pending situation I found uncomfortable. I find most pending situations uncomfortable. Virginia calling her husband's death *this matter* was especially jarring, although I could not immediately analyze its relevance.

"I can understand your decision, but we have made considerable progress and expect to have an answer to your question within twenty-four hours," I said.

"Twenty-four—" Ms. Washburn began. Apparently my suggestion had come as a surprise to her, which was understandable.

"It doesn't matter," Virginia said. "I don't want you to go forward. I'll pay your fee." She reached into her purse and pulled out a wallet. She searched for a specific credit card.

I did not bother to inform her, as we had specifically stated in our client intake form, that Questions Answered does not accept credit cards. We are simply not equipped to do so. "That will not be necessary," I told Virginia. "If we do not answer your question, we do not require payment."

Ms. Washburn must surely have expected that response from me, given that it has always been my policy. If the client no long wants the question answered, we will cease work on the research and there will be no charge because there has been no answer provided. Ms. Washburn has argued that our work is valuable and that we should bill by the hour as attorneys do, but I am still the proprietor and my initial decision has not been overturned. Still, now Ms. Washburn gasped a little as if what I'd said had been a surprise.

Virginia stopped reaching for her credit card. "Really?" she asked.

"That is our policy. I would advise against this, but the decision is yours."

She did not stop to rethink her statement. "Fine, then. You'll stop trying to find out who killed Brett."

"If that is what you have concluded," I answered.

"Samuel," Ms. Washburn said quietly. I looked at her but did not respond. There was nothing else to do.

"That's what I've concluded," Virginia said.

"You realize we will report any findings we've made to Detective Monroe," Ms. Washburn said. "And we'll have to tell him you asked us not to solve your husband's murder. That might make you seem like a more logical suspect."

Virginia glanced at her and shrugged. "I'll take my chances," she said. She turned and walked out of the Questions Answered office while Ms. Washburn, mouth slightly open, watched her go.

Once Virginia had gotten into her car and driven out of the parking lot of the strip mall where our office is located, Ms. Washburn rolled her desk chair closer to my desk and looked at me. "So what do we do now?" she asked.

I looked up from my screen, which displayed a listing of people who had died in Leonia, New Jersey, in April of 1884. "I don't understand," I said. "We have been asked to stop researching Ms. Fontaine's question. So we will stop researching that question and go back to the questions we were trying to answer before she hired us. You've done this before."

"Yeah, but this is a murder and her firing us came out of nowhere. Aren't you curious about why she did that?" Ms. Washburn was looking at me intently, trying to convince me of something.

"The subject matter of the question has no bearing on our policy, Ms. Washburn. The client is no longer employing us. We have no reason to continue working on her behalf."

There was a promising listing on my screen, a woman named Nathana Brookins who had been only thirty-four years old at her death. No cause was listed in the perfunctory obituary I had found. I wasn't sure it was the one I was seeking, but Nathana certainly had all the necessary qualifications so far.

"Doesn't it seem to you that she might have fired us because we were getting too close to finding the killer?" Ms. Washburn asked. "That maybe she was the murderer after all?"

"That is not our concern." Nathana Brookins had been the wife of Richard T. Brookins for eleven years before her death. She had two children, a son named Richard Jr. and a daughter named Elizabeth.

"Samuel, there are times I don't get you at all. I understand how you're thinking, but I can't fathom that you don't care."

I turned my attention back to Ms. Washburn and tried to consider, as Dr. Mancuso has urged, how she might be feeling. But the issue was so clear in my mind that her suggestion seemed irrational. "Ms. Fontaine has, as you said, fired us. Who would we be working for if we decided to continue with our research?"

Ms. Washburn crossed her arms. "For Brett Fontaine," she said.

"I doubt he will be available to pay our bill." Richard Brookins Jr. had married a woman named Samantha Taylor in 1902. They'd had no children. But Elizabeth Brookins, who married Francis Benson-hoff in 1905, had a son named Arthur.

"Is that what this is about?" Ms. Washburn asked. "The money? Isn't the question itself the reason you get involved? I've seen you turn down a hundred questions because you didn't find them interesting and those people would have paid us. What is it about this question that makes you so quick to quit?"

Tracing the lineage of Nathana Brookins was going to have to wait. I looked at Ms. Washburn. "This isn't simply about money. It's about the order of things. This is a business. If we start researching questions simply because we want to know the answers, we should do so during our free time, not while we are working here."

Ms. Washburn's eyes narrowed. "Really. What are you working on right now?"

I brought up the email client on my screen. "I am reading through my emails," I said. I don't know why I did that, except that Ms. Washburn was about to find a hypocrisy I was perpetrating and I did not want to diminish myself in her eyes. That must have been the motivation.

It didn't matter because that is the moment my cellular phone rang.

I did not find it unusual that the call was coming on my personal phone and not the landline we have at the Questions Answered office. That was particularly predictable when I saw the caller was Reuben Hoenig. I debated answering but could not summon an appropriate reason to ignore the call.

"Hello?" I do not know why the greeting on a telephone is always presented as if it were a question, but that seems to be the norm.

"Sorry to bother you," Reuben responded. "But I think I've been taken hostage."

THIRTY-TWO

"The only things we can be certain of about this question are that there are two factions who are trying to keep us from finding the answer, and they are not communicating with each other."

Ms. Washburn looked at me from the driver's seat of her Kia Spectra and shook her head slightly. "Aren't you the least bit worried about your father?" she asked.

"There is no reason to worry about Reuben at this moment," I told her. "He has been taken against his will and that is troublesome but I do not believe him to be in much danger at all right now. The kidnappers think he is their best bet to get us to abandon the question. What I don't know is why they think we are so close to answering and how it will affect them negatively."

"But he's so scared." The light turned green so Ms. Washburn refocused on driving.

Reuben had sounded shaken when he called; that was true. "I'm pretty sure they took me because of something you're doing, Samuel," he told me. "I can't think of anything I'm doing that anybody would care about."

It occurred to me that my mother might have discovered something about the women Reuben had known during the years he was away from New Jersey, but the idea that she would therefore have him abducted was absurd so I discarded it. "What happened, exactly?" I asked him.

"I came out of the CVS and there was this van parked next to my car." He meant my mother's car but this didn't seem the time to emphasize the distinction. "It had its back doors wide open and I was afraid I wouldn't be able to back out of my space without hitting them. But I didn't see anybody by the van. So I walked over to see if there was anyone in the back. As soon as I got there somebody put a dark canvas bag over my head and shoved me into the van."

"Did you see the person who attacked you?"

Ms. Washburn, sitting next to me at our office workstations, widened her eyes with surprise. "What's going on?" she asked. I could not answer and discuss the situation with Reuben at the same time so I made a rare choice and decided against responding to Ms. Washburn.

"No," Reuben answered. "I saw the inside of the van and then the inside of the canvas bag. It could have been anybody."

"Was it a man or a woman?" I asked.

"You're not listening. It could have been Kim Kardashian for all I know. I didn't see anything. By the time I got this bag off my head they'd closed the doors of the van and locked it. All I can see is the inside of a van. It's not very interesting."

"What about the voice of the person who took you?" I suggested. "Male or female?"

"Nobody said anything. I was outside then I was in the van. I heard the doors shut. That's it."

My best guess was that I could have found nine things in the back of an empty van that would be helpful in identifying it or finding a way out, but again there was no point in discussing that with Reuben. "Where are you now?" I said.

He sounded exasperated. "I'm in the *back of a van* and it's going somewhere. Every once in a while we turn and I lean one way or another. That's it. That's all the information I have."

The man was impossible to deal with. "Did you take note of the license plate number?"

"What am I, a robot? I don't remember every license number I see."

Ms. Washburn was suddenly at my side looking concerned. I did not feel especially tense; this was clearly not a very well considered plan. Anyone who believed they could influence my actions by taking Reuben simply wasn't doing much research into the personalities involved.

"All right," I sighed. It was clear I wouldn't be getting much information out of Reuben. "Have you called the police?" The idea that the kidnappers had left Reuben with his hands untied and his cellular phone in his pocket was another indication that we were not dealing with the most experienced professionals involved with this question. A theory was beginning to germinate in my mind.

"And tell them what? That I got thrown in the back of a van but I have no idea where I am right now? I don't think that's going to help them find me much."

"No, I agree," I said. "I believe I will be hearing from your abductors very soon and then we will have a plan of action. Conserve your battery power." I disconnected the call.

"Samuel!" Ms. Washburn shouted. "Did you say your father has been abducted?"

"Yes." I explained the situation to her with the meager information I had been given by Reuben. "The only thing to do now is to wait for a phone call from the person or people who took him. At the moment we don't even have conclusive evidence that the question of Brett Fontaine's murder is the reason Reuben was thrown in the van."

Ms. Washburn looked at me with an incredulous expression. "What other reason could somebody have to kidnap him?" she asked.

"He has a rather checkered past," I noted. "Any number of people might hold some grudge against him. But I agree that the Question of the Dead Mistress is most probably the cause of this abduction."

"We need to call your mother," Ms. Washburn said.

"There is no need. Reuben has his phone and he will contact her. No doubt my mother will be calling us within a matter of minutes. In the meantime, can you please look into the possibility that the homeless woman who vanished before Melanie Mason supposedly died was about the same age and height as Melanie?"

"Samuel, your father has been kidnapped. Doesn't that mean anything to you? I know that you have the same emotions as other people; why am I not seeing them right now?" Ms. Washburn was leaning over the edge of my desk to look into my eyes. I had never wanted to kiss her more.

But I simply didn't have an answer to give her. Reuben Hoenig meant very little to me emotionally, although Dr. Mancuso had recently been hinting—he never actually suggests anything—that I had issues with Reuben over his abandonment of my family that I had not completely resolved. That was valid, but it was not helping me at this moment.

"I don't know," I said. It was the closest thing to an accurate answer I could offer.

Now in the Kia Spectra Ms. Washburn found an appropriate time to speak but did not look in my direction. "What makes you think there are two separate groups involved with Brett Fontaine's murder, and why do you think they're not talking to each other?"

"We saw Anthony Deane on the phone to someone as we left his office," I said as Ms. Washburn continued driving. While I am not enthusiastic about talking to her while she drives, it is better than her talking to me. "Virginia Fontaine arrived at our office almost immediately upon our return to demand that we stop working on her question. Then Reuben was abducted. This leads me to a theory."

I thought that explained my thinking sufficiently but apparently Ms. Washburn would not have agreed. "I get the chronology," she said when she had stopped behind a fifteen-year-old Buick letting a passenger in illegally in the middle of the road. "But how does that lead to all those conclusions?"

"My reasoning is quite simple," I told her. "I believe Anthony Deane was calling someone involved in this question as we left. Either it was Virginia Fontaine, whom he was informing that we had made some progress that could be damaging to her, or it was someone else, either Melanie Mason or an ally of hers, who immediately decided to kidnap Reuben in the rather dim hope that it would force us to stop asking questions about Brett Fontaine's murder."

"And they're not talking to each other because…?"

I felt my anxiety level rising a little. "Please watch the road, Ms. Washburn."

She nodded her understanding rather than say anything more.

"Thank you. I surmised that the two groups, if they are groups and not individuals, are not in communication because there would be no reason to abduct Reuben once Virginia withdrew her question and we accepted. If they were in touch with each other, the assault on Reuben would have been aborted. I believe we are dealing with two factions here and they probably do not share the same agenda."

When the car had stopped again Ms. Washburn asked, "What about the theory you said you had reached? Was it about getting your father back?"

"No. I had reached this conclusion before I knew he'd been taken. The fact is, I believe you and I were being used by Virginia Fontaine in an attempt to murder her second husband Brett, but that she had not managed to do so because others did so first."

"Hah?" Ms. Washburn grunted more than spoke because she was driving again.

"Ms. Fontaine discontinued our contract immediately after Brett's body was found and she was surprised. When she appeared to be the most logical suspect in his murder she engaged us again in an attempt to clear her name. She wanted to ride with you on the surveillance of her husband, whom she suspected of cheating. She was carrying a gun in her purse she did not want you to see. The research she was asking us to do was something she could easily have completed herself, given her background and skills. But she chose to come to us. I believe she wanted you to find her husband being unfaithful while she was there so she could use you as a witness when she shot him in what would have been presented as self-defense."

Ms. Washburn said nothing. I'm not sure if it was because she was driving or because she looked stunned, but either way I hoped her attention was on the road.

My mother had indeed called while we were in the office, sounding frantic and demanding that Ms. Washburn and I—particularly I—do something about Reuben's abduction. I had suggested that Reuben was not in any immediate danger but Mother had not taken that piece of information as the reassurance I had intended it to be. So Ms. Washburn had suggested we call Reuben back for more information. His cellular phone immediately placed my call in the voice mail system. I saw no reason to leave Reuben a message.

Less than one minute later my cellular phone had rung showing an unfamiliar number as the caller. The voice on the other end of the call, clearly filtered through a simple electronic device, was not Reuben's.

"We have your father," it said.

"I am aware of that," I had responded. Ms. Washburn listened in as closely as she could from a few feet to my right. "What is your purpose in abducting him?"

"You have to stop investigating Brett Fontaine's death," the voice said.

"We have already done so. Our client has rescinded the offer to pay us for an answer to the question so we are no longer continuing our research." I thought that information alone would be enough to secure Reuben's release.

The caller, however, did not seem to process my statement completely. "If you don't stop asking questions your father will die."

It occurred to me that Reuben would die whether I continued the research or not because all living things die at some point. My mentioning that to the person on the phone hardly seemed advisable, however. "You are not listening. We have already ended our inquiry. There is no advantage to your holding Reuben Hoenig. The best course of action for you is to release him immediately."

Ms. Washburn had nodded her approval.

"If you want to prevent your father from pain and death you must follow our instructions precisely."

I pressed the mute button on my phone. "I believe we are listening to a prerecorded voice on the phone," I told Ms. Washburn.

"Why would they do that?"

"Either for technical reasons, to best mask the voice so we would not recognize it, or for time," I said. "It might have made more sense to their schedule to have the demands recorded ahead of time. I think it possible no one is listening on the other end of the call."

Ms. Washburn absorbed this and then her eyes widened. "So they don't care if you follow their demands or not."

"It is true. Their plan could be in place no matter what the outcome of this gambit might turn out to be from their perspective."

Ms. Washburn had leaned on the end of my desk. "So they're going to kill your father either way."

I considered that. "Possibly. It's more likely they were never going to kill him either way."

"If you want to prevent your father from pain and death you must follow our instructions precisely." Apparently the kidnappers, having received no verbal response, chose to replay a sound clip they had used once before.

I then released the mute button from my phone. "What are your instructions, other than to do something I have already done?"

The recording seemed satisfied with that question, probably since a prerecorded answer had already existed. "Come to the PC Richard store on Route 22, the one that looks like a boat. Be there in an hour. Bring all your research into the death of Brett Fontaine. Do not contact the police. Any variance from these instructions will result in the death of your father." The call was disconnected from the caller's side.

Ms. Washburn and I left the Questions Answered office sixteen minutes later.

Now we were three minutes from our destination, a strangely shaped building with a very long and odd history. The Flagship began its existence as a ship-shaped nightclub in the 1930s and had gone through any number of incarnations since, including a complete tear-down and rebuild in the same shape as a large cruiser. It has been an outlet for various electronics chains for at least two decades.

"What should we expect?" Ms. Washburn asked me.

I understood her feeling of urgency but the conversation while the car was in motion on such a treacherous stretch of highway was too stressful for me. I did not reply until she had parked her Kia Spectra in the Flagship parking lot.

"I think we will see a panel van of some sort pull up. A woman will most likely get out of the passenger side while the engine remains running," I said. "The woman will demand our research. We will make it clear that we have no intention of doing any further work on Ms. Fontaine's question. Then we will see how the woman and her compatriot in the van react."

"What if they react badly?"

"I sincerely doubt they will react well."

The white van, marked with the logo of U-Haul, appeared at that moment. Ms. Washburn pointed to draw my attention but I had already seen the vehicle and was tracking it with my eyes. "I think it would be best if we got out of the car," I told her.

Ms. Washburn had opened her driver's side door before I could open mine on the opposite end. We stood in the parking lot among other cars and in view of shoppers entering and exiting the PC Richard & Son store until the van had parked as unobtrusively as possible about ten yards away from us, too far to rush the van but close enough that our interaction would not draw attention from anyone else at the store.

"There will be no violence here," I said to reassure Ms. Washburn. "It is far too public a space."

Ms. Washburn did not acknowledge my words. She was focused on the van. As I'd expected, the passenger door opened and a woman stepped out. I did not recognize her face from Brett Fontaine's memorial service, although she might have been the woman who laughed at Anthony Deane's remarks. I did recognize her from online photographs I had studied.

"Who's that?" Ms. Washburn asked.

"That is Melanie Mason." I did not advance toward the woman, preferring to have her as far from the van as possible. She did not seem to have any strategic agenda in regard to her placement from the van, which made me wonder if Reuben was indeed in the cargo compartment in the back.

"Mr. Hoenig," she said when she had reached Ms. Washburn and me.

"Ms. Mason. I would say it is nice to meet you but we have met in a sense twice before and besides, this is not very nice. You have a man confined in that van and you will get nothing from me before I see him."

Melanie Mason was a woman of medium height with brown hair and a tight smile with no amusement in it at all. "Your father is unharmed, Mr. Hoenig. So far."

"I will need visual confirmation of that statement."

Ms. Washburn, I could tell, was sizing up (I believe the expression goes) Melanie Mason and finding her less than admirable. Melanie would not have known that, but having studied Ms. Washburn's facial expressions for some time I could make the judgment easily.

"You're not going to get it," Melanie Mason said.

"Then our business here is concluded," I said. Ms. Washburn's face, turned toward me as I spun on my heel, registered astonishment. I started back toward the Kia Spectra.

"You're condemning your father to death," Melanie suggested.

I had only a few steps to reach the Kia Spectra but I did not turn back to face my adversary. "I do not believe I am," I said.

"Believe it."

This time I did stop and regarded her carefully. "Prove it," I said.

Ms. Washburn gasped. Her voice was audible only to me, standing only a few feet to her side. "Samuel."

I thought of Reuben and his behavior over the past twenty-seven years. I thought of my mother and how devastated she would be if any harm came to him. I thought of Virginia Fontaine and her odd plea for us to stop investigating her question. And I thought of how angry I was at Melanie Mason for causing all this. I took three steps back in her direction so she could hear me snarl at her.

"You created the illusion of your own death by killing a perfectly innocent homeless woman in a car. Was it just for the insurance money? Have you been in touch with your husband all this time? What makes a person behave the way you do? Is it a simple disregard for the feelings of others? They tell me I'm supposed to be the one who has trouble with empathy but as far as I can tell, Ms. Mason, you are as empty emotionally as anyone I have ever met. Now open the back of that van and show me my father or I will drive away and tell the New Brunswick police everything I know about how you killed Brett Fontaine."

Melanie Mason waited two seconds and then began to applaud very slowly. "Very impressive, Mr. Hoenig. I'm really very taken with that speech. Were you preparing it all this time or was that spontaneous? You'll see your father when I say you can."

"Then say it or we'll leave." Ms. Washburn's determined look would have been enough to convince me.

It did not seem to have that effect on Melanie Mason, however. "You're not scaring me," she said. "All you have that I want is an assurance and some documents. I have a person."

"You have overestimated that person's value to me," I told her. "Do with him as you will if you are not satisfied."

I saw Ms. Washburn flinch but she said nothing.

This stalemate might have continued indefinitely but for two factors: First, I was fully prepared to leave the scene if Melanie could not immediately produce Reuben (and I was fairly sure she could not). Second, that was when the driver's door of the van opened and Leon Rabinski stepped out of the vehicle.

Rabinski's presence certainly was not a shock. Ms. Washburn's mouth twitched a bit when she saw him. But Melanie Mason looked positively livid.

"Didn't I tell you to stay in the van?" she demanded when Rabinski had made his way to our group. "You're drawing attention to yourself!" I did not see how Rabinski was doing that but Melanie was clearly creating more of a scene, as Mother would call it, than her supposed widower.

"How long are you going to be?" he asked. "You should have been done with this by now. Did you get the stuff you wanted?"

"Not yet. Get back in the van." Melanie pointed at the van, presumably worried that her husband did not realize which vehicle she meant.

"How hard is this?" Rabinski seemed exasperated. He turned to me. "Give me the documents you have about Brett Fontaine's murder."

"Not until I see Reuben Hoenig," I repeated for his benefit.

"See?" Melanie said, using her open palm to gesture at me. "He won't do what he's supposed to."

"That has always been a problem of mine," I admitted. "There was a time in school when I would not line up by height order because it made no sense. Children of shorter stature do not walk more efficiently."

"Enough!" Rabinski shielded his right arm from the view of the PC Richard patrons and produced a gun from his jacket pocket. "Now hand it over."

The weapon was not pointed at either Ms. Washburn or myself; it seemed that Rabinski was using it as a threat rather than an instrument of violence. He had it aimed between us and probably would hit a 2014 Chevrolet Tahoe behind us if he fired. Ms. Washburn gasped a little but not as much as she would have before having started working at Questions Answered, I would have wagered.

"As I understand it, the demand was that Ms. Washburn and I refrain from doing any further research and produce any documents we have regarding the murder," I said. "Is that accurate?"

"That's right," Rabinski said. "So hand them over."

I looked past him at Melanie Mason. "Please listen very carefully because I have told you this more than once and I want you to understand. We have already stopped researching our client's question because she has rescinded her contract. Now let me see Reuben Hoenig. Open the back of that van." I did not point because I was sure everyone gathered there knew which van I meant.

"We won't," Melanie said firmly.

"You can't," I countered. "Reuben is not in the van. You have him in another such vehicle near here to ensure my cooperation. But that will not be effective because I will not agree to any terms until I have visual proof of life—and no, a phone call will not be sufficient."

Rabinski looked at his wife and put up his hands, palms up. "Well, this was your idea."

Melanie Mason looked disgusted. "Fine. Go get him."

Rabinski drew a heavy sigh and walked to the initial van, which he turned off. He left it where it was parked and walked to the other side of the ship-shaped store, out of our view.

Ms. Washburn looked at Melanie with contempt in her eyes. "You killed Brett Fontaine. How did you manage that with me following him the whole time?" Ms. Washburn clearly had not stopped taking that detail of this question personally.

"Trade secret," Melanie said, making Ms. Washburn's expression that much more annoyed.

"They lured Mr. Fontaine into the warehouse we had found while you were waiting outside," I told Ms. Washburn. "No doubt there was some business matter Mr. Rabinski could mention or something less professional that Ms. Mason could offer. In any event, Mr. Fontaine was bludgeoned to death inside the warehouse fairly quickly while you waited for him outside the rental property. Mr. Rabinski, aware that you could see him only from the waist down, made sure to wear the same type of shoes and trousers Mr. Fontaine had on that day. After they managed somehow to place the body in the car's trunk he walked out, probably through the back yard of the rental property, and let you follow him to High Street. He noted that you'd had to stop in traffic and set that property up as the place where Mr. Fontaine's body would be discovered."

"You knew?" Ms. Washburn asked.

"Some of it is conjecture, but it fits the facts," I said. "Is my account accurate, Ms. Mason?"

Melanie puffed out her lips. "So you can record me confessing to a murder? I'm not saying a word, Hoenig."

"And it was so you could have control of Brett's business?" Ms. Washburn said to her. "Just for that? What was so great about a tiny real estate firm?"

"Hardly tiny," Melanie told her. "In two weeks it'll be sold to Century 21 for more than six million dollars." She fixed her gaze on my jacket, assuming (I suppose) that there was a recording device concealed there. "But I'm not saying we killed him for that or any other reason."

"I am not recording this conversation," I assured Melanie. "You may speak freely."

"I'll bet."

Another white van turned the corner of the ship and headed toward us. This one bore no logos or advertising on its exterior. It had no windows except in its cab, where Leon Rabinski was clearly visible driving. There was no one in the passenger seat.

It was reassuring that this van, the one surely bearing Reuben Hoenig, had been parked so close to the place of the rendezvous. That was an indication that the plan all along had been to return the hostage and not to do him harm. Mother and Ms. Washburn would have been very upset if anything negative had been done to Reuben.

Rabinski parked the second van closer to where Melanie Mason, Ms. Washburn, and I were standing. He got out and with an air of impatience opened the rear doors of the van and gestured at them with his left hand. "See?" he said.

We got a very brief glimpse of Reuben, sitting on an overturned bucket and looking rather surprised to see other people. He almost stood before Rabinski slammed the van's back doors again.

There was something about the way he'd looked. Frightened, helpless and confused, Reuben was no longer the man who had left my mother and me. He was a man who needed my help. I could not explain it then and I cannot explain it now.

"We held up our end," Melanie Mason said. "Now hand over your research."

"I can't," I told her.

I felt Ms. Washburn move closer to my left side and stand by me. Her shoulders were positioned a little more squarely than usual as she projected an attitude of defiance. We had discussed this possibility before leaving the Questions Answered office.

Rabinski reached into his pocket again, no doubt planning to brandish the handgun he had there. "What do you mean you can't?" he growled.

"There are no documents. There is no printed research," said Ms. Washburn, pointing to her head. "Everything we have we have here."

I nodded mine in an attempt to be less obvious.

"You're lying," Melanie said.

"We're not," I assured her. "We sometimes take notes but most of our research is done online and we do not print out the results until we have an answer. We did not reach a definitive answer on the question of who killed Brett Fontaine until you confessed it to us here in this parking lot."

"I confessed nothing," Melanie told me. "You made some accusations but you're not getting me to speak into your recorder."

I closed my eyes and shook my head slowly. "There is no recorder, Ms. Mason." I opened my jacket to prove there was no device in any of my pockets.

"Brett Fontaine deserved to die," Rabinski said. "He was obsessed with my wife and he stood in the way of my success. Him dying did nothing but good."

"For you," Ms. Washburn pointed out.

"Why not for me? I worked for that guy for ten years and all I ever heard was how I wasn't good enough. Well, now I'm good enough. I run his company and I'm doing it better than he did. I worked out the way to cash in Mel's insurance policy and get some working capital and all that happened was an old drunk died in a car accident. What do you know, a half a bottle of bourbon in her and she couldn't make it on Route 22. Go figure. Right over there." He pointed at a spot in the distance next to an outlet of the Home Depot.

"Shut up, Leon," his wife said.

"Why? They're not recording it and they can't prove anything. Yeah, Mel and I killed Brett with a grappling hook in an old warehouse and we dumped his body where you'd find it, lady." He gestured at Ms. Washburn. "Some people improve the world when they die."

"How and why did you make such a spectacle of the false ghost at the gravesite where you are clearly not buried, Ms. Mason?" I asked.

"The cop wouldn't leave the accident alone," Rabinski answered. "He kept coming by and staring at the headstone like he knew something. And we wanted Brett to think the ghost of his old girlfriend was coming back for him. So we set up a few little electronics and played a game. Got the cop to go away and shut up, and it got Brett hooked. Then you showed up." Rabinski scowled at me. "You didn't see the cameras because they're so small but we saw you." I had assumed there was some sort of Wi-Fi device operating visual surveillance equipment but had been unable to locate it on the scene.

"For the love of—will you shut up, Leon?"

That was when Ms. Washburn stepped forward. "We already know all this," she told Melanie. "What I don't understand is why. Why did you concoct this elaborate ruse just to get Brett Fontaine to follow you into a warehouse? You probably could have gotten him just by wearing the right sweater."

Anger flashed in Melanie Mason's eyes. "It wasn't like that," she said.

"I'll bet. Then what was it like?"

"He loved me but he was married to…*her*. And he wasn't going to cheat on her. But I was dead as far as he knew. We did that for the insurance money. I was living in an apartment in New Brunswick that Leon found for me, not one of those dumps Brett put the students in. Since I was dead, it wasn't really cheating, was it? So he followed me right into that warehouse thinking he was with a ghost, and when he came out, he was a ghost himself."

That was all I'd needed to hear. "Grapefruit," I said into my collar, and within seconds sirens were audible in the near distance. Three patrol cars and an unmarked unit bearing Detective Monroe were surrounding us almost immediately.

Melanie Mason looked at me with fury. "You said you weren't recording the conversation."

"I wasn't. Detective Monroe was." I walked to the van and opened the doors. Reuben, looking none the worse for wear, stepped out and I helped him down. "He put the wire on me before we drove here."

Monroe nodded toward Melanie and Rabinski and the uniformed police officers from one of the cruisers began the process of putting handcuffs on them. "We told you not to call the police," Rabinski said.

It seemed a moot point at this moment but I was bound to answer. "I didn't," I said.

Melanie glared at Ms. Washburn. "She wasn't supposed to either."

"I didn't," Ms. Washburn said. She smiled a bit; she was enjoying watching Melanie being taken away, alive and guilty as per her own confession.

"Then who did?" Rabinski demanded.

"I did," Reuben said. "Samuel texted me the time and place of the meeting. You shouldn't have left me in there with my phone." He held up his cellular phone for emphasis.

"A lesson learned," Ms. Washburn said. "What do we have to do next?" she asked me.

Before Monroe could say we had to go to his headquarters to make a statement, I said, "We have to go save Virginia Fontaine's life." Then I looked at the detective and added, "So that you can arrest her."

THIRTY-THREE

VIRGINIA FONTAINE'S HIGHLAND PARK home was still a work in progress. Although construction on the building had clearly ended some months previously and the walls and floors were all completed, there was remarkably little Virginia (and presumably her deceased husband) had done to personalize the living area.

Our goal at this moment, however, was not to assess the décor. Ms. Washburn and I had broken into the house, after it had been agreed that Detective Monroe would be occupied for some time while he helped process the two prisoners taken into custody at the Flagship. We were searching for some sign that Virginia might have left behind as to her state of mind and her intentions.

But so far our search had been fruitless. Everything in the house was in its place and nothing was particularly idiosyncratic.

"I wish I knew what I was looking for," Ms. Washburn said. She was speaking to me from the master bedroom upstairs, while I was searching the living room beneath her.

"If we knew what we were looking for, we would have already found it," I answered.

"Why do you think Virginia's life is in danger?" Ms. Washburn appeared at the landing above me and opened the door of a linen closet. She did not touch anything inside.

"Because someone has been trying very hard to make her seem responsible for her second husband's death and that person or those people could be very upset seeing their plans disrupted now that Ms. Fontaine has discontinued our employment." There was not even a thin coating of dust on anything in the living room. Virginia had not been gone long and was a very meticulous housekeeper.

"Not to mention the two arrests that have been made in that murder," Ms. Washburn pointed out. She moved to the end of the hallway upstairs and opened a door to a second bedroom.

"The people angry with Ms. Fontaine have probably not heard about those just yet," I said. "Have you tried calling her again?"

Ms. Washburn emerged from the smaller bedroom and closed the door behind her. "Yeah, her phone is still going right to voice mail. Why don't you think it was the same people? How come Leon Rabinski and Melanie Mason didn't want to frame Virginia? It would take the suspicion off them. And if she was arrested, Leon would get pretty much full control over Fontaine and Fontaine."

"Because the rage, as we can tell by the phone call from Anthony Deane to Virginia Fontaine that resulted in her terminating our contract, was not about the death of Brett Fontaine. Are there any antidepressants in the medicine cabinet?"

Ms. Washburn looked down at me. "I was sort of shy about looking. And I'm not a pharmacist."

I was relatively sure no such medications would be found anyway, but confirmation would have been helpful in disposing of the notion. I was about to start for the stairs so I could check the evidence myself when the side door opened and Virginia Fontaine walked into her house.

Ms. Washburn and I made no effort to conceal ourselves. In fact, Ms. Washburn walked down the stairs, noting Virginia's shocked expression, and stood by my side.

"What are you doing here?" our former client gasped.

"I believe there might very well be an impending attempt on your life," I told Virginia. "It is our intention to remove you to a safe place until the threat can be neutralized."

Virginia did not seem to fully absorb the information I had given her. "How did you get in?" she demanded.

"I picked the lock on the back door," Ms. Washburn told her. "We looked for a spare key but you didn't seem to have one anywhere."

Virginia put down the bag of groceries she was carrying on a side table in the front hallway. "Right, because I didn't want anybody except me to get into the house when I'm not around," she said. "You broke into my house."

I walked toward her. "I believe you are missing the point," I said. "Someone might very well be planning to kill you as we speak. It is necessary for us to leave and go somewhere they would not expect to find you."

"Nobody's trying to kill me," Virginia said. "You're just trying to get me to hire you again. I'm going to call the police."

"The police are aware of this," Ms. Washburn told her. "And we're not trying to get you to do anything except leave so you can stay alive."

Virginia stopped walking and stared at her. "The police know you broke into my house?"

We had agreed with Detective Monroe that there would be no acknowledgement of any activity Ms. Washburn and I might undertake before he arrived on the scene. Mentioning the awareness of a law enforcement agency was a misstep on Ms. Washburn's part. "No! Um…they just know…that someone's after you," she told Virginia.

That did not placate our former client. "Why would someone be after me?"

I was certain we would be alone with Virginia for only another few minutes now. "May we please discuss this in the car?" I said. "Time is very much a factor here." I pointed toward the front door. "Please come with us and we can keep you safe."

Virginia did not respond as I would have hoped or expected. If someone had informed me that my life was in danger if I did not leave the premises, I would not have to be told more than once. I had already mentioned that very circumstance to Virginia three times and Ms. Washburn had referred to it once. But our former client merely stood in the room with her hands on her hips looking defiant.

"I'm not moving until I get an explanation about all this. For all I know you just want to pack me into a car and take me somewhere for your own reasons." That made virtually no sense at all but there was no time to debate the point with Virginia.

I spoke very quickly, which is not my typical rhythm. Because I usually concern myself with speaking in a socially acceptable set of parameters, I tend to speak slowly and think more carefully about each word than most people do. But in this case I felt the pressure of time and wanted to simply satisfy Virginia's curiosity enough to convince her she should come with Ms. Washburn and me.

"We have no intention of abducting you for any reason," I said. "But once Anthony Deane explained to us that he'd been with you when your first husband died accidentally I knew there was a very good chance that someone would come to take revenge upon you. And now that you are no longer a viable suspect in the death of your second husband there is no reason for the person holding a grudge to anticipate your arrest and imprisonment. So as they say the clock is ticking and I am very concerned that we might already have waited too long. Please come with us."

"Wait," Ms. Washburn said. "This hinges on Tony Deane saying he was with Virginia when William Klein died? What's that got to do with Brett Fontaine's murder?"

"Nothing." I started toward the front door hoping the two women would follow me simply due to the power of my implied suggestion but they remained rooted to the spots where they stood. "It was only because Rabinski and Melanie Mason wanted there to be more circumstantial evidence against Virginia that they even conceived of staging Mr. Fontaine's murder at the scene of Mr. Klein's."

"Wait," Ms. Washburn said again. "William Klein was murdered?"

"Hang on," Virginia said simultaneously. "Melanie Mason isn't dead?"

It was going to take far too long to explain everything. "I promise all this will become clear but it is *imperative* that we leave now. Please follow me." I looked out through one of the small panes of glass in the rather ornate front door and saw no threats. I reached for the doorknob and opened the door.

At that moment a shot rang out.

I was unable to see the shooter or even accurately pinpoint the angle of the shot but the report of the gun was unmistakable. It was probably a rifle, which was odd. This street did not seem to have any natural points where a sniper could set up without being observed.

None of that seemed to matter at the moment I heard the shot, however, because the first thing I saw was Ms. Washburn falling to the floor.

I slammed the steel door—which honestly could be expected to offer little protection from future gunshots other than to hide the people inside the house from the assailant outside—and immediately rushed to Ms. Washburn, who was lying on the floor at the base of the stairway. I was thankful there was no blood visible on the floor or an obvious wound on Ms. Washburn's body anywhere I could see.

"Where did it hit you?" I asked when I reached her.

She looked up. "Hit me?"

"You are not shot?"

Ms. Washburn shook her head. "No. I just dropped to get out of the way." She started to scramble to her feet.

"Wait," I said. "We can't be sure the shooter is unable to see us, or might not fire blindly into the door. Stay down." Ms. Washburn sat on the floor.

"*I'm* shot," said Virginia Fontaine. In my haste to reach Ms. Washburn I had run past Virginia and paid her no attention. "In the shoulder. Is it bad?"

I could think of no way to answer that question. Is a gunshot ever good? I pivoted from my position next to Ms. Washburn and attended to Virginia, who was indeed showing signs of a wound in her left shoulder. The bullet had probably entered through the back and had either lodged inside or gone through Virginia entirely. I was not a well-enough trained observer to determine which of those things was the case and I was not inclined to turn Virginia over to check for an exit wound.

"Please call 911," I said to Ms. Washburn. "We need an ambulance and police officers here as quickly as possible." Then I turned my attention toward Virginia. "Who is out there?" I asked her.

"How would I know?" Her voice included a tinge of pain but the wound was probably not life-threatening.

I resisted the impulse to roll my eyes in exasperation. "This is no time to be coy," I said. "Someone is shooting at us and has wounded you. You must know: Who would have been angry enough at you for killing William Klein that they would want to exact revenge at this late date? Is it Anthony Deane?" He would have had enough time to drive here from his office, but I had no idea how he would have gotten news of the arrests made at the Flagship.

"You think I killed William?" Virginia wailed.

"Of course you did. Your alibi was that you were at your job when your husband accidentally fell off the fire escape outside your apartment. But the bolts on the railing had been loosened and Anthony Deane, whom we know was infatuated with you and might feel obligated to protect you, offered an alternative alibi when none would have been necessary if you'd actually been at work. You wanted to leave William Klein but for some reason you felt divorce was not an option and murder was. So tell me: Who is it out there who wants you dead because of that?"

Virginia moaned, ostensibly in pain but probably for dramatic effect. Ms. Washburn crawled to my side. "The police and EMS are on their way," she said. "Probably the cops will get here first. It'll just be a few minutes, Ginny."

Our former client did not respond except to look pained. A second shot rang out. A hole appeared in the front door and I heard the bullet whiz at least two feet above our heads. "Stay down," I said. "Whoever is shooting doesn't know we're on the floor."

Another shot was fired, resulting in a hole lower in the door and the destruction of a vase on a table to our left. Virginia raised her head. "Hey," she said. "That was a wedding present."

I pushed her head back down toward the floor without comment. But I was wondering which wedding she was referencing.

"Maybe we can use that table as a shield," Ms. Washburn said. She pointed at the dining table, which was large and appeared quite substantial.

"I'm not sure we can move it quickly enough to avoid further gunfire," I mused aloud. "We could be putting ourselves in harm's way as we would be attempting to protect ourselves."

The shooter seemed to be newly emboldened because another shot rang out and destroyed a small bowl that had fallen to the floor four feet to my right. "Can we make it upstairs?" Ms. Washburn asked. "He's not aiming up there."

"I don't think I can," Virginia said. "I'm shot." Apparently she thought we were not aware of her injury.

I raced through my mind for the probable identity of the sniper outside. Since I could not safely get a panoramic view of the street to determine a likely point from which the shots were being fired, I felt this was the most efficient road to ending our situation without any further loss of blood from anyone in the room.

Leon Rabinski and Melanie Mason were in custody. Unless they had staged a spectacular escape, which no doubt would have resulted in a message from Detective Monroe, I thought it impossible either of them was responsible for our current plight. And given that the attack was seemingly aimed at Virginia Fontaine more than Ms. Washburn and myself (the shooting had not begun until she had arrived through the attached garage, which made it more difficult for the shooter to aim at her before she was indoors), I believed my initial assumption that it was a form of revenge for the death of William Klein was correct.

That simplified the problem considerably. "Who would be especially upset about the death of William Klein?" I said.

"William's been dead for years," Virginia said. The loss of blood or shock might have been affecting her judgment.

Ms. Washburn clearly followed my line of reasoning. "Not Debbie Sampras," she said. "She was a high school friend of Brett Fontaine, and probably never met Virginia's first husband."

"True. And while it is probably a physical possibility that Anthony Deane could have driven here in time to take up position outside the house, it was he who called to warn Virginia that we were asking questions about Mr. Klein. If she hadn't been shot, I would suspect Virginia herself of trying to eliminate us."

"Hey," Virginia said. Then she lay her head back down on the carpet.

I heard sirens in the distance. "Perhaps the shooting will stop when the emergency medical service vehicle and the police arrive," I suggested.

Another shot rang out, causing no visible damage. "Maybe not," Ms. Washburn said.

My cellular phone rang. The screen indicated the call was coming from my mother. No doubt Reuben had found his way home. This was probably not a good time to take the call. I texted a message to Mother indicating I could not respond at the moment.

"As I see it, there is only one suspect left who might be angry enough to want Virginia dead," I told Ms. Washburn.

"Who?"

The front door lock exploded and the door swung open. Once it did my suspicions were confirmed.

"Peter Belson," I said.

"Peter," Virginia murmured. While her wound was not by itself life-threatening, the time it was taking for her to receive treatment was no doubt leading to a serious loss of blood.

Belson tried to kick the door closed behind him but he had destroyed the latch and the lock when he fired at it with the rifle he held with his right hand. It would not close, so he reached behind and secured it somewhat with the chain mechanism that had been left intact.

Ms. Washburn looked at me. "What's our play?" she asked.

I did not understand the idiom. We were certainly not going to perform a theatrical presentation while being held hostage by a vengeance-driven car salesman. I wished again I had been able to see his hands when Belson and I had communicated via FaceTime. I might have anticipated his obsessive drive. I assumed his favorite Beatles song was either "I Will" or "Run For Your Life."

"What does that mean?" I asked Ms. Washburn.

"She wants to know what strategy you're going to use to get away from me," Belson answered as he advanced toward us holding the rifle. I saw a pistol strapped to his hip. The sirens were much louder, indicating the emergency vehicles were either parking or already parked outside Virginia's home. "And no matter what you're thinking, there's no way you're getting away."

I felt it best to appeal to his sense of justice, as that was driving his obsession. "Virginia is going to be arrested and tried for the death of her first husband," I told Belson. "I have already spoken to the detective in charge of the case. He is no doubt on his way."

"Huh?" Virginia barely looked up.

"Too little, too late," Belson said. "Juries acquit people. She killed my brother and she's going to die for it."

"Your fraternity brother?" I asked. The term had been bandied about rather loosely in this matter and I felt it best to clarify the terms we were discussing.

"My *brother*," Belson corrected me.

That was confusing. "William Klein was your brother?" Ms. Washburn asked. I was relieved to know she was puzzled as much as I was. "But you have different last names."

Belson gestured wildly with his free hand. "Okay, my *half* brother! You happy?" He was obviously not in a very stable frame of mind. He pointed with the gun at Virginia. "And she killed him."

"She never mentioned that you were her first husband's half brother," I said, hoping to get Belson to move the barrel of the gun away from Virginia's head.

"Ms. Fontaine didn't know. Will didn't tell anybody about me. Because he was afraid it would hurt his mother."

"So William's father and your mother were not married," Ms. Washburn said.

"No! I'm a bastard, okay?" Belson was clearly in a state of agitation, which was not terribly surprising considering that he had shot Virginia and blasted his way through her front door. "But that doesn't mean we weren't brothers!" No one had suggested they were not.

We were not able to make that point because there was sound from outside the house. We could hear footsteps, probably people wearing boots, approaching from the front and spreading out to encompass both sides. It was probable there were officers in the back of the house as well but that was too far away for us to hear them.

The amplified voice of Detective Monroe came through next. "You inside the house." Clearly they were not aware of the shooter's identity yet. "There are officers on every side of you. You can't get out. If you open the door and come out without a weapon, hands on top of your head, you will not be hurt."

Belson seemed to find the message amusing. He did not laugh out loud but smiled and shook his head as if acknowledging a ridiculous statement. "Do you hear this guy?" he said to the prone Virginia. "He thinks I'm coming out so they can shoot me."

"No," I countered. "He said if you go outside without a weapon—"

Belson turned to me with a furious expression. "I wasn't talking to you!"

Ms. Washburn caught my eye with a look that indicated I should not try to correct him. I trusted her judgment and remained silent.

"You in the house!" Monroe said again through his bullhorn. "We know you have hostages in there. Send them out and we can talk about this!"

This time Belson did laugh. Again he addressed Virginia, who might have been unconscious. "If I send you three out, what leverage do I have?" he asked her. I do not know if he expected—or perhaps heard—an answer. "You're not going anywhere. I'm going to shoot you and then shoot myself."

"They never get the order right," Ms. Washburn mumbled.

Belson spun. "What?" he shouted at Ms. Washburn.

"I didn't say anything."

"Yes, you did!" Belson took two steps toward Ms. Washburn and pointed the barrel of his rifle toward the floor. "What did you say?"

"I said you should let us go and turn yourself in. It's the only way to save yourself."

"Weren't you *listening*? I *said* I'm going to shoot myself after the three of you are dead!" He looked at Virginia again. "Honestly, some people."

The situation, from my point of view, was deteriorating rapidly. Monroe was unlikely to successfully negotiate Ms. Washburn, Virginia and me out of the house. If Belson intended to shoot us and then turn the gun on himself, he could not be reasoned with by emphasizing his own survival.

I stood up, taking a chance that Belson would not fire at first movement. He did not, but looked at me with wonder on his face. "What?" he said. "You need the bathroom?"

In retrospect it might have been useful to say I did need to use the restroom, but I did not think of it immediately. The thought of using a bathroom in an unfamiliar house was so distasteful to me that I rejected it reflexively. "No," I said. "But I would like to call my mother and say goodbye if you are going to kill me."

Belson's eyes widened as he comprehended what he was being told. "You have a mother?" he asked. The thought never seemed to have occurred to him.

I had not done enough research into Belson's background to know the answer to my next question and that made it emotionally (and possibly physically) dangerous. "Yes," I said. "Does your mother know what you are doing today?"

Ms. Washburn inhaled sharply, understanding I had taken a chance. If Belson's mother was deceased, he might react badly to the suggestion. If she were alive and would approve of his actions, that might embolden him to the task.

Instead his face seemed to sadden. "No," he said. "I didn't tell her I was going to kill you."

"Don't you think she will be sad if you do that?" I asked. "And if you were to turn the gun on yourself, that would be her last memory of you."

Belson's eyes moistened. "No." That was all he said.

"That would be very sad." Ms. Washburn stood up and took my arm. "I bet she would tell you there are still possibilities as long as you don't do what you're planning."

From outside Monroe said, "I'm going to call you on the phone in there. Answer the phone and we can figure a way out of this."

I looked at Ms. Washburn. "Did you see a land line in the house?" I asked. She shook her head.

My cellular phone rang again. Caller ID told me the call was coming from the New Brunswick Police Department. Belson leveled the gun in my direction.

"Answer it," he said.

Before he could reverse his decision I pushed the section of my iPhone screen to accept the phone call. "Detective Monroe," I said immediately.

"Hoenig. Who's holding a gun on you in there?"

"There is a wounded woman in this house who murdered her husband some years ago, but she needs medical assistance as quickly as possible," I said, deliberately not answering his question. "Are there emergency medical technicians with you?"

"I'm not letting them in," Belson said.

"Your mother would want you to let them help her," Ms. Washburn told him.

Belson did not answer but I saw a tear emerge from his right eye. That seemed to be the most effective avenue to explore.

"They're here," Monroe answered. "But I'm not sending them into a room with an armed man who could endanger their lives as well as yours. Who's the gunman, Hoenig?"

Again I did not respond directly to Monroe's question. I looked at Belson. "Suppose we ask the detective to call your mother so you can explain your motives and say goodbye," I said. "Can you give me her telephone number? What is your mother's name, Peter?" I felt that calling him by his first name might be a better way to establish a rapport with the man holding the rifle.

Belson did not blink or move. "Patricia. Patty."

When I spoke into the phone again I made an effort to lower the volume of my voice. "Find a phone number for a Patricia Belson, Detective. Call her Patty and tell her that her son needs to speak with her."

"Her son? Who's her son?" Monroe had clearly not considered Belson a suspect. I did not answer him. After four seconds he asked, "What town is she in?"

"Where does you mother live?" I asked Belson.

"South Brunswick. Why?" His attention seemed to be fixed on a far-off point but he was staring at the floor and the prone body of Virginia Fontaine.

I informed Monroe of Patricia Belson's location and it took 68 seconds for him to speak to me again. "I have Patty Belson on the line," the detective said.

"Your mother is on the phone, Peter," I said in what Ms. Washburn would later confirm was a soothing tone. "She'd like to speak to you." I held my cellular phone out to him, a gesture that was difficult.

I don't like to have people touching things personal to me. But the circumstances demanded it and I told myself I could clean the phone or replace it later.

Belson looked at the phone and seemed to come to some level of awareness that I was addressing him. "Mom?" he said. I nodded. Belson looked at the rifle in his right hand and the ammunition he was holding in his left. He seemed confused.

I put out my other hand and gestured toward him. Belson seemed to understand but was still not completely present mentally. Naturally right-handed, he reached for my phone and then thought again.

He handed me the rifle and took the phone.

I tried not to watch as he put it to his ear. "Mom?" he said again.

I looked at Ms. Washburn, whose eyes were studying the pistol resting in a holster strapped to Belson's left hip. She looked up at me and I assessed Belson's positioning. He chose that moment to turn slightly to the right, instinctively trying to make his conversation that much more private. I nodded at Ms. Washburn.

She reached over quickly and removed the pistol from Belson's holster. Her movement was so swift and fluid that Belson did not seem to notice. I heard him quietly say, "No, I don't want to leave you, but she killed Will and now I can prove it."

Ms. Washburn handed me the pistol. I had attempted to determine how to remove the ammunition from the rifle and decided I was not well versed enough in firearms to make a safe attempt. Instead I moved away from Belson and placed the rifle across the seat of one of Virginia's dining chairs. Then I sat on it, careful to keep the barrel facing the wall. I looked at Ms. Washburn, whose cellular phone was already in her hand.

Police officers and emergency medical technicians were rushing through the door seven seconds later.

THIRTY-FOUR

"HE DIDN'T EVEN COMPLAIN while he was being arrested, except that he had to give Samuel his phone back." Ms. Washburn leaned on the side of my desk in the Questions Answered office and shook her head in wonder. "I'm not even sure Peter knew he was being arrested, even with the Miranda warning."

My mother, sitting in her usual easy chair in front of my desk, reached for Reuben Hoenig's hand. Reuben was seated in a folding chair Ms. Washburn had put out for him when he and Mother had arrived at the office. Once I'd gotten in touch with her to let her know Ms. Washburn and I were all right—a message Mother hadn't known was necessary before it was delivered, as it turned out—both she and Reuben had insisted on seeing us in person to get the final story on the Question of the Dead Mistress.

Indeed, Detective Monroe had bounded into Virginia Fontaine's home after four uniformed officers in protective gear had cleared the area and seemed disappointed to meet no resistance at all from the armed man who had come to kill three people and ended up wounding only one, badly but not in a life-threatening manner.

"I don't get it," the detective said to Ms. Washburn, as he appeared more eager to talk to her than to me. "You knew the crazy lady had killed her first husband." He said this as Virginia Fontaine was being wheeled out of the house on a portable gurney.

"The missing bolts from the fire escape indicated it was a calculated murder, a staged accident," I told him. I had no compunction about talking to Monroe. "The fact that Virginia had established two conflicting alibis indicated she had something to hide. When we discovered that William had in fact been cheating on his wife and that Virginia had actually engaged us to confirm her second husband was doing the same, it became apparent she wanted the information to justify killing Brett Fontaine. But Melanie Mason and Leon Rabinski beat her to the action."

"I don't get it," Monroe repeated. "She wanted to kill the second husband but she couldn't do it until she knew he was fooling around on her?"

"That's right." Ms. Washburn spread her hands to indicate she did not comprehend the motivation either. "When she saw the papers transferring part ownership of Fontaine and Fontaine to Rabinski instead of her, Virginia was incensed. But she needed that extra push, the thing that had put her over the line the first time. She wanted to be in the car with me when I followed her husband so she could kill him if we found him with his mistress, alive or dead. That's why she trumped up a picture of Brett with an empty car and told us it was him driving away with his dead college girlfriend."

"Meanwhile this guy was carrying a grudge because the first husband was his half brother," Monroe said, pointing in the direction of Peter Belson, who was still muttering to his mother as he was led out of the house. He had no phone but that did not seem relevant to Belson.

"Not according to his mother," Ms. Washburn, who had spoken to Patricia Belson, told him. "She says they met in college and Peter somehow came to the conclusion that they were related through his father. But she says he never cheated on her."

"So it's all about husbands messing around." That was Monroe's assessment of the situation.

"I guess so," Ms. Washburn said. She looked at me with a warm smile, something I had been hoping for the past few days.

"The poor man," Mother said now in the Questions Answered office, referring to Peter Belson. I thought her sympathy for Belson—who had intended to kill Ms. Washburn, Virginia Fontaine, and me with a rifle—might have been misplaced, but Mother has always been more understanding of others than I am.

"I know," Ms. Washburn said. Perhaps this was a type of thought that was gender-specific, although I tend to believe such things are myths. The human brain is essentially the same for either sex.

Reuben looked at me with a befuddled expression, indicating he did not understand the women's interpretation of the incident either. "So I'm trying to sort this out," he said. "The dead mistress was never actually dead, and she killed the second husband?"

"She and her husband, Leon Rabinski," I said, nodding. "They had already defrauded her life insurance policy and in the process essentially murdered a homeless woman. The lure of a lost lover was apparently enough for Brett Fontaine to follow."

"But she also fooled Officer Palumbo with the same technology and then got you and Mike to go there so she could play ghost," Mother said. "How did she get the message into your office papers?"

"Ms. Washburn and I had interviewed Rabinski that day," I reminded her. "He must have slipped the note into my stack while we were there without either of us noticing."

"And the half brother was waiting all these years to get revenge on the wife, so he waits until you two are in the room to run in with a gun?" Reuben had a way of simplifying concepts that made them sound foolish.

"That's about right," Ms. Washburn said.

My mother shook her head in wonder. "This was all about money. It always seems to be all about money."

I stood up and walked to her. I patted Mother on the shoulder. "Neurotypicals are motivated by odd things," I said.

"Don't try and hang this all on us," Ms. Washburn told me. "Anybody can do something stupid for money. But sometimes it's about love, isn't it?"

"I don't see how this question was about love," I told her. "Perhaps I'm missing something." It would not be unusual.

"Virginia Fontaine didn't have to come to us at all," Ms. Washburn said. "She was so upset by the idea that her husband cared more about his college girlfriend than he did about her that she exposed herself to danger and eventually ended up getting shot and almost dying because she couldn't bear the thought."

"She's going to be all right?" Mother asked.

Ms. Washburn nodded. "She lost some blood but the wound itself wasn't that bad. She'll be in the hospital for a couple of days and then Detective Monroe says she'll probably be out on bail until she faces trial."

"They're going to take the word of a man who busted into the house with a couple of guns and tried to shoot the two of you?" Reuben said. He seemed confused by the notion.

"There is more evidence than simply Peter Belson's testimony," I assured him. "The police reports from the time indicated the loose bolts in the fire escape. And there will be the testimony from Anthony Deane, whom I assume will be subpoenaed, about his giving the police a false alibi for Virginia LoBianco Klein during her first husband's death."

"Tony Deane—another example of how love blinds a person, Samuel."

"You think Anthony Deane is in love with Virginia Fontaine?" I asked. "Even though he's currently married. To a man."

She held her gaze on me for a moment, which I took to mean she was trying to formulate a response I would understand. "I can't think of any other motivation for him to do what he did," Ms. Washburn said.

I could think of six but I had to admit to myself that none was as compelling. "It is a very odd way of showing one's affection," I said.

Ms. Washburn's face took on the inscrutable expression I'd seen a number of times recently. "People have a lot of ways of showing their love."

Mother stood up, slowly but not as painfully as she would have before she had the inorganic knee joint installed in her leg. She looked at Reuben. "I think it's time for us to go," she said. "Maybe we'll go crazy for dinner tonight and get a pizza." Mother turned to look at me. "Plain." She knows I will eat pizza but not when it has been heaped with other foods incompatible with its own composition.

"There's more to the story," Ms. Washburn said.

"I imagine there is," Reuben said. "Perhaps we'll hear it another time."

"Perhaps you and I could meet for lunch one day," I said.

The three of them turned and stared at me for a moment. "I would like that," Reuben said.

With that, Mother and Reuben left the office, both shaking their heads and looking back at me as if something extraordinary had occurred. The fact that I had offered to have lunch with Reuben was not all that special. He had been living in my mother's house for months now. It was certainly time to understand him better.

Ms. Washburn stood and looked at me as if assessing for three seconds. Then she turned and walked back to her desk.

I considered her facial moods of late and the fact that she had occasionally been less accepting of my personality traits than usual. It all seemed to start at the time we had been disagreeing over the disposition of Virginia Fontaine's request that we prove her bizarre ghost story. I went over the conversation in my mind for some indication of what might have engendered such uncharacteristic behavior from Ms. Washburn.

"I did some research into your cemetery spirit," I told her as I resumed my normal work position. "The gravestone you were considering was that of Nathana Brookins, I believe. She was born on the same date and died on the same date, exactly one hundred years before you were born."

"You're going to tell me I saw a trick of the light?" Ms. Washburn said without looking up. "Or do you think she also faked her death and then set up a series of tin cups and string to speak to silly young people who passed by?"

"I have no explanation for what you saw," I told her. "I am certain that you saw it, but I can offer you no theory."

Ms. Washburn looked sharply at me. "Samuel, are you saying you think I saw a ghost?"

That was the crux of the argument we'd had the day her odd behavior had begun. "I am saying that I trust your judgment and your word. I do not believe there are ghosts. But I believe that you do and that you are entitled to hold that belief."

Ms. Washburn snorted a tiny laugh. "Nice of you," she said and turned back toward her computer display.

I stood up and walked to her side. I had replayed the conversation from that day in my mind and had a suspicion of its importance. Some words are not simply meant to be understood between people, no matter how obvious. They need to be said aloud.

"Ms. Washburn. I love you too," I said.

THE END

ABOUT THE AUTHORS

E. J. Copperman is the author of the Haunted Guesthouse series, with more than 220,000 copies sold (so far), the Mysterious Detective series, and the Agent to the Paws series.

Jeff Cohen wrote the Aaron Tucker and Comedy Tonight mystery series. He is also the author of two nonfiction books on Asperger's Syndrome, including *The Asperger Parent*.

31901063802641